Between

Gayle C. Edlin

ISBN-13: 978-0-9909736-3-8
Printed by CreateSpace

This is a work of fiction. Names, characters, businesses, places, events, and incidents are either the products of the author's imagination or are used in a fictitious manner. Any resemblance to actual persons, living or dead, or actual events is purely coincidental.

Cover design by Fred Dye (freddye.com)

Between the unforeseen devotion of unexpected friendship lies ... everything.

Stricken

J ess was nursing the swelling mass that would surely leave her with a black eye—rare, visible evidence of Lucas' abuse—when Lucas pulled over again.

"Goddamn fog." He threw the truck into park and reached toward her.

Jess flinched reflexively, but Lucas only opened the glove compartment.

"Relax, will you? I said I was sorry. It's not a big deal."

It's not a big deal.

Those words would have rubbed at Jess once, chafing and forming malevolent blisters that swelled until they popped, spewing out the gooey mess that marks infection. Those words would have galvanized her to respond with words of her own, delivered with a stiff spine, flashing eyes, and sincere belief.

Now Jess simply cowered, knowing that inaction was most likely to prevent another strike, though nothing she could do guaranteed her safety.

Lucas rooted around in the glove compartment, single-minded in his focus as Jess sat cringing. She might as well have not been sitting there at all. Underneath the sting high on her cheekbone and the dullness of her reflections, she realized what he must be looking for just before he spoke.

"You got my cigs?"

"No." It came out crackling, the sort of popping sound that couldn't be helped by clearing one's throat because its source was emotional rather than physical.

"Well, help me find them!" Lucas slapped the steering wheel, hard enough that Jess almost pitied the thing, except that it was blessed with an abundant lack of sensation.

"Did you try the ..." Jess began, pointing, and Lucas reached up to the visor, tipping it.

A smashed pack of Marlboros dropped into his lap. Only the best for Lucas, though he could scarcely afford generics.

"Ha! Don't need your help. Found them myself."

Jess leaned back in her seat, thinking again how upset she should be—as she had been, once—and wondering how she could have ever turned into this ... this *person* ...

This vanishing person.

Her temple continued to throb, and she wondered if she might get a migraine out of the experience, too. She no longer had a prescription for the only medication that ever helped those rare, sick headaches, but it wouldn't matter if she did ... she wouldn't dare to take it now.

Now that she was pregnant.

The thought sent bile surging into the back of her esophagus, though goodness knew how long it had been since she'd eaten anything. When the vomiting started, she'd told Lucas it was the flu, picked up at Benji's, the diner where Jess worked in Bozeman, the last town in which they'd both been employed. The conjoined twins of plausibility and Lucas' supreme confidence that she would not dare tell him anything but the truth supported her lie.

But she'd known. She'd known right away that the one thing with any potential for good in her life was happening again.

And this time, she wouldn't—*couldn't*—tell Lucas. This time, Jess knew not to tell Lucas, because he'd hit her last time. Hard enough that even if she couldn't prove it, she knew he'd killed the baby.

My *baby*.

2

The stench of cigarette smoke filled the truck's cab, and Jess leaned toward her window, feigning sleepiness as she sought the thin stream of fresh air trickling into the truck. This midnight hour was resplendent with a fog that made itself comfortably at home in Wyoming's central basin, though Jess couldn't imagine what right fog had to inhabit such an arid place.

"Feeling any better, babe?" Lucas' nicotine fix made him temporarily solicitous.

"Much." Jess smiled. She had to make sure her smile was perfect—not too bright, not too dim—because Lucas abhorred anything that deviated from his idea of how things should be. Fresh from another Lucas-induced injury and fearful for the new life sparking inside her, Jess was simultaneously over-cautious and terrified.

The combination exhausted her.

"Good. Get over here." Lucas beckoned, stretching out his arm, and Jess unbuckled her seat belt and slid to his side.

It was her penance, behaving the way Lucas wanted her to, she thought. That avoiding another potential strike meant she'd have to endure the foul smoke without letting it affect her pregnancy-sensitive stomach seemed, to Jess, one more punishment meted out by the universe in retribution for the major crime she could not recall. One more fact that proved people who led charmed lives made up the notion of karma.

People with lives where elusive Fate cared about her minions, not lives like Jess'.

"Goddamn fog," Lucas said again, his arm around Jess tightening. She let herself be held close, let Lucas' arm grip her waist—thankfully not yet thickening—as if she wanted to be there, relaxing into the awful comfort of the half-hug.

How had she ever believed him to be her rescuer, her one true love? He was more of a jailer ... almost a pimp in the way he demanded her paychecks from the string of diners she'd worked in since they'd "found each other." Aware now—peripherally, like the light fighting its way through the fog from across the road—Jess knew Lucas had been the one to find her, searching as he had been for a victim on which to foist his "affections."

But she couldn't imagine how she could escape.

She had no money. She had no car, having sold that upon agreeing to travel with Lucas when he hadn't found work in Jess' hometown.

And she'd failed to get away before. Her demoralizing lack of success and Lucas' fury each time she'd tried, forged iron shackles around her limbs as surely as those in any stone dungeon.

"What the hell is that? A bar?" Lucas peered out the window, ahead and to the left, following the flickers of light barely penetrating Jess' sad reverie. "That's great! Get me a go-cup. And something to eat."

"But ..."

Ignoring her barely-formed protest, Lucas shrugged out of the embrace in which he'd been holding Jess and extracted a crumpled $50 bill from his pocket. Lucas liked to carry large bills.

"Go on, and for Christ's sake, don't tip like you did last time. We don't have any money to spare."

Jess no longer dared express the notion that bar tips were not far removed from the restaurant tips that composed most of her wages in the years since they'd met. Likewise, she held in the chastisement she longed to deliver: Lucas should never purchase a go-cup he fully intended to consume the moment he held it, rather than waiting until he arrived at his destination as the law required.

Of course, when one had no destination ...

She reached for the money, and it seemed as if the fog crawled into the cab with them to slow her movements. It felt like fighting an insurmountable inertia, even as Lucas began to twitch the bill at her, his eyes flashing.

"Come on, I'm tired, too. I'm the one doing the driving; you can sleep."

Not that it would be possible for Jess to sleep through the country music Lucas "needed" to keep him awake on the all-night pilgrimages upon which he insisted. The thought came automatically, deprived of any vigor it should retain. She could not argue with Lucas.

Not ever.

When Jess finally took the money, Lucas leaned over to kiss her, as he always did, and smacked her across her buttocks as she exited the truck, as he always did. Jess smiled again because it was expected of her, but she was grateful for the fog and the dark as her tears—forbidden, disallowed tears—flowed, silently defying Lucas' prohibition against them.

She crossed the road carefully, though it would have been easier to hear any traffic if Lucas turned off the ignition instead of letting noisy truck's motor idle. But the truck, like Jess, limped along in life and once stopped, it might not start, particularly on a night as thick with moisture as this one.

The mist swallowed Lucas waiting in the truck behind her. He switched on the radio, though, so she knew he was still there. And he sang lustily along with whatever hideous song happened to be playing, "la-la-la-ing" his way through the parts he didn't know, which were many and arose with discomforting frequency.

Pavement gave way to gravel as Jess honed in on the dull light streaming from the fixture hanging over the painted sign on the windowless building ahead—no, there was a window, but it was boarded up. Injected with a shot of adrenaline as she noticed this unwelcoming fact, Jess halted her forward progress, looking as closely as the swirling soup of fog permitted.

The sign proclaimed "Between Bar & Gri l," the first "l" having lost its grip at some point in its life, apparently on account of vagaries of weather and time; the lonely remaining "l" seemed near to joining its twin. Like the rest of the building, the lettering looked unreasonably old to Jess. She couldn't fathom how a restaurant, even one boasting an accompanying bar, could sustain itself out here in nowhere's dark heart.

"Between" seemed like a good name for the place, at least. Jess could not remember the last town they'd passed through and had no idea what town lay ahead, so she couldn't say what it was that the bar stood between.

Unease oozed between her shoulder blades, massaged by the tenuous fingers of the pervasive fog. Lucas "la-la-la-d" his way through the chorus of the twanging song on the radio and the $50 Jess clutched tight in her cramping hand felt damp, listless. She pushed the money into her pocket and then wrenched her barrette—the last thing she had left of her mother's—out of her hair, letting overgrown bangs fall down over her damaged face, camouflaging the swelling remains of Lucas' wrath.

Jess knew Lucas wouldn't let her get away with not entering the bar on the strength of mere worry. Lucas was thirsty and hungry too, and she had to go in and get him what he wanted. This was the way of things in Jess' life now and as much as she knew in her heart—the part of her to which Lucas had, all unknowingly, relinquished any claim the first time he struck her—she couldn't see a way out of her situation, not even for love of her child.

And she did love her baby. She did love her baby, she did!

Brushing away the tears and tugging her rumpled hair into place after she did so, Jess walked straight toward the foreboding door of Between Bar & Grill. Housed in a recessed, off-center square of the building and resembling nothing so much as a gaping maw as she approached, even the doorway denied welcome to its unlikely patron. Jess ran her thumb over her barrette's smooth, pearly edge as she went, stroking it like a worry stone, using it like the talisman that she dreamed it could be if she ever brought herself to run away from Lucas again.

So focused was Jess on getting into the place that she nearly stepped on the black cat curled up underneath the limited shelter of the entryway's overhang.

When the cat hissed, Jess let out a little shriek and dropped her barrette. She was on her knees in an instant, prompting the cat to issue another hiss, but the urgency of not losing her last tie to her mother overrode Jess' concern about the cat. Thankfully, the barrette did not stray far from gravity's design, and Jess closed her fingers around it, breathing in little gasps.

"Mama." The word was like prayer to Jess, and her voice slathered its simplicity with the devout purity of love both childish and mature.

Something in her tone must have appealed to the cat, too, because it immediately switched from violent oaths to a sweet, kittenish mewl. It sounded like a cry for help long after the promise of assistance vanished. It felt like hope switching on a porch light when the electricity hadn't worked in months.

"Hey," Jess said, keeping her voice as gentle as she could. "I won't hurt you. I'm sorry I scared you."

The cat regarded her, its eyes the only defining part of it as it crouched, black fur in black shadows. The eyes disappeared under a blink, and then tipped slightly.

As Jess' own eyes became accustomed to the dim light cast by the single bare bulb above, she dared to stretch out the hand holding her mother's barrette. And the cat bravely extended its nose to both offerings. Jess expected whispers of breath as caressing as the fog, and the absence of that sensation was like shouting into a canyon and hearing not the slightest echo in response.

Realizing she couldn't hear Lucas singing anymore either, Jess startled into standing, frightened into scuttling toward the door again. The cat jumped away, though it refused to leave the meager protection provided by the bar's entryway, and reverted to hissing.

7

"I'm sorry. I have to go."

Before her paltry concerns about what might lie beyond the door had a chance to override her certainty about the atrocities sure to result from taking too long to find out, Jess pushed her way inside Between Bar & Grill.

Death

While the inside of the bar looked the part, it sounded like no bar in Jess' experience. No music played—there wasn't any jukebox she could see, actually—and two men sat silently at the bar. Jess scanned the room even as she eased her way up to the lazy corner of polished wood nearest the door; she spotted only one more person, slumped over one of the round tables scattered about the open area.

The pair at the bar stared at her, but not in a threatening way. Rather, their gazes held surprise bordering on shock, as if Jess were a ghost. The idea was so intense, she fought the urge to check to see if a specter snuck into the bar behind her, stealthy as fog.

After an indeterminable expanse of frozen time, the grizzled man turned to speak to his companion.

"Regular."

"You're an idiot," responded the other man—clean-shaven and wearing a suit, the better to contrast with his slovenly drinking partner. His words were flat and certain. "I'll take that bet."

"Dumbass." The unkempt individual transferred the cigarette he'd been holding to the ashtray before him and stretched out his hand to the other man.

They shook, and each drank from their respective glasses. Then the heavily whiskered man raised his voice and called out, seemingly to the bar at large.

"Barkeep!"

In the stillness that followed, Jess heard the tiny sound of footsteps—so faint as to seem distant—and down the hall past the person draped over the lone, occupied table came a petite woman, smaller even than Jess. The woman's hair was white, and as she lifted the gate at the far end of the bar and stepped behind it, Jess saw wisps escaping the otherwise neat ponytail that hung to the middle of her back.

"'What will it be.'" The scruffy man enunciated carefully and nudged the man in the suit.

"Obviously." Languid disinterest coated the suited man's reply. "No contest there."

The bartender approached Jess, her slight smile apparently warm, but Jess noted a strange flickering as the ancient eyes studied her.

Ancient eyes?

Jess fidgeted with her hair, hoping it was sufficiently thick to cover Lucas' damage. As if triggered by her notice, the throbbing behind her left eye seemed to intensify.

"What will it be?" The trilling of the bartender's voice raised the fine hairs on the back of Jess' neck. Jess felt this response before, to certain piano music that resonated with her in some indefinable way. She hadn't had the sensation since meeting Lucas.

She found it entirely unnerving to have this response to a voice.

One of the men seated along the bar snickered. Jess spared a glance in the duo's direction, finding the suited man smiling as he stretched up to look over the grungy man's head. The man he peered over was ... if not also smiling, at least attempting to do so.

"Sweetest sound in the world." The suit raised his glass to the bartender.

"Cryin' shame we don't hear it much," the slob agreed, lifting his glass as well.

10

They clinked glasses and watched Jess and the bartender. Who, Jess realized, still awaited her response.

"I ... umm ... I need a go-cup, whiskey sour, and ... a cheeseburger, I guess? Also to go."

The bartender extracted a cloth from underneath the bar and polished a swath of the blemished—but shiny—surface in front of Jess. After depositing the cloth back underneath the counter, she nodded, as if finally agreeing to Jess' order.

She pulled a pad and paper from her apron, wrote briefly and with flourish, and then, whipping the paper away from its brethren, began to move. After depositing Jess' order in the window behind the bar, she rang a bell on the counter there.

The bell made a harsh, metallic demand, especially grating in the present quiet of the bar and following the melodic sound of the bartender's voice. As the bell's ring faded, Jess heard more footsteps: this time, the heavy tread of a much larger person.

A hand—so massive it reminded Jess of a bear's paw— reached up into the window and plucked the order from the ledge.

Jess shifted uncomfortably, thumb racing over her mother's barrette. She wasn't willing to sit on one of the many available stools. Though worn, they looked comfortable enough to tempt Jess, except for the disquiet she currently experienced. No, it wasn't her body that needed rest and healing.

Except for her eye. There, pain continued to pulsate. Not escalating, but not ebbing, either.

At least she wasn't feeling nauseous, too. Jess heaved a small, relieved sigh and watched the bartender, who almost seemed to float as she moved, preparing the drink Jess requested.

Again, the silence of the bar struck Jess, making her shuffle her feet, perhaps to deepen the shallow pool of sound around her. Noises emanated from the kitchen—the feet that had nearly shaken the bar earlier now relegated to smaller movements, sliding a bit as their owner began to cook. Jess heard the sizzle when the cheeseburger met the grill to which the bar's broken sign had referred.

The smell of cooking meat sharply countered the muted bar sounds, and Jess almost felt hungry as it permeated the air. Hunger, while it would be a fortunate change from nausea, wasn't entirely welcome as the burger was destined for Lucas. Well, perhaps he would let her have a bite; she could blame the flu for her slight appetite and maybe ... maybe everything would be ...

No.

It wasn't going to be "all right." *Nothing* was right in Jess' world. Nothing except her baby. Jess clutched the barrette tightly, its metal edges biting into her fingers.

The bartender finished mixing Lucas' drink and poured it into a disposable cup. As the last droplets rejoined the flood which preceded them, Jess met the bartender's eyes again.

She found something definite but unfathomable there, something knowing and sure. Even Lucas wasn't that certain of anything in life, though he was excessively comfortable imposing his will on the world in general and Jess in particular; Jess struggled with simply asserting herself. Realizing this diminutive bartender had more confidence—no, more self-possession, even stronger than assurance—than Lucas, the most commanding personality Jess knew, shook her.

As the bartender approached Jess with the go-cup in hand, Jess fumbled in her pocket. She placed the money gracelessly on the bar just before the cup joined it there.

The bartender smiled but this abbreviated warmth did not extend to her eyes, dark points of contrast to her nearly transparent hair. Those eyes, Jess thought, absorbed every facet of the world around their owner, transferring all they saw in exquisite detail to the razor-sharp mind directing them.

Unsettled, Jess went back to stroking her barrette, thumb sweeping back and forth in double-time. She hoped the grill heated exceptionally well so the burger would cook at a record pace.

The bartender plucked the $50 bill from the counter and glided toward the monstrosity of a cash register near the window to the kitchen. The register, an ancient model with a glass window on top for the monetary designations to appear when one or more of the many keys arising from the machine's curving front depressed, was noisy as well as imposing. When the cash drawer ejected, it made a racket so grating that Jess winced.

She twisted her head away from the bar, scanning the wall opposite. There, she noticed something else unusual—something she hadn't seen earlier. The wall, composed of vertical wooden planks, was covered with writing ... no, carving! Jess squinted, and the etchings clarified into names.

Names and dates.

Many of the names were explicit, specifying first, middle, and last. Sometimes the date noted only a year, was absent entirely, or appeared semi-presently as a question mark. Jess drew closer, eyes widening, thumb stilled on her barrette. She felt as if she couldn't breathe at all as she approached the wall and raised her free hand to trace one of the largest names: "Warren Wolford, 9/26/1972." Immediately underneath Warren's name was another, scratched even larger and apparently by the same hand, though not as smoothly: "Sandman, 9/26/1972."

She noticed the names appeared more evenly formed than the dates; many names seemed to be written rather than carved, but all the dates were roughhewn. When warmth—the wall felt ... alive!—penetrated her musings, Jess withdrew her hand.

How could a wall be alive? She must be imagining things.

At least a hundred names adorned the wall, perhaps two hundred. Jess scanned the expanse, more easily visible now that she stood closer to it. The oldest date she spotted was "17

December 1873" and the stilted slant of the name above it made her shiver because it looked right, matching writings Jess remembered seeing ... somewhere. Perhaps a field trip when she'd still been in school ...

"Order up!" The call echoed deeply across the stillness and Jess whirled, finding the two men at the bar watching her as she stared at the wall. They observed her with shuttered eyes, Jess thought, and while it didn't frighten her, exactly, she didn't delight in their notice, either.

"What are the names for?" Jess asked, wanting to change the pair's focus as she stepped back to her position at the bar. She willed her voice to remain steady, and it almost did.

The two men exchanged glances before turning back in their seats. In the mirror, Jess saw the sloppy man lock his gaze on the wall behind the bar, somewhere around the vicinity of the kitchen window, where a neat square container had appeared. He picked up his barely-smoldering cigarette and sucked the smoke away, while the orderly man next to him feigned a cough.

"That's going to kill you one day, Joe." The businessman's jesting tone warred with the severity of his words.

Joe fingered the sagging pack before him, rustling its plastic casing.

"With just one left?" Joe ran his words together, dropping the occasional consonant, as if he didn't care to expend effort on enunciation. "Don't think so, dumbass." He added the insult casually, like an afterthought.

The businessman grinned broadly and nodded to Jess. "To answer your question, young lady, those are the names of Between's regulars, and the dates they arrived at this fine establishment."

"Oh." It seemed an unlikely tradition to Jess, particularly all the way back into the 1800s, but she didn't have time to think it through. The bartender had deposited the container with Lucas' burger next to the go-cup and change she'd placed on the counter while Jess had been lost, pondering the wall.

Jess felt overwhelmed by an urgent need to leave this strange place and its odder occupants. Even Lucas' company seemed almost preferable to remaining a minute longer inside the weird walls of Between.

Almost.

"Thank you." Jess slid two dollars and change back to the bartender. The bartender inclined her head toward Jess and smiled that barely-there smile once more.

"You are welcome," she said, and her musical tone made the hair on Jess' neck and arms stand at attention again.

Jess tucked her barrette and the rest of the cash into her pocket. She fumbled to pick up the go-cup and the container holding Lucas' burger, noticing peripherally that the atmosphere of the bar changed, becoming ... expectant. Joe sat up straight, and the man in business attire—an older style of suit, Jess thought— seemed ready to leap out of his seat.

Joe moved first. The other man turned away, calling out, "Eli!"

Before Jess could decide if she should be threatened by Joe's approach, hampered by his efforts to light his last cigarette with the remains of its predecessor, he spoke.

"Lemme get the door."

"Oh." Jess was flustered by this chivalry, from such a gruff and unkempt source, too. "Thanks."

"Eli, there's a customer on the way out." The suited man raised his voice, even as Joe and his attendant cloud of smoke intersected Jess' path to the door.

"Watch the step," Joe said, his voice anticipatory.

Jess thought of holding her breath as she passed through the smoke. Was this a special cigarette brand, that it didn't seem to bother her? But then Joe opened the door and all Jess could do was stare.

It was as if the world outside had been devoured, swallowed whole by a brilliance that superseded the sum of every lightning bolt in history. Jess looked outside Between's door and saw only a suffusion of flaring light, jagged flashes of blinding nothingness overlapping, intertwining, and searing even in the profound silence that accompanied them.

The black cat Jess met earlier shrieked, shooting off the step and into the bar past Jess and Joe, who still held the door. The cat's feet scrabbled away, harsh and loud in comparison with the silent chaos outside.

Jess faced a cold and brilliant madness; she'd never felt so alone.

"What ... what is that?"

Instead of answering the question Jess hadn't intended to ask, Joe scrutinized her closely. Then he asked his own question, speaking breathlessly around his flaring cigarette.

"What do you see?"

"What do I see?" Jess looked from Joe to the light and back again. "Don't you see it, too?"

Joe plucked the cigarette from his mouth, but before he could speak, a new voice—a voice a chasm deep—answered instead.

"We all see death differently."

Regular

"Shut the door, Joe!" The businessman cried, urgent to the point of frantic, and Jess turned to see someone new, a giant of a man who must have come from the kitchen.

The big man positioned himself slightly behind Jess and Joe, between them and the suited man. He did not stand near enough to be imposing, except that he would be impressive across a canyon. He was both tall and broad; though not particularly muscular, he had to be strong by virtue of his size alone. He watched Jess with an unnerving calm, particularly strange with white nothing flashing out of the corner of Jess' wounded eye.

Death?

"She sees a white death," the large man said in his booming voice. "It beckons her."

"What?" Jess realized she'd transferred her gaze back to the immensity of light outside the door, and dimly wondered where the cat had gotten to.

"*Joe, shut the door!*" The man in the suit strode around and behind Joe, intent obvious in every taut muscle of his body. He tried to shove the door shut as Joe fought to hold it open.

"She's got to choose for herself, Warren. You know that."

Joe released the door and pushed Warren away. He moved quickly, catching the door before it closed again. Warren stumbled, landing in a heap in front of the wall of names.

"Tell her, Eli!" Warren sounded wild. He pointed a shaking finger at the large man and repeated his directive, terror rising and dividing the tendrils of his words, a cacophonous vocal hydra. "Tell her!"

"I see a white death, too," Eli said then, his voice even. As much as the luminosity, scintillating and surging outside the bar's door hypnotized Jess, Eli's voice possessed its own appeal. She tore her eyes from the empty brightness, turning to the source of replete sound.

"I am Eli Winter."

"Jessamy Buccholz." Though Jess hadn't used her full name since Lucas nicknamed her, she fell into the formality of the moment, standing there on the edge of ... something ...

Jess scanned the room. She found Joe watching her intently and Warren—still on the floor, but now with his back full against the wall—pressing his head on his bent knees. Eli dominated the bar's foreground like a curious statue and the bartender moved about in the background, stacking glasses and straightening bottles as if nothing untoward was happening.

The cat was nowhere to be seen.

"What's going on? Is it ... a lightning storm?"

"It's not a storm!" Warren's voice crackled, emerging hollowly from his lowered head. "It's what Eli said it is. It's death!"

Death.

"That doesn't make any sense."

Joe snorted. "You got that right. You see light, I see dark. Don't make sense, none of it."

Joe planted one foot in front of the open door and reached for Jess' burden. "Here. Give me that and take the door. Make your choice."

Obedient—Lucas taught her well, after all—Jess stepped closer to the maelstrom of white light, grasping the door's outer handle and finding it icy. Or perhaps it was her hand that was cold?

"You stay in Between, or you go to meet the death you long for," Eli said.

Jess recoiled, her free hand pressing against her belly.

"I don't want to die!"

Eli's eyes were twin fires, raging in the ocean of his broad face.

"A white death does not greet you unwelcomed."

"But ..."

"Do you know what I see?" Warren said in a rush, the pitch of his muffled voice rising like an escaped helium balloon. "I see fire and demons; I see straight into Hell! Shut the door!"

Jess glanced from the swirling abyss to Warren. If he truly saw demons outside, no wonder he hid his eyes.

Then she shook her head.

"This can't be real. I'm leaving."

Even as Joe moved to return the go-cup and cheeseburger to her, Eli inserted himself in Joe's path.

"Death will not leave you untouched if you change your mind." And he lifted his right arm, extending the stub of his hand to Jess.

Jess hadn't noticed the disfigurement earlier, and it was horrifying to behold. Eli's fingers were stumps and while the scars were jagged and stretched tight—in the way of such markings— there was an obvious bluntness to the wounds, as if ...

As if Eli stepped just outside Between, stood on its threshold, and extended his hand, inserting it into the white death beyond.

"What ..." Jess felt an urgency, a burning need to know. Her fingers clenched on the door's handle, cold surging through her as if conducted by electric current. "What does it feel like?"

Eli blinked, rotating his hand to stare at its palm, apparently considering the question. Behind him, Joe snorted.

"Like fire." Eli shrugged, lowering his mangled hand. "Like ice. Like death."

"Yeah, like death. Another whiskey on the rocks." Joe moved away and shook his head as he went. "Warren. Warren, relax, man—she ain't going nowhere." He set Jess' order on the bar and waited as the bartender prepared his drink.

"Shut the door!" Warren pleaded, voice strained to its limit, brittle nails working a jagged chalkboard.

Jess looked away from Eli, staring into the abundant, shimmering void.

"Why is it pretty?" she asked.

"Pretty?" Warren laughed, breaking across the border to hysteria.

"The surface of death is a reflection of what we expect to find in it," Eli said.

"Then ... what's underneath?" Jess looked back at the dancing brightness. "Isn't ... isn't it Heaven?"

"If Heaven is cold fire that consumes flesh and bone," Eli raised his voice, pulling Jess' eyes back to him, "then that is Heaven."

Jess stared, confusion holding her in a tight, clammy embrace. That this situation made no sense did not deprive it of its reality; she felt it in her bones, just as she'd recognized the bartender's agelessness. Eli's odd injury, Warren's terror of what lay beyond Between's door, and even Joe's current, feigned disinterest—the bewhiskered man was now deep into his whiskey—all buffered the truth of what Jess saw with her own eyes ... preposterous, unprecedented, but still real.

Heaven ... Heaven would be where Jess' mother was, and Jess took one step closer to the white abyss before she relaxed her grip on the door's handle and turned away. A cry escaped her as the door clicked shut, smacking like a coffin's lid.

"Looks like we have another regular." Joe articulated with care and barely preceded the bartender's echo of his words, the measured music of her speech sounding melancholy and distant to Jess.

"Told you, Warren." Joe slapped the bar. "Barkeep, next round's on him."

Jess found Warren watching her, solemn. Eli nodded to Jess and walked away, his heavy steps fading as he went. Back to the kitchen, Jess supposed, her thoughts fuzzy and slow.

"What am I supposed to do?" she asked no-one in particular.

"Belly up to the bar and drink!" Joe roared, all apparent geniality. "What's in this cup of yours?"

Jess froze, hysteria rising in her as a delayed reaction, the realization that Lucas waited for her ... what Lucas was like when he had to wait ...

"Hey. Hey!" Warren scrambled to his feet and had his arm around Jess' shoulders in an instant, sending Jess into the chasm of her rising despair. She cringed away, and Warren stepped back, raising both hands.

"I'm not going to hurt you. You just ... you look like you should sit down. Sit down, have some water. Or some food?"

"She don't got to eat here," Joe groused. "Nobody got to eat here."

"Shut up, idiot," Warren spoke to Joe but locked eyes with Jess. The trembling that started when Warren touched her escalated, and Jess moved blindly back toward the bar, scrambling onto the nearest stool.

"Great, she's losing it. Like we need another of those."

"Shut up!" Warren repeated, raising his voice further. It was the proverbial straw, and Jess gave in to her sobs, lowering her head to the bar and pressing it against stable solidity of the wood there.

What am I supposed to do? What am I supposed to do?

"Bartender, an ice water. And a cold cloth, too."

"And another whiskey for my 'friend.'" Joe banged his glass on the bar and made Jess jump, popping up her head.

"Joe!"

"Fine, I'll sit with Sandman and leave you to your mothering."

Warren sighed, settling onto the stool next to Jess as Joe crushed his lifeless cigarette into the ashtray and stomped away. Warren glanced over his shoulder, and Jess followed his gaze. Joe chose the chair directly across from the slumped figure. In pointed opposition to the collapsed heap of a man facing him, Joe's back was straight and rigid; Warren sighed again, this time with palpable pain.

The bartender slid a glass of ice water into Jess' peripheral vision and she reached for it, willing the shaking to subside so she could drink. She managed a few sips before the bartender returned, this time with a small cloth bag, instantly reminding Jess of the sort of thing a heroine in an old movie would press against her head after a faint.

"For your eye." Warren's voice softened, and Jess couldn't look at him.

"I walked into a door," she said, delivering the obvious falsehood without enthusiasm.

"Of course." But Jess knew Warren didn't believe her. The agony of someone *knowing* rose up, slapping at Jess like a bird with razor-blade feathers.

She reached for the bag and placed it over her eye. Cooler than the bar's wooden surface by far, the bag emitted a soft scent—roses, Jess thought, though she hadn't smelled a rose since her mother's funeral. Her mind swerved away from the idea, dodging it like the gaping hole to a wounded heart that it was.

"It won't help, you know," Joe called from the back of the bar. "It'll never help here."

"It'll feel better with ice," Warren replied. He spoke evenly once more, with an edge of humor as if the sliver of a joke no one else knew constantly tickled his funny bone.

"What does he mean?" Jess asked, searching for something—anything—to take her out of the maelstrom of fear, disbelief, and confusion inside her head.

"As long as you're in Between, as far as we know, you don't change from how you came in. You don't age. You don't need to eat or drink. Bruises—injuries—they don't heal."

"But what about Eli's hand?"

Warren turned to the bar and picked up his drink.

"If you hurt yourself while you're here, it heals. And it heals fast."

Jess directed her good eye at Warren and stared as he took a sip of whiskey, imparting nonsense in lieu of believability. "I must have fallen. I must have fallen and hit my head and I'm dreaming all of this. All of you."

Warren grinned over the rim of his glass, and this time, it frightened Jess.

"Denial is a long way from acceptance, but it's a step on the path."

Jess shuttered herself from the bland pronouncement, shifting her body away from Warren and the rest of the bar.

"Denial," Warren said again, this time loud enough that Joe heard.

"To denial!" Joe responded.

Jess refused to look at them, but the ice swimming in their glasses, clinking against the edges as the beverages shifted and were received in communion, revealed that the distant toast happened regardless of her rejection.

She looked back at Warren, opened her mouth to speak ...

As if Warren waited precisely for her gaze, he whirled and threw his glass against the wall of names. It happened so fast that even as her body jerked in surprise, Jess could only watch it. She listened, held immobile by shock, as the glass fell in bits and pieces, shards and splinters. Warren grinned—wickedly, it seemed—and then dashed over and scooped up a handful of glass, clasping it tight in his fist.

"What are you doing?" His behavior alarmed Jess to the point of action at last. She abandoned the bag she'd been clutching in favor of the towel the bartender was using on the edge of the bar, snatching it up and rushing to Warren's side. Blood seeped between Warren's fingers; aghast, Jess knew that he purposefully ground the glass into his hand, fingers squeezing tight and shifting as he drove the spiky fragments deeper into his flesh.

As she tried to wrap the towel around his hand, he jerked away and opened his fist. Behind the pieces of glass sparkling like malevolent glitter, Jess saw skin knitting and binding, pushing the encroaching fragments out like an amoeba rejecting an alien invader, forming thick scars right underneath her stunned scrutiny.

"And just like that, it doesn't hurt anymore." Warren spoke triumphantly.

"To not hurting!" Joe sang out, even as Jess' eye ached, denying another supernatural incident with every pulsation.

In mere seconds, Warren's open palm healed, though a patchwork of shiny scar tissue remained. He flexed his hand experimentally, and met Jess' blank stare with a quirk of his brow.

"You get used to it. Eventually, you get used to all of it."

"But this is crazy!"

"That it is, girl." Joe appeared at Warren's side with a broom and dustpan. "Clean up your mess, dumbass."

"It's your turn next time," Warren told Joe as he took the broom.

"Yeah, yeah. All this time and you still twitch."

"How long ..." Jess began, and flinched as Warren slapped his newly-healed hand against the wall behind him.

Warren Wolford, 9/26/1972

"That's not possible. You've been here ... you're saying you've been here ... almost 50 years?"

"What does it take to convince kids these days?" Warren shook his head as he took the dustpan from Joe, who still waggled it at him.

"Don't know, dumbass."

"Where's my drink, idiot?"

"Get it yourself," Joe said without rancor, shuffling over to the bar.

Warren grinned at Jess and she realized her mouth was hanging open. She closed it.

"Go sit down. Ice your eye. You came in with that, so it's going to keep hurting. Lucky for you, this place rarely runs out of anything and it's never short of ice. It won't help much, but ... it's better than nothing."

And then Warren bent to clean the shattered, bloody fragments of glass and melting ice marring the floor. Left with no other option she could conceive, Jess moved to follow his suggestions.

Revelation

Time didn't mean anything when it stopped. Jess pressed the soft, scented ice bag against her head, sipped her water, and even picked at the burger Lucas would never receive. The burger grew cold and the bag, warm; when Jess set it down, the bartender took the bag away and brought it back—returning it with fresh ice, Jess supposed, though she couldn't say for certain as she wandered in her thoughts until utterly lost.

In a place with all the apparent time in the world, nothing existed to track it.

"What time is it?" She asked the question once, without thinking. Joe guffawed loudly in response; Warren only shook his head.

"Hey. Hey, what's-your-name?" Joe said now, and Jess peeked out from the ice bag—which wasn't doing her much good—to look at him.

"'Jessamy', she said," Warren told Joe before Jess could bring herself to respond.

"Jessamy. That's … a mouthful." Joe leaned back on his stool, as if considering. "So, Jessamy, you want to get your name on the wall before you forget what day you got here?"

"Why …" in spite of the lethargy that time's absence inspired in her, Jess was interested. "Why would I forget the day I got here?"

"Don't know." Joe shrugged his answer, like the question bothered him. "People forget things all the time."

All the time.

"Do people forget things here? More than ..." Jess wasn't sure how to refer to the world outside Between.

"Dates go fast," Warren said, his voice a soft counterpoint to Joe's. "Most other things stay. For a while, anyway."

"I ..." Jess looked at the wall and tried to imagine her name there. A new thought intervened, trampling all else in its urgency. "Wait. Wait! There's so many names ... only just the four—five— of us ... where ..." She stood up, almost toppling her stool in her haste. "Where are they?"

Joe smirked. "They got tired of waiting! Went out the door."

Jess froze, horrified.

"Out ... into ..."

Warren punched Joe on the shoulder.

"Some people go out into ... whatever it is they see, it's true. But most people stop seeing ... that. Eventually, they see what they left."

"What do you mean?"

Now Warren shrugged.

"They just stop seeing ... death ... and see the regular world again. So they go back to it. Literally, back to it. Bartender!" Warren drained the remains of his drink and rapped his glass against the bar. "Another."

The bartender was nowhere in sight, and Warren rapped his knuckles against the bar next.

"Here, the girl ain't drinking this." Joe grabbed the abandoned go-cup and eased it across the bar to Warren.

"Thanks." Warren nodded to Joe and to Jess, removing the cover and drinking with vigor, if not outright enthusiasm.

Jess looked back at the wall, wondering how many of the people marked there survived their time in Between ... and how many hadn't.

Light steps announced the bartender's return and Jess moved back over to the bar.

"New girl's not ready to get on the wall. But Warren needs another whiskey, and I'll take the dice."

The bartender quirked one eyebrow and produced a worn, lined cup from behind the bar, handing it to Joe before stepping back to the bottles to prepare Warren's drink.

"You play poker?" Joe asked Jess, rattling the dice in the cup. "Don't matter. We'll get Eli out here sometime and teach you— have a *real* game."

"Euchre would be better than poker," Warren opined.

"Euchre? Old man's game." Joe continued to shake the dice. "Call."

"Beats 'high-low' and if you count Between years, I'm almost 90."

"Girl's lying." Joe spared a disparaging glare for Jess. "Has to be lying. No way it's so long since Zane come in. Call!"

Warren shook his head elaborately.

"Low."

Joe ejected the dice from their container at last, silencing the sound that had begun to make Jess think of a crippled rattlesnake.

"Ten. Dumbass."

"Who's Zane?" Jess asked as Joe collected the dice and replaced them in the cup.

"Zane's upstairs," Warren said.

"Zane's always upstairs," Joe muttered. "So's her."

The bartender brought Warren's drink. He nodded to her, and she tipped her head slightly in response. The bartender looked over at Jess, inquiring without words, and Jess shook her head, flicking a gaze up at the worn ceiling tiles.

"There's an upstairs to this place?"

"Yeah." Joe resumed his agitation of the dice, wearing on Jess' already strained nerves.

"High," Warren said this time, and Joe promptly rolled a six.

"Dumbass, right?" Warren winked.

"Now that you got right, dumbass."

"Aren't there supposed to be more than two dice?" Jess asked.

Joe favored her with a raised brow, and then turned a smug smile to Warren.

"Suppose she thinks a deck of cards got more than 47, too!"

Warren shook his head, giving Jess an apologetic smile.

"Where are the stairs, then?"

Warren pointed down the dark hall at the back of the bar.

"Stairway on the left, bathrooms on the right," Warren waved. "Not that you'll need the bathroom now that you're a regular." He smiled, and it warmed his whole face. "We don't need to eat, we don't need to drink, and we don't need ... well, we don't need to 'go,' either."

"Or sleep. Or breathe," Joe added.

"You're kidding."

"Joe once held his breath for ... well, we think it was for a day at least, but it's hard to tell."

Jess shook her head.

"That's impossible."

"You see 'white death' out the door," Joe jabbed his finger, sharp opposition to Warren's gesture in both style and direction, "you watch Warren break glass in his fist and heal right up, but you don't think I can hold my breath for a day?"

"Well ..."

"It's all unbelievable," Warren said, placating. "But after you try it—after you see it for yourself—believing is all that you can do. Just hold your breath sometime, Jessamy, and you'll see. Let me roll, Joe."

"Nuh-uh, not until you call a seven right. You know the rules!"

"Your 'rules' I know, yes. But I never learned the real rules."

"My rules are the real rules."

"Idiot."

"Dumbass."

Their voices faded as Jess walked toward the hall, though the bickering continued unabated. When Jess spotted the indentation of the rising stairway, she glanced back. Joe and Warren each had one hand on the dice cup, intent on their argument, even though it seemed more like well-practiced script than improvisation.

The bartender, unblinkingly somber and polishing a glass that shone like a beacon in her hands, watched Jess. The look sliced through Jess as certainly as the shards had carved into Warren's hand, making the deep ache behind her eye seem like a paper cut by comparison.

Jess held the bartender's stare for a moment but she looked away first, of course. She hadn't the strength to try or the will to win against the enigmatic bartender with the angelic—if rarely used—voice.

As Jess began to mount the steep stairs, holding onto the shaky railing to her right as a courtesy, not a safeguard, the idea of the bartender as primordial stayed with her. It was absolute, not a musing, Jess thought, that the bartender was ancient. But this knowledge was esoteric—utterly impractical—as far as Jess could see.

The stairway bent at 90 degrees before Jess glimpsed the floor above. Though the shadows cast at the junction portended a better-lit second story, Between's lighting remained dim at best.

And all together, it held not a single candle to the brilliance Jess had seen outside the bar's front door.

She shuddered, hurrying up the remaining steps, and found herself at the end of a hallway with four offset doorways visible along its length. The three farthest doors were shut tight but the nearest stood open, with its doorway occupied.

The crouching woman in the open room's entrance wore a loose blouse and a long skirt. Her thick golden hair, streaked with gray, formed a halo around her head. She was watching something inside the room.

Jess hesitated by the stairwell.

"Hello?"

"Shh!" The woman's voice was raw, like Janis Joplin but without any lyrical quality. "Go away. Eclipse is scared."

"'Eclipse?'"

"I said, 'Shh!'" The woman raised her voice, then clamped both hands over her mouth. "She's back under the bed. I almost had her out."

"The black cat?" Jess kept her voice quiet this time and continued to hold her ground near the stairway.

"Black with white on her neck, yes. Eclipse. It's her name."

"Okay."

"This is my room." The woman stood. Her feet shuffled toward Jess and then away, in a jerky, unstable dance. "I can share, but not with you. With Eclipse."

"I don't want to bother you." And Jess didn't, particularly not in light of the woman's erratic movements. It looked something like withdrawal to Jess. "I'm ... new here. I just wanted to see the upstairs."

"What color is your death?" Intensity gushed from the woman's eyes when she looked at Jess, though she didn't look at anything for long. Her line of sight shifted again, now making Jess think of a bird, constantly alert.

"It ... it's white."

The woman nodded, as if this was as it should be, and seemed to settle from her former flightiness.

"Matches your aura," she said then, favoring Jess with a slightly longer stare. "Mine is bright colors and broken, like a smashed church window."

Jess shivered.

"This is my room," the woman said again, and this time, she pointed. "Mine and Eclipse's, if she wants to share. Zane's is all the way at the end. You can have one of the others."

"Nobody's in the others?"

"Nobody now. Drew went back to the regular world. Larry went to his death. It was black, but Larry didn't care. I guess he liked the dark."

Jess found her shiver had been premature and shuddered outright.

"Go on. I need to help Eclipse. She came to meet me first. Before you." The last two words were added with more vehemence than Jess could tolerate.

Jess rushed past the woman, hugging the wall opposite and glimpsing the plain room beyond the open door only briefly. She opened the next door, across the hall from the woman, and ducked inside, closing the door behind her as fast as she could after flicking on the lights.

The room appeared much the same as the one she'd just seen. Windowless, lit by two plain lamps—one with a tired lampshade listing to one side and the other a bare bulb only—the room held a bed and a desk. There were two doors in the far corner, which Jess investigated: one opened to a closet empty of everything but a lonely wire hanger, the other revealed a tiny bathroom with a toilet, sink, and standing shower stall.

Though the shower seemed inviting to Jess, even in its dingy state of half-cleanliness, she didn't linger in the claustrophobic bathroom. She lay down on the bed, atop the worn patchwork quilt there, and stared up at the watermarked ceiling, wondering why she wasn't more ... something.

Afraid? Disbelieving? Angry? Lost?

The thing was, if she felt anything, it was ... relief. And that, more than the incredible situation in which she found herself, scared Jess.

She lay there, awake and aware, vibrating with deep concern that she was almost comfortable here, almost at peace trapped by the white death waiting outside. It surely wasn't the right way to feel, though Jess couldn't imagine what someone should feel or do when confronted with such a situation.

Was anger appropriate? Who caused death to appear outside? Even the bartender, Jess felt, wasn't the source of Between's strangeness. If the bar's "regulars" did see different forms of death outside Between, their confinement would seem to be something of their own making, really.

It's my fault. This, like everything else.

A small voice in the back of Jess' mind—one which had long been silent—piped up then, offering a counterpoint to blame's omnipresent derision.

That's Lucas talking.

Once more, relief poured over Jess like a cool breeze on a crisp day: gentle, caressing, comforting.

Safe.

Whatever Jess could believe by reality's strength of presence, she considered herself and her baby to be safe now, here in this static place, this stagnant time. Whatever Between might be to anyone else, it was first and foremost protection to Jess. She remained on the bed—not sleeping, not moving, and for a long time, not breathing.

Joe was right. Anything related to the messiness of living outside seemed to be unnecessary in Between's bonds. Jess checked her wrist for a pulse and found nothing. Impossible, of course, but nevertheless true.

As far as Jess could tell, she was already dead.

Already dead.

Dead, in Between, with no time to track her absence, and ...

Jess gasped, sucking needless air into uncaring lungs.

What was it Warren said? About people going back ... something specific ...

"...they go back to it. *Literally,* **back** *to it.*"

"Literally!" Jess whispered the word aloud, realizing its significance with physical shock.

She flew from the room, past the other woman's now-shut door and down the stairs. She thundered over to the bar but she didn't gasp for breath. She didn't need to.

"Warren!" Jess managed, tormented by unfathomable confidence that she was right in this, too. "You said ... you said people go *back*, outside, when they leave. You mean ..."

Warren stared, his eyes pitying. And Joe, frowning sternly, answered.

"If you stop seeing death, you start seeing exactly what you left. Exactly what and exactly where and exactly when."

Jess gasped, again taking in air she didn't need for purpose she didn't have—perhaps never had. She fled the bar, returning to the room upstairs that was no longer the sanctuary she'd thought it.

Her life, as she'd left it, would simply wait until the day she exited Between, hovering like a vulture over road kill. Every blessed minute of reprieve in Between was forged not on heavenly

34

safety but on the hellish foundation of false security. Jess could leave the bar to join an immediate death, or could await a more violent one of no less surety at Lucas' hands.

This knowledge—this awful, painful awareness—broke Jess, skipping her over the intervening stages of grief like a rock across water. She dropped into the bottomless lake of depression and curled there, fetal position around the still and silent namesake life within her.

And she mourned.

Love

Knocking on the door behind her pulled Jess back into awareness of her surroundings some time later, but she couldn't force herself to sit up until she heard the door opening.

"Don't cry."

Jess turned and found the woman from the hallway watching her through the half-open door. The woman's hand, at first resting on the doorknob, began moving up and down as if she could not decide whether to hang onto the protrusion.

"Am I scaring the cat?" Jess scrubbed at her dry eyes, wincing when she brushed too hard against the bruised one.

"Eclipse. No. She's fine, sitting on top of the bed, like she should. Like you."

Jess met the woman's eyes, insight striking her as furiously as Lucas ever had.

"Am I scaring you?"

The hand near the doorknob became claw-like, gripping tightly, releasing furiously. The woman drew her hand up to her chest, touching the neckline of her blouse there. Tapping, pressing … again, Jess thought of a frightened songbird.

"A little."

"I'm sorry."

"It's okay. Can I come in?"

Jess wondered why anyone would want to come in to a room where sorrow veiled all the furnishings, including the human sort—wondered why she would let anyone come in, much less this particular person—but she nodded.

The woman extended her wavering hand.

"I'm Love. Love Hummingbird."

Bemused, Jess shook the offered hand, finding a surprisingly firm grip and returning it as best she could.

"Jess. Jessamy Buccholz."

"'Jessamy' sounds pretty. I would always use 'Jessamy'—not 'Jess'—if I were you. But I'm not you. You do what you like."

"Thanks," Jess said, addressing the first part of the short speech. She hoped this woman was glad to be who she was, quivering hands and all. Jess dropped her gaze to her own hands, staring at the motionless pulse points on her slim wrists. As silence stretched with elastic flexibility, she wondered if her heart would ever beat again.

"I don't think Eclipse wants to stay with me."

Jess tore her gaze from her limp arms and looked back at the woman—Love, or so she'd said, and Jess supposed no one could challenge a name here, even an obvious pseudonym.

Love stared toward the door. Jess followed her line of sight, and saw Eclipse regarding them both.

"I think she wants to stay with you."

Now why would she want do to that?

Jess found herself shaking her head.

"But she wants to, look."

Love slipped onto the bed, opposite yet next to Jess. She pointed and withdrew her treacherous hand twice, then three times, before speaking again. "In a place like this, you're lucky to have someone who wants to be with you. I know … I've been here a long time."

Jess looked at Love, and to her dismay, began choking on dry sobs.

"If cats make you sneeze outside, don't worry; that won't matter here."

Jess shook her head, cleared her throat.

"My mother had a cat. Ruthie. She died."

"Oh, poor kitty!"

"No, my mother died. Well, Ruthie died, too, I guess. They took her away."

Love stared, and Jess felt the accusation in those bright eyes. Or maybe Jess felt the accusation she'd always leveled at herself.

Rightfully so.

The moment of supposed judgment passed, slipping into the timelessness enveloping Between. Love set her hand atop Jess' and Jess was startled anew.

Love's hand did not shift this time.

"They took her away?"

Jess nodded, then tried to explain.

"When Mama died, Ruthie mostly stopped eating. She wouldn't eat hardly anything, not even the baby food Mama gave her as a treat. And Mama had been sick so long, we—I—lost the house. I let them take Ruthie, too. But I shouldn't have." Jess' words caught, trapped by grief. "I shouldn't have let them take her."

"If she stopped eating, she was ready to go. She didn't want to be without your mama."

Jess heard the emphasis on "be" and nodded again, though she didn't understand. As if she knew Jess missed her point, Love elaborated.

"None of us want to be. Not really, or we wouldn't get stuck in Between. Wouldn't see what we see."

"What?" Aghast, Jess, pulled her hand away from Love's.

"Well, that's what I think," Love said, raising her voice a little. Her hand began its shifty dance again, emphatic against the yellow square of the quilt onto which it had fallen when Jess moved.

Like her own unknowable knowns of late, Jess knew that not wanting to believe Love's theory didn't make the other woman's idea less accurate. Before she could think of anything to say, Eclipse jumped onto the bed and stepped between Jess and Love, bumping up against Jess' knee just as Ruthie had done.

Just as Ruthie had done when she'd wanted to live.

"She likes you," Love said, mournful. "I wish she liked me more, but you can't argue with cats. Cats know what they like. Cats know who they like."

As if taking her prompt, Eclipse began to purr. The small sound amplified in the quiet space where not even breathing existed to compete with it.

Mesmerized, Jess stroked the cat from head to tail, and then offered her fingers to Eclipse to sniff, as she'd done at the bar's entryway.

And then she realized … whatever else the cat was doing, Eclipse wasn't breathing, either.

"She's …" Jess raised horrified eyes to Love, and found the woman nodding.

"She sees death outside, too."

"How … how can this be happening?"

Love sighed, and Eclipse pressed against Jess' hand, prompting her to resume petting the cat.

"How, why … are you someone who cares about that? I'm a who and what person."

"What?"

"Yes, that's right. I care about who people are and what happens to them. Not how and why. How and why take too much thinking, have too much space around them. I get lost in that space and I don't understand. I talk to people about who and what and then I understand. I don't want waste time with how and why. Which I can't understand a lot, anyway."

As Love explained it, it seemed a sufficiently coherent philosophy. Jess felt badly that all she could muster only a single syllable in response.

"Oh."

"We had people here who cared about how and why. There was a ... fizz ... fizz ... it sounded like the other word for a doctor. He talked about worms and holes, times and spaces. I told him there isn't time here, but he said something about singing. I think it was singing. I didn't understand. I told him he has to care about who-what, at least for a while, but he only cared about how-why."

Jess thought she knew, but she still asked the question.

"He went to his death?"

Love nodded, sage.

"He went to his death. His name was Robert Dickinson and he didn't understand, either, even though he thought he did. So he went to his death. His was gray. He's the only one I know who said it was gray. Gray with strips of... whatever he said they were. It sounded like rainbows to me."

"Rainbows," Jess echoed. She'd found her "white death" pretty; how much more beautiful would rainbowed death appear?

And though she thought "how" and "why" were questions worth asking—and couldn't imagine not asking them—Jess understood with excruciating intensity why Love preferred "who" and "what."

Or in any case, why she preferred them here and now.

Jess chose her next words carefully.

"What made you come in Between?"

Love looked up from Eclipse, who Jess still stroked lightly, and the smile that spread across her face transformed the worn features, sparkling up through her washed-out eyes.

"I followed Joe. He's my brother. He told me to wait in the car but I saw he was mad and I wanted to tell him not to be mad, so when he didn't come back, I followed him in. And then we were both trapped, him by blackness and me by broken colors ... they cover everything, from the ground I can't see all the way up to the sky, if there is a sky anymore."

Love's smile faded as she spoke and this time, Jess covered Love's hand with hers.

The other woman moved her hand away quickly, but Jess' touch seemed to restore Love's fragile happiness—however temporarily—and Jess felt a rush of gratitude.

She wasn't alone. She'd been alone with Lucas ever since the first time he'd struck her, but she wasn't alone now.

"What made you come in Between?" Love asked, and Jess took a deep breath.

"Lucas did. He wanted something to eat and drink. And he told me to go get it for him."

Love looked straight into Jess' injured eye.

"He hit you." Though it wasn't a question, Jess answered it when she turned from both the Love and the purring cat. "He shouldn't do that. That's wrong."

"I know."

"But you stay with him."

Jess drew an unnecessary breath, more out of habit than anything, she supposed, and chose to affirm again.

"Yes."

Love placed her trepidant hand on Jess' shoulder this time—touching, moving away, touching again.

"Leaving is hard. If it was easy, I guess none of the bad men would have any women to hit, and they'd just have to hit each other."

It was an oddly satisfying thought, and Jess smiled at Love.

"Why was Joe mad at you?"

"Why!" Love clamped her lips tight over the word.

"I mean, what made him angry?"

"I did. But he shouldn't be mad at me. I can't help the way I am. The doctors tried to help but the medicine cost too much … so I drank. I drank and I drank and I drank. I drank too much, so Joe was mad. I don't drink here. I've never had a single drink in Between. Now it's Joe who drinks too much, not that it helps. You can't drink things away in Between."

"You can't drink things away outside Between, either," Jess whispered.

"No," Love agreed, though she didn't need to—and from what Jess could tell, didn't want to. "But you can drink them away for a little while out there. In here, you drink, but you never get drunk. Warren told me."

"Then why … what makes them drink?"

Love shrugged.

"It's something to do."

Jess thought about that.

"What do you do here?"

"I talk to people. The ones who come upstairs. It's easier to talk upstairs. Most times, only regulars come up here."

"Regulars … the ones like us? The ones who see death outside?"

"Yes. The others come and go when they want. They stay in time and place—they don't have spaces in between."

In between or in Between? Jess wondered, and then decided it didn't matter.

Love sighed in the quiet that fell anew, a heavy blanket covering them both with its weight. Eclipse curled into a ball and licked one paw. It made Jess think a hot shower might feel good, even in a small and somewhat grimy shower stall.

"Wait. You said ... the people who aren't regulars, they 'stay in time *and place*.'"

"Yes."

"What do you mean?"

"I came in Between on November 11, 1994, just outside Las Vegas."

"Las Vegas! But we were in Wyoming, out in the Basin somewhere ... "

Love nodded, but Jess wanted to shake her head, hard, like a wet dog would. She wanted to throw off the drowning, cloying dampness of the insanity endeavoring to swallow her whole.

"This can't be real!"

Jess didn't think she'd said it out loud. Close to pure panic, she barely recognized thought at all; instead, she was caught up in a crashing wave of pure emotion, one that pounded her onto stark terrain so foreign it might as well have been on another planet.

And maybe, just maybe, it was.

"Ouch!"

Jess jumped up and away from Love, who had pinched her hand, hard. The abrupt and violent motion sent Eclipse surging from the room via the unique levitation only frightened felines achieve.

"Did that wake you up? No. No, it didn't, because you're not dreaming. Now I have to go find Eclipse and calm her down all over."

"Would I wake up if I was pure crazy?" Hysteria gave Jess' voice a cutting edge and granted her the power to project it like a weapon.

"You're not crazy. You're just in Between."

"I ..." Jess looked down at her hand, which had—an instant ago—sported the bright mark of Love's nails, and found it smooth and unblemished. Her eye started aching again and as she tried to will herself not to sob, Love moved to exit the room.

But she stopped in the doorway, nodding to another person passing by there.

"Zane. We got a new girl. She thinks she's crazy. Want to meet her?"

A thin young man peered past Love, shaking his head. Jess caught a glimpse of brilliant blue eyes underneath a shaggy head of hair. Those eyes met Jess' when the hair's movement permitted but there was no change in the purpose behind them, no registration of Jess as a deterrent to whatever mission this man was on.

"Not now," he said, solidifying Jess' impression. He walked past Love, and Jess noticed his hand slapping rhythmically against his thigh, steady as a metronome. The cadent sound of Zane's hand could not outdo the weight of his tread—a heavier noise than his slight body seemed capable of generating—as he descended the stairs.

"Zane looks outside every day. Well, he thinks it's every day. What's a day in Between, anyway? I need to find Eclipse."

Then Love left too, closing Jess' door softly behind her.

History

J ess didn't know how long she stood there, alone and
motionless in the room above Between that had somehow
become hers for as long as she chose to avoid her waiting
death. She heard Zane come back upstairs, his feet falling even
heavier on his return, and she understood this meant he continued
to see his own, customized oblivion lurking outside.

She noticed Zane pause, ever so briefly, near her door—in
that tiny resting space, she imagined he put a hand on her door
before resuming his gloomy advance back to his own room. She
felt a surge of panic at her impression's clarity, but when she
walked over and touched the door, it remained reassuringly solid,
not the least bit diaphanous.

She shuddered.

And she decided with foolhardy determination that if
Between's doors and walls shifted to transparency, she would not
walk but would run out into her bright death, welcoming it. If
matter—the one thing that didn't seem to defy all known laws
here—began to disintegrate, too, there really would be no reason
to cling to this ... this ...

Jess still didn't believe it. She moved back from the door,
looking around her with the clutching despair that so frequently
stalks powerful fear. She felt for her non-existent pulse, first on her
wrist and then on her neck, and next pressed her hand against the
frozen fetus inside her, thinking of it abstractly for perhaps the first
time.

This baby would never have the slightest chance of life, Lucas or no Lucas, if Jess didn't find her way out of Between alive. The potent realization grounded her, restoring her mind's gravity, pulling her out of the unbalanced, swirling vortex.

This wasn't just about her. She had someone else to live for again.

Jess dug for the barrette in her pocket and held it close to her face. Along the tarnished metal edge, she could see a hint of her reflection, marred by Lucas' fist. Though the pain of impact remained with her always in Between, it swelled now, as if thriving on her recognition. It occurred to Jess that since attempting to hide the injury was getting her nowhere, perhaps exposing it would lessen some of its Between-enchanted potency.

She clipped her hair back, sparking the smallest remnant of the defiance she'd had in abundance as a child—the daring she'd started to lose when her mother got sick, and which Lucas smothered entirely.

Funny how this fire needed not air to resurrect, but Between's dead space instead.

Not that Jess had any real expectation of surviving here, since she was all but deceased herself. She moved back to the bed, sinking down onto it and curling atop the covers as she'd done before Love's knock. Recalling the scene, and the fact that her meltdown had drawn Love into her room, Jess straightened, and sat back up.

She didn't know what she should do here, but she had already established crying by herself as a singularly bad idea.

Clinging to the vestiges of her fast-fading resolve, Jess went to the door and opened it. The hallway was empty, the other doors shut tight except for Love's, which stood slightly ajar. Jess considered her options: Love was undoubtedly seeing to Eclipse's comfort, and Zane ... well, she didn't really know Zane yet.

Yet?

She couldn't possibly be thinking of getting to know Zane—or Warren or Joe, either—any better. Why, Lucas would be so enraged, he ...

Standing there, her hand on the doorknob, Jess felt sudden lightness. Between was a prison, yes, but as much as it confined her, it also offered reprieve. However temporary this odd respite might prove to be, Lucas wasn't here now. And he'd never know how much she talked to any of the men here, or have anything to say about it.

The rash thought brought a smile to Jess' lips, and while it wasn't a large expression by any means, it exercised muscles which had scarcely performed such a workout in almost two years. Jess still smiled as she pulled the door closed and headed purposefully toward the stairs.

Descending, Jess heard the new arrival before she saw her. The woman's high-pitched voice was cringe-worthy, and she enhanced its power with volume.

"Is everyone in this bar deaf? Or are you all just dumb, like your bartender?"

"She asked you what you wanted to drink," Warren pointed out as Jess stepped out of the stairwell. He raised his glass to Jess as she drew near.

"Look who's back!"

The woman standing too-close beside Warren turned, and Jess found her just as jarring to look at as to hear. The new woman wore garish makeup and brightly-colored clothes that featured a paucity of fabric.

"So?" The woman continued to speak loudly. "Are you?" She looked expectantly at Jess, waiting for her answer.

"Am I what?"

The woman heaved a dramatic sigh and took a long drag off the cigarette she held, advancing to blow its smoke directly into

Jess' face. Jess almost coughed before she remembered: smoke wouldn't affect her here.

"Are you all deaf, or are you just stupid?"

Jess shrugged, and heard a loud laugh behind her. She looked, and found Joe coming down the hall, presumably from the superfluous bathroom there.

"That's telling her," he said, stopping short of the decidedly un-merry group at the bar. "Barkeep!" He pounded the bar once, though the bartender stood nearby, watching the scene. "Whiskey."

"I'll have a whiskey, too." The new arrival closed back in on Warren, leaning across him to flick her cigarette into an ashtray. Her strategic movement brought her breasts close to boiling over their flimsy covering, judging by the path Warren's eyes tracked.

"Ain't a regular," Joe said to Jess as the bartender poured the requested whiskey.

Please, not a regular!

Joe winked, as if Jess had spoken aloud.

"Not even pool or darts? What kind of place are you running here?" the obstreperous woman demanded, taking her whiskey from the bartender and sucking down a long draught. "And why," the woman went on, slamming her drink down onto the bar so forcefully that some of the remaining alcohol sloshed over the edge, "can't any of you hear that noise?"

"It just doesn't bother us, I guess." Warren's attempt at placation failed.

"It'd bother the dead," the stranger opined, prancing over to the bar's door and yanking it open. "Hey! Hey!"

Warren slid out of his seat and moved to Joe's far side, knuckles whitening around his glass.

"Shut the door!" Warren's cry edged on urgency, escalating with each word.

48

"Why?" The woman redirected her belligerence back to Warren, but only for a moment. "Hey! You little bastards knock it off right now; you'll light the whole canyon if you keep this up!"

Warren downed the remainder of his drink and signaled for another, keeping his face determinedly forward. Jess glanced at Joe, who looked toward the door, and then directed her own eyes at the brilliance she saw outside. She noticed the light cast sharp, brittle shadows off the woman who stood seemingly within it, barking vague threats and blatant obscenities at occupants of a world only she saw.

Or heard.

"Ain't a regular," Joe said again.

"Thank God." Warren muttered this under his breath, devout as a new postulant.

"Are you kidding me? No signal here, either?" Still standing in the open doorway, the woman conjured a cellular phone from somewhere within her unsubstantial garments.

"No, and having the door open won't help!" Warren shouted now.

"What's your fucking problem?" The woman waved the phone about, presumably looking for the signal she'd already determined to be absent.

"Yeah, Warren, what's your fuckin' problem?" Joe turned to Warren. "Zane was just here and you're fine."

Warren shot Joe a baleful glare, one made all the more grim by the blanched whiteness of his face.

"Zane's quick about it." He lowered his voice with obvious effort. "And I just hope she leaves by closing time. I don't want a repeat of when the drunk frat boys almost hauled me out of here."

Something flashed in Joe's eyes, something as close to terror as Jess had seen in the grizzly bear of a man.

"Okay, okay. But she's just one, and we got Eli now."

"I mean it ... I'll call the cops! It's barely June, for Chrissake!" The woman screeched, finally letting the door fall closed. "Who's Eli?"

"The cook," Warren answered.

"And bouncer," Joe added.

"This place doesn't look like it needs a bouncer. It needs a lot of things, don't get me wrong, but a bouncer doesn't seem like one of them. Excuse me, old man, but I was talking to Warren ..."

So saying, the woman batted her eyes at Warren and firmly inserted herself between him and Joe.

"Here, take my seat, *lady*." Joe infused his voice with sarcasm even as he removed himself from his barstool and waved with feigned chivalry.

"Thanks." The courteous response fell flat on delivery, since the woman had eyes only for Warren. "And where were we?" Her hand fell to Warren's where it rested on the bar—or where it held him up using the bar.

Joe rolled his eyes.

"What're you drinking, girl?"

"Water, I guess," Jess responded, following Joe's lead to a pair of seats near the door.

"Water? Why the hell ..." The question broke off, and Joe's eyes dropped, appraising Jess' belly. When his gaze moved back up, no question remained.

When he spoke again, Joe's tone moderated, like sandpaper stripped of its grit.

"It don't do nothing to you in Between. Drinking."

Jess nodded.

"I know."

Joe frowned, less from disappointment in her answer, Jess thought, than out of convention.

"Water," he finally told the bartender, who nodded in response.

The peacock woman next to Warren paused in preening him, sparing a disdainful glance for Jess.

"Live a little, girlfriend," she all but sang. "You might as well do it now. Your life ends when the kid's born."

Jess absorbed the contempt, the judgment. It seemed as if it passed right through her and not just because her life already ended, more or less, when she entered Between.

She'd heard many anti-child sentiments over the years but she'd understood them to be typically spawned on account of what proponents experienced with their own parents. Jess' mother taught an entirely different lesson; while Jess hadn't learned everything well, she had internalized the idea of babies as blessings so thoroughly that it was inseparable from fact.

Even under her current circumstances.

The bartender placed Jess' water squarely in front of her and Jess whispered her thanks. It earned a tip of the head from the bartender, though not a smile. Then the bartender walked toward the back of the bar.

"Where does she go?"

Joe shrugged, and drank deeply of his whiskey. Jess could smell the alcohol's fumes, hear the ice chattering in the glass with the disturbance of motion, but it seemed as far away as the Moon … surreal.

"She's never far off. Guy a while back thought maybe she was part of the place, like she come in and out of the walls or something. Who knows?"

Jess sipped her water and thought of her earlier fancy, of structure dissolving and becoming translucent. Was it something in Between that made people think this way? Or did the struggle to make sense of the senseless naturally inspire imagination?

"It doesn't make any sense," she said.

"Yeah. Why do the sluts go for Warren?"

"What? No, not that!"

"What then?" Joe didn't sound as if he cared, but Jess thought she saw a spark in the older man's eye when he spoke.

"Any of it. This place. Why ... none of it makes sense!"

Joe shifted his body toward Jess, enhancing the physical barrier between her and the other woman.

"Keep your voice down. You start talking about what Between's like for a regular when someone like that one can hear and crap really hits the fan. What Warren said ... "

Intensity electrified Joe's face now, filling each crag and brushing up against every whisker with taut sincerity, fervent warning. He set his glass on the bar and leaned closer.

"Bunch of college kids come in once and not one of them saw what we see. I was new then and started talking. Didn't think about it, just started talking about the color, the demons, the stuff we see." The volume drained from Joe's voice as he spoke, though he'd not been loud when he'd begun. "The drunkest one asked me who saw demons and when I told him Warren, he tried to get his boys to pull Warren out with them."

"Oh!"

Joe nodded, finishing his whiskey in a gulp that likely would have choked him outside Between.

"I just about killed Warren because I was new and stupid. Now we call Eli when someone's leaving and we don't talk about what this place's like if folks don't see with their own eyes."

Jess realized her hand around her glass tightened like a hawk's talon gripping prey and pulled it away, wiping condensation on her pants. The flatness of her pocket reminded her that her mother's barrette was in her hair, which made her think of her eye, which promptly started to throb.

Again, Joe seemed to follow Jess' thoughts.

"Eli can teach you to fight."

"What?"

"Fiiiiight." Joe drew out the word as if Jess simply failed to understand its meaning. "Fight back."

"Fight back? I couldn't."

"You should. Any man hits a woman, bastard should get hit back."

"But ..." Jess couldn't find any words worth speaking. Every platitude she recited, every excuse Lucas ever gave ... they were all lies. She'd always known, but since she'd lost the last baby—the one she'd named Madeline in her mind, after her mother—Jess felt deserving of each strike because she hadn't managed to save her child.

She had to save this one. Somehow.

Settlers

Jess never learned the peacock woman's name. The woman left Between without incident though not without annoyance, crooning and pleading for Warren to come home with her right down to her last few seconds in the bar.

No one—not even Warren—seemed sorry about her eventual exit.

"About time," Joe groused when the door clicked shut, muffling the sound of the woman's voice. After she'd cooed her last cajoling plea to Warren, she'd opened the door and gone right back to shouting, turning her attentions to the parties unknown who were lighting unsanctioned fireworks in her part of the real world.

The shouts stopped the instant she crossed Between's threshold.

Jess sighed, hopping off her bar stool to stand. Not that her legs cramped or her back ached.

She was just bored.

Joe nodded to Jess and moved to rejoin Warren.

"For the love of Pete! She was loud."

"But she had those ... uhh, those ... colors ..." Warren fumbled, awkwardly altering his statement as he caught Jess' eye. He looked so uncomfortable, she had to smile.

"Real big colors." Joe slathered sarcasm over the poor substitution. "Take an eye out with those colors."

Warren favored Joe with a daunting frown, which started the other man laughing so hard that he nearly spilled his drink.

"How can you keep drinking like that?" Jess realized when the words were out how brash the question sounded. "I mean ..." Faced with Joe's and Warren's blank stares, she floundered. "I mean, don't you have a ... a crazy bar tab?"

"What else are we gonna do? Anyways, Warren's loaded." Joe elbowed Warren and winked at Jess.

"Shut up, idiot." Warren swiveled in his seat to face Jess. "When you become a regular, you can keeping getting your last order, whatever it was, even if you're out of money. Think of it as free refills for regulars."

Joe held up his drink as Warren spoke, rattling the cubes with quick tilting of the glass, and grinning unrepentantly.

"Got to pick smokes off those what leave them behind, but I get whiskey forever."

"But ... you were going to order for me ... before ..."

Joe shrugged.

"I might've asked you what you wanted, but I wasn't gonna pay for it. Barkeep knows I'm broke. Warren's holding out, though; don't let him tell you nothing else."

Jess couldn't think of a witty reply, but she did request another water when Joe ordered his next whiskey.

Warren turned back to Joe.

"It's not even good whiskey. You should've at least gotten a decent brand."

"And leave old Jim Beam alone? Never."

"Idiot."

"Dumbass."

"Wait!" Jess stepped closer to the bickering pair. "How can this place not run out of drinks?"

Warren sighed.

"I'm beginning to think Love's got a point about how and why."

"Her name's Iris," Joe bit out.

"Like it matters." Warren matched Joe's tone exactly. Joe glared over the rim of his whiskey and then set the glass down with a bang. He scrounged a cigarette from the mangled pack lying on the bar and lit it as Warren watched.

Warren inclined his head toward Jess, though the hunch of his shoulders did not lift this time.

"She," and his eyes led Jess' to the bartender, "gets supplies every now and then. There's a man who makes deliveries. I don't think it's ever alcohol, though. I've never seen a bottle's level go down, not in all my time here. Not even the whiskey."

"But ... but if the bar moves ..."

"Delivery guy talks even less than the barkeep, but he's got the same voice," Joe offered. "Magic-like, I mean."

"Oh," Jess said, as if that explained everything. And perhaps it did. "So ... they ..." She lowered her voice, glancing toward the bartender and back to Warren and Joe.

"She don't care what we talk about." Joe raised his voice. "Her and the delivery guy, they're running this place, I know it. Maybe they make us see what we see, maybe they don't. Still trapped us, some way or another."

Warren nodded. The bartender, when Jess looked back to her, remained apparently absorbed in polishing the glass she held.

"It doesn't make any sense!" Jess' voice took flight with her confusion, high-pitched and brittle.

"So?" Joe raised one bushy brow along with his drink, and then lowered both, a counterpoint to Jess' hysteria, which continued to escalate.

Jess knew herself to be no poker player, but she didn't want to wear her every emotion as the peacock woman costumed herself in colors. She fought to restrain her spiking fear.

"Whatever makes sense anyways?" Jess latched onto the tenuous security of Joe's monotone speech, noticing how his eyes didn't reflect the blandness of his voice. His eyes drilled into hers, into her. "Does being alive make sense? Maybe it makes sense to know you're gonna die and you got to live your life with knowing it? Does little kids starving to death make sense or maybe people going crazy makes sense, or how about 'men' beating women—that make sense?"

"Joe ..." Warren spoke softly, as if he didn't have the strength to cut through the spell Joe wove.

"Don't!" Jess cried. "That's not fair!"

"Exactly. Don't none of it make sense and it ain't fair, neither. Not fair how some walk in and out of the bar and don't see death waiting for them, even though it is—even when they don't see it like we do. Not one thing in Between makes sense and it ain't fair, and way I figure, that makes it fit with the rest of life."

"But ..."

"But what?" Launched and predatory, Joe's voice now soared. Peripherally, Jess saw Eli's face as the big man bent his head to peer through the window behind the bar.

"Joe."

"What?" Joe's neck would have cracked, if it could, with the rapid-fire turn he forced on it as he traded his line of sight with Jess for one with Eli.

"Joe's riled up, that's all." Warren laid a hand on Joe's shoulder.

Joe shrugged it away.

"People need time, Joe."

"Time, we got," Joe bit out, and Jess sank onto the nearest bar stool, relieved that Joe kept looking at Eli. Her hands shook, and she tucked them into her pockets, searching for the barrette she'd forgotten she'd placed in her hair. "Time, we all got. For now."

Eli spoke, his voice as level and worn as the bar.

"Jessamy's path is not your path."

"Eli, nobody got a path here. Nobody walking nowhere; we're all stuck!"

"Jessamy," and the realization that her name sounded beautiful when Eli said it felt caressing to Jess, "does not see the death you see. She does not feel what you feel. That is the path I mean."

And you know it. The unspoken chastisement hovered in the air like smoke on a cold and still day.

Eli nodded and turned away as the absence of spoken words following his own stretched, pervasive and thorough. Jess could hear the slightest squeak as the bartender continued to scrub the glass she held. Eventually, Eli's heavy footsteps punctuated the quiet, and the bartender set one glass down and picked up another. Warren swirled the ice in his drink, and Jess tapped her fingers lightly against the barrette in her hair.

A muscle in Joe's jaw pulsed as he and Jess resumed staring at each other. This time, Joe's gaze lacked the intensity suffusing it earlier. Jess forced a blink to break the spell and it worked—Joe looked away.

"Buy you a drink?" Jess said then, her voice cracking only a little.

Genuine confusion coated Joe's voice, knit into the wrinkles that deepened across his whiskered face.

"What?"

Warren grinned and slapped Joe on the back.

"Lady's offering to buy you something better than that swill you've been drowning yourself in, Joe. Can't imagine why she'd waste her money on you, but there it is."

Jess wasn't sure what drove her, either, but the smile quirking Joe's lips proved that at least some of her instincts were still good.

"I like old Jim Beam here," Joe said. "Wouldn't part with him for all the wax on the bottle Warren keeps pointing me at."

Warren snorted.

"Of course not. Because you're an idiot."

"Shut your hole, dumbass." Joe delivered his line without inflection and signaled the bartender. "I'll take the dice."

Time continued its meaningless plodding. Had she been able to measure its pace against goalposts that weren't an eternity away, Jess would have said she spent the rest of the night playing dice.

"I think she's got the rules down," Warren said. "Your version of the rules, anyway." He winked at Jess behind Joe's back.

"Rules, shmules. Like you know better."

"If this place had a rulebook, at least ..."

"Yeah, and if it had steaks instead of burgers."

Warren frowned.

"What?"

"What-what?" Joe lifted his head then, sliding the cup of dice back to the bartender. She whisked it away, tucking it underneath the bar.

"If this place had steaks instead of burgers, what?"

"We'd eat better, that's what."

"Idiot." Warren slapped the bar with his hand, making Jess jump. Her movement drew Joe's attention, halting his response to Warren and furrowing his bushy brows. And Jess steeled herself for whatever blow she was about to receive.

She used to wish Lucas used words more than his fists, believing the old adage about "sticks and stones." But she'd already learned Joe could throw words as effectively as Lucas threw punches. And the words embedded themselves, festering, in a way that none of Lucas' blows had ever done.

Except the one that took her first child. And the one currently gracing her face.

59

Jess realized she'd raised her hand to the aching spot around her eye and brought it back down.

"Nobody's gonna hurt you here, girl." At Joe's rough-edged words, Jess felt her face crumple in spite of the fact that her eyes were currently incapable of leaking tears. "Aw, don't do that. Barkeep—napkin!"

The bartender promptly produced a cloth napkin and held it out to Joe, who pointed at Jess. Jess, who hadn't seen a cloth napkin since the church ladies hosted a luncheon following her mother's funeral, lowered her head in a pointless attempt to hide her pain.

She fumbled for the napkin and pressed it like a shield over her face. And she gave in to the sorrow welling out, forcing its way through all the cracks wrought in her soul since her mother's death, since Lucas' fists, and since she'd entered Between.

Even tearlessly, her sobs wrought a release of sorts.

After a while, Jess became aware of someone awkwardly rubbing her back, a gentle pressure that faded in and out just below her neck. She couldn't believe it was Joe, even though she'd been sitting next to him while they played dice, so she peeked over the curtain of the napkin.

Joe was indeed her comforter, and he looked uncomfortable—in fact, he looked like he was in pain.

And just like that, Jess found giggles squeezing out between her dry sobs. Joe froze, staring, and Warren leaned around Joe to watch the spectacle.

"Women!" Joe retrieved his hand and rubbed it against his pants as if he'd gotten dirty.

"Oh, I'm s-s-s-sorry. I r-r-really am," Jess choked out, surprising herself by catching Joe's arm just above the wrist. She released him just as quickly, and busied herself with the napkin, drying her already-dry face—habit proving more powerful than the vagaries of supernatural reality. She winced when she brushed too hard against her sempiternal bruise.

"Women," Warren echoed, in a tone much more amused than Joe's.

"It's just ... this is crazy. It got to me."

"It gets to all of us," Warren said. "That's why we keep drinking."

"If you're saying I'd bust out like that," and Joe jerked his head in Jess' direction, "if I didn't drink, you're fuller of crap than I thought."

"Sure. Idiot."

"Dumbass!"

The chorus set Jess off again, this time, tipping her fully into laughter's terrain. She was grateful to leave the badlands of misery behind, if only for a little while. Although ...

"Bartender?" Jess called, and the woman abandoned her incessant cleaning, favoring Jess with her even, unblinking stare. "Can I have a bag of ice please?"

After the briefest pause, the bartender gave a sharp dip of her chin and moved away in her elegant, eerie glide. When she returned with the ice, she set it gently on the bar in front of Jess.

"Thank you," Jess said.

"You are welcome." The music of the bartender's short sentence did not fail to bring a pleasant chill to the back of Jess' neck.

"For the love of Pete!" Joe exclaimed. "You got her to talk again."

Jess, engaged in positioning the ice against her bruise, paused and frowned at Joe. When Joe ignored her, Warren explained.

"She doesn't speak often, and she only ever says five things." Warren began to tick them off on his fingers. "'What will it be,'

'You are welcome,' 'Looks like we have another regular,' 'Time for you to go,' and ... wait, what's the other one, Joe?"

"You're kidding."

"'You're kidding?'" Jess repeated, unable to imagine the bartender using that phrase.

"No, he means ... oh. Of course." Warren shook his head, raising his hand with the pinky finger still extended, awaiting the final phrase. "'Thank you for visiting Between.' She only says that when a regular leaves."

"She don't have much chance to say that."

"You could hear her say, 'You're welcome' more often if you'd just ..." Jess began, but Joe cut her off.

"Nuh-uh. She'd say, 'You are welcome,' not 'You're welcome.' And it don't matter what we do; she don't talk to the two of us no more."

The innocuous statement, delivered as simple fact, made Jess sit a little straighter. She felt as if the air gained electricity, like lightning was about to strike.

"Why doesn't she talk to you anymore?"

Warren smiled, but it was a grim effort, and Joe looked down into his glass. Just when Jess thought neither man would answer, Warren did.

"Maybe we've just overstayed our welcome."

Depositions

J ess laid on the bed, one hand absently stroking Eclipse,
who'd slipped out of Love's room when she heard Jess
open the door to hers. The cat purred, a sound that made
Jess sleepy as a child. The soothing component of the purr—and
its underlying summons of sweet rest—hid underneath impotent
longing as sleep remained an impossible dream in Between.

Jess pretended for a bit, lying there with her eyes shut. First,
she shut them too tight and the pull on her facial muscles made her
bruise throb instead of simply ache. After that, she tried to keep
her face relaxed, but there was too much to think about and an
even greater surplus to see behind her closed lids.

How had she never considered the human eyelid, a fragile
surface incapable of shutting out all light, even for sleep? How had
she not noticed the patterns that appeared behind her lids, or
observed that shutting her eyes didn't lead to true darkness? Like
water heating in a black pot, the illusion of movement under her
closed eyelids mesmerized Jess, shifting and reshaping in
kaleidoscope shades of nothing.

Eclipse continued to purr, and Jess supposed the situation was
better for the cat. The cat wasn't worried about what would
happen when she left this place, about the fact that she wasn't
really alive at present. The cat had no cause to reflect on her life or
the static absence of aliveness existing in Between. Eclipse felt safe
now and that made her happy.

To judge by the constant vibration she produced, at any rate.

That was something good about being a cat, Jess decided. She didn't imagine she had any chance of emulating the furry creature who had taken such a determined liking to her, but she could keep petting her.

So Jess continued to caress Eclipse and Eclipse kept vibrating her appreciation. And the blending blackness with almost-purple undertones and not-quite-gray highlights continued to churn, starting somewhere deep within Jess' brain and ending at the peripheral screen of her eyelids.

Time—or was it timelessness?—dragged on, with precious little to fill it. Jess thought about praying but after thinking of things from Eclipse's perspective, she figured there really wasn't anything else she needed.

Except, perhaps, peace.

In all the times she'd wished herself away from Lucas, Jess never thought peace could possibly be lacking in such freedom. Temporary though her intermission in Between might be, it certainly felt permanent.

It also felt surprisingly unsatisfying.

The sound of a door opening and closing down the hall intruded into Jess' small world and though Eclipse continued her droning purr, Jess stilled her hand. Then she heard Zane slapping his own hand against his leg as he'd done the first time she saw him. The soft sound increased in volume, along with Zane's dragging footsteps as he moved down the hall. The noise decreased as he approached the stairs.

Jess noted the regularity of the sound Zane's hand made before Eclipse nudged Jess into her own rhythmic motion again. As she resumed petting the cat, it seemed to Jess that Zane kept time to a slow tune.

*Or maybe he just kept **time**?*

Jess sat up with a start and Eclipse voiced her disapproval with a single, disgruntled meow. When Jess remained frozen, Eclipse stalked from the bed and the room, slipping out the crack in the door, tail flicking in agitation.

After Eclipse's departure, Jess made her own way to the door. She wasn't thinking of ambushing Zane on his return so much as of confirming her suspicion about what he was doing. She started the count her mother taught her when she was too young to know her age, too scared of thunder to understand its relationship to lightning, and too much of both to realize lightning was what deserved her fear.

"One one-thousand, two one-thousand, three one-thousand, four one-thousand ..." she whispered, and then changed to tapping one finger against the barrette nestled in her hair. It was slightly askew from her time lying on the bed, but she didn't want to break the rhythm she established to correct its alignment.

And as Zane's footsteps heralded his re-approach, Jess found her pattern synchronized with Zane's quite well, though she was not exactly on his beat.

He's counting seconds.

She opened her door fully as Zane trudged past.

"Why are you doing that?" she demanded, prompting Love to call out from her room.

"Ugh. Not 'why' again."

"Zane!" In a burst of curiosity she didn't realize she could muster after her years with Lucas, Jess scurried up beside Zane as he reached his door. She caught herself before she grabbed his metronome hand, clasping both her own together to still the urge.

"What?" He stood there, motionless from the top of his shaggy head to the tips of his sneaker-shod feet, staring at the door before him. Perfectly still, except for his hand, pacing the passage of time that otherwise had no markers, meaning, or discernable purpose.

"Why are you keeping time here?"

"No more why." Love's voice sounded louder and Jess turned to see the woman's head shaking in the widened gap of her open door. Love pulled back, then popped out, still voicing her denial with her head's movement. "Why isn't important. And quit scaring Eclipse."

"I'm sorry," Jess said, and then looked back at Zane. "But it's important to me."

He looked at her now and those blue eyes seemed bottomless, as if he stared out of the pits of hell Warren saw. In the blankness of Zane's gaze, Jess had the distinct impression that he made the demons who kept him captive.

Jess held Zane's clear, empty stare.

"It's my sentence," he said finally. His words came out with unnatural regularity, paced to the beat of his hand.

"What?" Behind them, Jess heard Love heave a relieved sigh and her feet shuffled away.

Zane's eyes drilled into Jess' with the fierceness of necessity, as if by this strength alone he could bring himself to speak. After another extended silence, he did.

"It's my sentence. My sentence for killing the man."

Jess gasped, hands flying up to her mouth, eyes fluttering shut as if to deny the words Zane spoke. And as she severed their visual connection, Zane opened his door and shut it behind him. The wooden surfaces smashed together, sealing with a harsh report.

Stuck in a place between horror and fascination, Jess was not so befuddled that she didn't start anew at the sharpness of the sound. In the subsequent quiet, she could hear Zane there on the other side of the door, marking time with his hand against his thigh, increasing the volume of the tattoo as if his own agitation burned through him.

Jess stayed in place until her confusion abated somewhat, until she felt that lowering her hands and opening her eyes wouldn't hurt, somehow. Or hurt more? The throbbing at her temple reminded her Zane wasn't alone in pain and she frowned, wondering if the pulsation of her bruise was her own way of tracking time.

Of marking her own sentence.

A ridiculous thought on the surface, the notion caught Jess up like a wave with a deceptive and powerful undertow, dragging her down. She slid along the wall next to Zane's door, settling at the bottom with a thump and her hands made their way up to her face again. She covered as much of her head as she could, fingers stretching out, lifeless muscles taut.

It occurred to Jess that staying with Lucas was almost as good as attempting suicide. Worse, now that she was pregnant, it was almost like murder. What did they call it on television?

"Manslaughter."

She whispered the word aloud and it came out clearly—her hands shielded her visage but failed to stifle her voice.

This was something else she'd never considered. Perhaps something she never could have thought while caught up in the initial thrall of Lucas' attention and later trapped by the tales he spun about her dependence on him. The most terrible part, Jess suspected, was that it was all true ... from the fragile beginning when she'd been too innocent to see through Lucas' shiny facade, to the awful currency when she'd been too battered to escape.

But she had responsibility now, to her child as well as to herself. She had to find a way out: out of Between, and out of Lucas' deathly grip.

She couldn't keep pacing the passage of non-existent time the way Zane did. Couldn't let her bruise's pulsation—how unjust that it could pound on like it did, with no heartbeat to power it—track a sentence she hadn't truly earned.

"Meow?"

It sounded like a question, and Jess turned toward its source. Eclipse stood by Jess' door, staring at Jess.

"She wants you." Love spoke, and Jess redirected her line of sight. Love peeked in and out of her door, as she'd done earlier. Her tone—and recurrent expression—were matter-of-fact, and Jess wondered at her acceptance of situations she clearly didn't enjoy.

"I don't know ..." Jess began, but she stopped before uttering the anathema 'why.'

Love smiled into the silence, and Jess smiled back.

"Why doesn't matter. She knows. So it doesn't matter if you don't. You see."

Jess nodded, partly because Love seemed sure Jess understood, and partly because Jess began to believe that she did.

"You'd better go with her." Love nodded to Eclipse, who rubbed her cheek against the frame of Jess' door.

Jess nodded, and slowly stood. Then she looked from Eclipse to Love.

"Do you want to come, too? Pet Eclipse for a while?"

"You mean it? Yes! As long as Eclipse doesn't mind."

"I think Eclipse would love it." Jess willed her words to be true. "Maybe it's just my room she likes, anyway, not me."

"Oh, no. I'm sure she likes you."

Love left her door hanging open and followed Jess—and Eclipse, who preceded them both now that she was sure of their destination. "She was waiting for you to come back in."

They settled themselves on the bed: Eclipse first, and then Jess and Love on either side of the cat. The cat flopped gracelessly on her side and her purrs escalated as her minion poured adoration over her with their hands.

"She likes it here, that's for sure," Love said.

"She likes it here and she likes us both," Jess corrected, shy but certain. Love beamed, making Jess glad she'd spoken.

They petted Eclipse together and the cat relished their ministrations. It went on for a long time, or seemed to, and Jess wondered anew at the way Zane marked time with his hand. It must take a great deal of his attention to do so.

"Love?"

"Yes?"

"Did you know Zane is tracking time?"

"You mean with his hand?" Love tapped her own free hand alternately against the bedspread and her own thigh to demonstrate. "Yes. He thinks he deserves to be here. He said he killed a man with a car. He said he didn't mean to, but he drove when he shouldn't and hit a man walking. And the man died. Now Zane's here and he deserves it. That's what he says, anyway."

Jess considered her words carefully.

"He could have gone to the police. Jail couldn't be worse than this, could it?"

Love shook her head.

"Zane said he did go to the police but something happened— something wrong. Something wrong someone else did? And then, the person who was talking for Zane, he used the wrongness to make it all go away."

"They threw the case out of court?"

Love nodded vigorously.

"Yes, like that. So Zane was free but the man was still dead. So when Zane came here, he said it was punishment from God, or something big like God. He said he'd stay until the sentence he deserved was done. But I think maybe he's been here longer than he would have been in jail."

Jess thought about Zane's clothing but it seemed innocuous enough that it wasn't from too far bygone an era. Then again, Jess couldn't contend that she had a strong grasp of fashion.

"It's sad, isn't it?" Love said, when Jess didn't speak.

"Yes, it is. I don't think ... I don't think God wanted Zane to be here. I think if God sent people who should be in jail here, Between would be so full the walls would crack."

"Oh!" Love gasped, her eyes wide. "I didn't think of that."

"There's got to be more people who deserve to be here than someone who made a mistake." Jess dropped her gaze to Eclipse, who seemed oblivious to the serious discussion over her head. "I mean, if Zane made a mistake—and it was an awful mistake, but it was still a mistake—it's not like ... it's not like he did it on purpose, is it?"

Jess dared to look at Love then and found the woman watching her intently.

"Not like someone who hits someone else over and over on purpose. That's not a mistake. That's just bad. But the man who hit you ... he didn't kill you."

Jess let those words hang for a moment, like the guilt that descended on her in the hallway, coating her in culpability as thick as molasses.

The guilt wasn't all hers, though—not by a long shot. Most belonged to Lucas.

"He killed my baby." Jess squeezed the words out, widening her heart's already-gaping cracks. "I was pregnant and he hit me. And then I wasn't pregnant anymore. He'll do it again, too. If I ever get out of here."

Love's eyes shone bright, though tearless, and she reached across Eclipse to hug Jess. Jess had to hug Love back to avoid crushing the cat who continued to purr underneath them. The raucous vibration balanced Love's soft voice, speaking sorrowfully, though Jess didn't process a word. She absorbed both noises, or perhaps they passed through her, filling the room beyond their intended target.

In contrast to the robust resonance directed at her, Jess herself was unable to make a single sound in return.

Anger

J ess fell into a rut for the next ... well, for a long while after her expository conversations with Zane and Love. Not tracking her life became a habitual practice of its own because Jess knew she could count her days here, if only by the number of times Zane came down to open the bar's door. But it frustrated her to think of her time in Between as a "sentence," so she obstinately struggled to lose count.

In spite of her efforts, Jess frequently found herself thinking of time in terms of Zane's construct of it.

What she didn't realize—not in the beginning—was how angry it made her to think she was even slightly to blame for this supernatural predicament. While the idea percolated, she avoided the parties who contributed to formulating the unpalatable notion: Zane, Love, and even Eclipse. She stayed at the bar as much as she could, playing dice with Warren and Joe, sipping her ice water, and pressing the ice bag to her temple when newcomers paraded into the bar, which happened with far too great a frequency to suit Jess.

The arrival of newcomers presented another way to track the progress of time that otherwise effectively stopped, and Jess resented it. She quickly learned that she could avoid almost everyone by sitting at Sandman's table and adopting a surly expression underneath the shadow of the ice bag.

The mixed blessing of the situation was how she then overheard conversations at the bar, and thus knew when discussions diverted to her.

As they did today.

"What's her story?" Jess looked up in time to see a sandy-haired young man elbowing Joe and jerking his head in her direction as he repeated his question. She dropped her eyes when Joe turned, leisurely and unconcerned.

"Don't know. I figured her too tough to let some bastard beat her, but maybe not."

A barstool skidded provocatively, but Jess forced herself to stare down at the glowering shine of the table in front of her.

"That guy? He the one?"

"Sandman? Nuh-uh. He's been sleeping it off for ... "

"Seems like forever," Warren added, and Joe picked the conversation back up with a bite that indicated he didn't need Warren's help.

"Yeah. Forever. Nuh-uh. Whoever hit the girl, she don't talk about it much. Don't talk about anything much, just sits there."

Warren jumped in again, steering the conversation literally away as he asked the young man about his travels.

Jess almost laughed, driven to the edge of humor by absurdity. Regulars knew every person in Between traveled. Nobody who lived in the neighborhood where Between appeared ever entered the place—even Joe and Love had been in an unfamiliar area of their hometown when they encountered Between. The bar attracted a select few, and of those, fewer still saw death outside when they readied themselves to leave.

As the handsome man rambled on about places he'd visited, Jess hunkered down even further in her chair, glaring at the oblivious, sleeping Sandman. She'd ask about Sandman the next chance she got, and then Joe could complain about something other than her lack of conversation.

Jess was frankly amazed that Joe and Warren talked as much as they did. Jess couldn't think of much she wanted to talk about anymore, and yet Joe and Warren not only engaged the stray visitor to the bar, but they continuously talked to each other. Even their cozy insults were wearing thin for Jess, but not, it seemed, for the two men trading worn barbs.

"Seattle's not the capital of Washington, idiot. It's Olympia."

"Nuh-uh, dumbass," Joe growled back.

"He's right!" The young man's voice pitched even higher in his agitation. Without looking up, Jess couldn't tell which "he" the outsider supported in this argument, and she didn't care enough to bother. She also didn't care to tell the young man that Warren and Joe weren't actually angry at each other.

Or so she told herself.

"If there was a signal here, I'd show you," the traveler went on, still not giving Jess a clue as to whose side he'd taken.

"There ain't never signal here." No sign of concern—assumed or real—carried in Joe's tone.

Their voices, a drone when Jess' bruise pulsated, cleared as she pressed ice to her temple. She wasn't sure it was worth dulling the pain if she had to tolerate inanities like the current debate about state capitals.

The trio at the bar moved on to arguing about Oregon.

"Portland," Joe insisted.

"No, it's Eugene."

"You're both wrong, it's Salem," the young man crowed, and Jess felt a renewed surge of bitterness. How unimportant her battery was compared to state capitals!

Something pressed against Jess' ankle and she started, pulling back reflexively even as she realized "something" must be Eclipse. The cat looked up with wide eyes, and Jess felt chastised by the lack of accusation there.

She *remembers me.*

Well, it was more than Warren, Joe, and their wandering, would-be geography instructor could say, so Jess abandoned the ice bag on the table and moved out of the bar toward the stairs. Eclipse scurried past her at the corner.

"Was that a cat?"

"Cat?" Joe poured faux shock thick into his voice; it would have made Jess smile on another day. Today, she vibrated with anger and it separated her from humor's healing power just as certainly as Between's walls separated her from the living world outside.

Jess hurried up the stairs and into her room, shutting the door firmly behind her. Eclipse bobbed her head at the sound, her front feet pressing into the quilt on the bed to compensate for the motion.

"Sorry," Jess said, and though she sounded anything but, Eclipse seemed to accept the sentiment. She sat, meowed once, and then swiveled to wash her shoulder.

Jess joined the cat on the bed and was rewarded with a bump of the furry head against her arm and the sound of purring. The pairing soothed, a cool balm applied to frustration's heat, and the sharp edges of Jess' rage melted.

She didn't realize how tense she'd been downstairs, how awful she felt at being ignored. As she petted Eclipse and absorbed the pleasure of the cat's appreciation, Jess decided Joe and Warren did what they did to keep the young man from asking questions too deep for a non-regular.

She wondered anew at their dedication to this task.

"I guess they have to do it, huh, Eclipse? Because of Warren almost getting pulled out, I mean. They have to make sure nothing like that happens again."

And there was no better diversion than to get people talking about themselves, however dull the topic might become. Being bored beat being dead.

Did it really?

Jess shook her head, as if she could reject the sinuous thought so easily. It slithered past before when she sat listening to the small talk at the bar, but the notion seemed to sink tentacles into her brain now, delving ever deeper.

Death by boredom. Many children espoused such a philosophy while on summer vacation, but Jess never found summer so tiresome as she found Between.

Maybe that's why they do it. It's boring, but it's not as boring as not talking.

Jess felt the heaving of pent-in sobs, of the disconcerting need to cry with nary a teardrop—honest or false—available.

"Mrrt?" Eclipse must have felt something, too, for she looked up from the inelegant sprawl she'd succumbed to when Jess petted her. She looked up, and she blinked.

"Why do we do that, Eclipse? We don't need to blink. Why do we cry or talk or do any of it? What's the point?"

The cat, of course, didn't answer. She just kept on purring.

Perhaps habit explained everything. Goodness knew Jess went through the motions of life long before crossing Between's threshold put it on hold for real.

You do things because that's what people do, not because you really need to do them.

Though not alive, Jess could act as if she were, and so she did. So did Eclipse, and so did everyone else in Between, with varying degrees of dedication.

What was it Love said about "how" and "why?" There was too much space in them for not understanding? That was true, but Between itself possessed an abundance of space for the same.

Jess sighed, curling her body around Eclipse as if to nap. The simple struggle of being, never mind living, exhausted her ever since her brief talk with Zane. She'd even argued with Joe about adding her name to the wall, instead of waving away his escalating attempts to sway her.

"You got to! You just got to do it." In lieu of explanation, his hands swept broadly through the air as if to encompass the immensity of whatever he failed to mention. "And do it before you forget the day."

"I'll never forget the day I came in here!"

"Yes, you will." Warren's words sliced right through Joe's concurrent assurances. Even though Joe expressed the same idea, Warren's voice contained an acerbity that made Jess take notice.

"Yes, you will," he repeated when she turned to him. "You'll forget everything if you stay here long enough. Time is the first thing to go, but it won't be the last. Memory wears away here like sand on a beach out there. You'll forget your name if you don't use it. You will."

"It was May 20," Jess snapped, and then pressed her glass of ice water against her temple.

"Barkeep … ice bag!" Joe called out. "Ask her when you need it; she don't care if you yell."

"I'm not putting my name on that wall," Jess insisted.

"Yes, you will," Warren said once more.

That time, he sounded sad about it.

"Maybe I should," Jess told Eclipse now. "At least it would be something to do."

And whether or not she made an impression with the wanderer downstairs or with anyone else in the world, she could make an impression on the wall. Jess never attempted to carve her name into anything before; she wondered how long it would take.

"But that doesn't matter, does it?"

Jess' "sentence"—earned or not—throttled her, forcing tightness and pressure on her entire body … even her lungs, which needed no air to support her in the panic rapidly supplanting residual anger.

She forced herself to breathe because of how much she felt like she was suffocating. She couldn't possibly asphyxiate in Between! It was funny, really ... even Lucas couldn't hurt her here, at least, not any more than he'd already done.

Unless he shoved you out the door.

Jess transitioned again: from anger to panic and finally to chilled terror. Whatever caused Between's unbelievable stagnation, its power did not extend to emotions.

Eclipse, working to groom a troublesome spot near the middle of her shoulder blades, flopped over during her efforts to reach it, drawing Jess' attention away from her inner turmoil.

"Silly cat." That her voice only shook a little felt like a triumph to Jess.

"Meow," Eclipse responded, looking right at Jess. And then she resumed her bathing efforts, moving from the awkward spot to an easy-to-access paw.

"I might as well put my name on the wall. I haven't got anything else to do. No offense, Eclipse."

Not only was Eclipse not insulted, she didn't appear to be listening anymore. Jess gave the cat a few final strokes and journeyed down the stairs, peering around the corner and sighing in relief when she saw only Joe and Warren seated at the bar.

"Is he gone?"

"The state capital professor?" Warren replied, grinning. "He's gone, all right. Joe told him he should walk across the parking lot to get a signal so he could prove what he said, and he did."

Joe stared hard at Jess and frowned. She returned the look. "What?"

"Gonna do it?"

Words seemed as useless as air in that instant, so Jess nodded. There was no point in pretending she didn't know what he meant.

"About time!" Joe slapped the bar when he said it. "Barkeep, get the pick." Another slap to the bar, this one so boisterous as to make Jess jump even though she saw the motion coming. "Girl's gonna add her name to the wall."

The bartender, engaged in her perpetual glass-polishing, nodded and set down the one in her hand. She glided to the center of the bar and bent to the cabinets there, emerging with the wicked tool Joe requested.

She passed it across the bar handle first and waited, her hand steady on the business end of the ice pick.

Jess looked up from the pick and fell straight into the abyss of the bartender's eyes. Unfathomable, holding neither warmth nor coldness, those eyes were as direct as anything in the sum total of Jess' life experience. Jess plunged into an ambivalent staring contest as if hypnotized.

The indifferent spell broke when Joe snorted.

"You ain't gonna win with her, Jessie. Might as well have a staring contest with a cat."

Jess rounded on Joe, frustrated on one front, outraged on another.

"Cat got your tongue now?"

"It's Jess. Not Jessie."

"Ain't what you said before, *Jessie*."

"Jessamy," Jess said, not caring that she shouldn't care.

Only her mother called her Jessie, and with Mama gone, nobody else had the right.

"Jessamy." Joe enunciated carefully this time, but his drawl made Jess suspect he'd known the proper form of her name all along. "Your real name. That's what goes on the wall."

Walls

J ess found she wasn't ready to give in after all.

"What difference does it make? What does it matter if I write Jess or Jessamy or … or anything?"

"It doesn't make a difference," Warren answered. "Not really."

"Do too," Joe insisted, his words lashing Jess but apparently bouncing off Warren. "You don't put a name that ain't yours on a tombstone and this is what we got instead of tombstones."

Jess' eyes slid from Joe, falling on the slumped figure behind them all.

"What about Sandman?"

"Tell her, Warren," Joe demanded.

Warren sighed. It was obvious he didn't relish the task ahead, but before Jess could say anything to stop him, he spoke. The words poured out in the beginning as if well-rehearsed but Warren couldn't support their delivery—the stream slowed progressively until it stuttered to a stop.

"Sandman was asleep in the entryway when I came to the bar. I got him up, told him I'd get him a coffee, and steered him inside. He must have fallen asleep again when we crossed over. You … you stay the way you enter here … the way you enter Between. Sandman will … he'll never wake up … on his own. I … I think …"

Warren drank deeply as if his glass held the only fuel that would enable him to continue.

And Joe, clearly tired of waiting, finished the tale for Warren.

"He thinks there's no way out for himself so long as Sandman's asleep. And Sandman'll never see a way out because he's always asleep. So Warren thinks they're both stuck here—stuck here forever."

Warren's shoulders slumped.

In the following silence, Jess looked back at the bartender, who remained unmoved in every sense. Jess reached for the ice pick the bartender still held and thought she felt it tingle when she grasped its wooden handle.

The bartender released her own grip and the shimmering sensation vanished.

Holding the pick, Jess faced the wall.

"Did you check his pockets?" she asked Warren over her shoulder.

He knew what she meant.

"Yes. No ID."

"Using his real name wouldn't help him wake up," Jess said. This time, she was speaking to Joe, even as her eyes scanned the stoic wall before her.

"Of course not. Ain't gonna help with Sandman. But you can help yourself."

"Can I?"

"Maybe so, maybe no. But Jessamy's better than Jess."

Jess looked back at the bar then. She couldn't help it—it was as if she was being forced by heavy hands on her shoulders.

Joe, Warren, and the bartender all watched her. Movement near the door to the kitchen drew Jess' eye, and Eli stepped out there. He, too, came to watch the show.

"No television here." Warren sounded apologetic. "We take our entertainment where we can find it."

Jess felt that almost-smile pulling at her facial muscles.

"I can put my name anywhere I want?"

81

"On that wall," Eli purred in his smooth, deep voice. He pointed with the stump of his death-shortened hand.

"Do 'Jessamy,'" Joe urged. "Longer names are better."

Jess approached the wall and walked the length of it, appraising the empty spaces across its surface. In many places, the wall looked as if it had been filled from the bottom up. She pulled a chair from Sandman's table and positioned it beneath the widest space she could find.

"You set yourself apart," Eli noted.

"Who cares? Just so's she takes her time." Joe sounded almost breathless.

Jess climbed onto the chair and stood there as utter silence descended in Between. She could have heard a clock ticking, if there had been one present.

Jess placed one hand against the wall in front of her and raised the other, wielding the ice pick like a weapon.

"Hold it like a pencil."

Jess jumped, even though Warren spoke softly.

"You will only do this once," Eli added. "Be gentle."

Jess looked back and saw a line of serious faces taut with anticipation. All except the bartender, who wore the inscrutable, blank expression she perfected above all others.

The wood underneath Jess' hand felt warm and oddly soft. She lifted her hand from the wall to help adjust her grip on the ice pick and felt a distinct, ridiculous sense of loss. She wanted to ask what was happening but the urge to do what she determined to do was stronger than her wish to understand.

As was her desire to touch the wall again.

Jess settled her grip, and—now holding the massive pick as if it were a simple #2 pencil—pivoted back to the wall. She returned her other hand to the wall's surface and the feeling of being lost evaporated as if it never existed. Expectation buzzed in the room like bees swarming, emanating not only from the active, unliving people behind Jess, but also from the inactive, living wall under Jess' palm.

As understanding bereft of knowledge surged through Jess' motionless veins, she brought the tip of the ice pick down against the wall. Gently, as Eli instructed. The pick pierced the surface as if entering butter instead of wood, and a thin trickle of clear fluid ran down the wall.

Blood? Or tears?

If not for the music soaring out of the opening she'd created, Jess would have recoiled. An old sound she'd never heard before, the song united the bright promise of newness with the familiarity of comfort. It raised the hair on the back of Jess' neck like a perfectly executed psalm and flushed her face like orgasm's aftermath. It embraced and punctured, exhilarated and exhausted.

Burning without blistering and longing to stay in this ethereal, connective experience, Jess still retained enough self-awareness to note how the wall healed itself almost as quickly as she wounded it. And how the music it produced as she wrote upon it softened when she paused.

Jess moved with effort, retracing the "J" to a readable width, and then lifted the ice pick out of the wall and to the right, starting the "e." The wall's song progressed, and Jess knew Between itself spoke her name as she engraved it, communicating not what she was called in life but who she was beyond life.

It was as personal as it could be and also just as public.

It felt like communion: Jess accepting Between and Between accepting her. And its witness by those who shared an understanding of reality's supernatural convolution here only added to its mystery.

A mystery composed of knotted twists rather than tangled snarls.

As she etched her first and last names into the wall, Jess had the fleeting notion that the suspension of time—of life—was good again, as it had been when she'd realized she was free of Lucas.

The song coursed around her and through her, and Jess knew how a bird in flight felt. Rivulets of fluid continued to stream down the wall as she worked, but Jess noticed this with peripheral awareness that barely registered within the enveloping comfort of the wall singing her name.

Far too soon, she wrote the "z" and knew her melody would end on its note. The crest of the final swell of sound passed, its last vibrations lingered before fading away. Transitioning to writing the date proved a mundane rather than surreal experience and demanded significant effort.

This carving effort felt utterly futile. But even as the wall sealed her name into its treasury, Jess continued to move the ice pick, beginning work on her numbers.

"That was great," Joe rasped behind her. "See what I mean?"

Jess sobbed—a silent downpour of tearless heartbreak. She didn't look away from the wall. Metal scratching wood struck her as a feeble but appropriate conclusion to her name song.

"Give her a minute, Joe," Warren said. "It was the best one I've heard, that's for sure."

"Why didn't you tell me?" Jess choked out the words in time with the plain wood she now chipped from the wall.

"Why do you think? Crazier than not breathing, ain't it?"

"More impossible than all the rest," Warren added, and Jess nodded her agreement, though she still didn't turn around.

"But .. what else?"

"What do you mean, what else?" Though Jess still resonated with her name song, feeling effects like an audible version of an afterimage, Joe sounded like himself.

Jess looked over her shoulder then.

"What else aren't you telling me?"

Warren stared, but Eli and the bartender had gone back to their respective tasks, and Joe looked down into his glass.

"Nothing that will hurt you," Warren said. The smooth words chafed Jess' fragile sanity. She lifted the ice pick from the wall and pointed it at Warren, stabbing in his direction as she spoke.

"You think that didn't hurt? All that ... that ... whatever it was, that I'll never hear again? You think it doesn't hurt to have something so perfect and then know—how do I even know this but I do!—it's a one-shot deal?"

Joe whirled around.

"You had it! Mr. State Capitals didn't have it at all. Don't think of that, do you?"

Jess hadn't, and it chastened her, stripping the indignation from her body and the loss from her mind.

"No. No, I didn't."

"Look, Jessamy," Warren stood, arms out. "This place is crazy. When I wrote my name on the wall, I had no idea. What do you say to even begin to explain what that's like?"

"I don't know. But you should have said something. I wish ... it was over too fast. It was ... the most amazing ... and now it's over. It's all over."

"I think it's supposed to teach us something."

Jess lifted her slumping head, locking eyes with Love. Love leaned against the edge of the wall by the stairs, her fingers gripping the wood there like claws, as if to hold herself up.

"Here we go." Joe slammed his glass onto the counter. "Barkeep, another. A double."

Love's eyes jittered from Jess to Joe and back again.

"It's supposed to teach us."

"What?" Jess asked, her voice trembling.

"If she says 'be happy,' I'm gonna puke."

85

Warren bumped Joe's shoulder with his own.

"Shut up, idiot."

Love's eyes didn't waver this time; they stayed with Jess' as if secured by long-distance adhesive. When Joe remained silent, having resumed his in-depth study of his whiskey glass, Love spoke again.

"It's supposed to teach us there's good in our naming." Joe snorted, but Love continued as if his disbelieving explosion was inaudible as well as immaterial. "There's good in our naming and good in us."

"And that's why the wall let you write made-up nothing instead of your real name?" Joe shook off the cautioning hand Warren laid on his arm and stood, shouting at Love. She blinked, but did not recoil. "Bull!"

Love held her ground, though her fingers tightened their already-impossible grip on the corner of the stairway.

"It is not. It's true."

"Just because you believe it don't mean ..."

Love's quivering surged, tremors increasing like gusty wind, but she interrupted Joe's words anyway.

"Names are only what we call ourselves. I don't have to keep the one someone else made up."

"*MA* named you 'Iris!'" Joe was nearly screaming, though he hadn't moved any closer to Love.

"But she called me 'Love.' All the time, she called me 'Love.' Like she called you 'Bear.'"

At that, Joe's expression wiped clean as if rage never clouded it. He stood, turned, and fell back a step, staggering into his barstool. He checked himself visibly, and eased back down onto his seat.

As Love's fluttering slowed, Joe's entire body went rigid; the former seemed stabilizing—the latter, rejecting.

"She called me 'Love' and she called you 'Bear' and I'm 'Love' because that's all she said I knew to do and you're 'Bear' because she said you were strong and would fight to protect your family."

"Stop!" Desperation, not anger, carried Joe's words now.

"Okay." Love frowned, but she nodded. "Okay." She retraced her steps back upstairs.

Warren shot a glance at Jess that she couldn't interpret and then slapped Joe on the back. "Drink's here, idiot." He nudged the glass closer toward Joe's hunched body.

Joe did not move, solid isolation wrought through the tension entrenched in his neck, shoulders, and quite possibly every other muscle in his body.

Jess, still holding the world's deadliest pencil, turned from the bar to the wall and resumed her carving. The date, difficult to create, came out slightly larger than her name. If she tried to embed this script in wood outside Between, she would be sore by the time she finished. But here, while her eye ached as it had since she entered the bar, she knew no additional pains could linger.

She carved for a long time, wood grit and other particles she ripped out of the wall falling down in lieu of tears—hers or the wall's. Between's extraordinary oddity reverted into ordinary strangeness, and Jess cried alone ... a familiar situation, in spite of its present aridity.

By the time Jess finished her work and climbed down off the chair, the ice melted in Joe's glass. As for Joe, he remained motionless, though he now covered his head with his hands, compact and crumpled as if broken by Love's words.

Especially by the one word that conjured a vision of a small boy, standing as tall as he could, fiercely protective and basking in pride because his mother recognized his inherent power. There was no sign of that boy now, but Jess could imagine him.

She wondered if Joe could.

Ambivalence

As Jess moved toward the stairs, the bartender intercepted her, hand outstretched.

"Oh."

It was all Jess had to say, and all she could say; she knew what the bartender wanted. She rotated the ice pick she'd forgotten she carried and lowered it carefully into the bartender's palm. This time, she distinctly noticed the tingling sensation—painless electricity—as the handle contacted the bartender's skin. Jess held the metal end of the pick for a moment longer, absorbing the unusual sensation, but then she let go.

The bartender tipped her head and turned away, her motion rote and apparently unconcerned.

Jess trudged on to the stairs, hoping Eclipse would join her at the top. She felt physically tired for the first time since she'd entered Between, and it seemed an odd malaise … how quickly she'd grown accustomed to the absence of such sensations!

Except for that awful throbbing at her temple, there was little to physically feel in Between. Jess thought about going back to retrieve the ice bag when she reached the landing halfway up the stairs but decided she could not spare the expense of such a journey.

Even knowing she wouldn't sleep, she almost felt as if she could. When she found herself alone at the top of the stairwell, Jess' exhaustion deepened, thickening her movements. She practically staggered into her room.

Eclipse lay on the bed in a decadent sprawl.

Behind Jess, Love spoke.

"I let her in." Love kept her voice soft and Jess was grateful, though she hadn't the energy to jump even if Love shouted. "She heard your name song, too. She liked it. I could tell."

"I'm glad," Jess replied, and meant it. She made it to the bed and slid alongside the cat.

Love followed her in and stood next to Jess' collapse and Eclipse' elegance.

"I told you 'Jessamy' is prettier than 'Jess.'"

Jess didn't feel like she had to answer that, so she didn't. She lay next to the purring cat whose efforts definitely demanded a response. Jess drew an unnecessary breath and began to pet Eclipse.

"I told you."

Jess realized she'd been mistaken about a response not being required.

"It's just a name," she sighed.

"Oh, but it's not!" Love's hands knit themselves into a knot and raised up over her heart. "Don't you see? There's good in our naming. Well ... there can be."

Jess' tiredness faded, draining like a water tower struck by a cannonball.

"Wouldn't the wall say any name beautifully?"

Love didn't even need to pause to consider the question.

"Between talks like the bartender. It's always pretty, but when it means something—when it's good—it fills you up like a whole Thanksgiving dinner and all the Christmas cookies you ever saw."

"But ..."

"Everybody knows when it's good. Everybody feels whole, like they matter."

Jess felt her body tighten, as if preparing for a blow.

"Do I matter?"

Love nodded furiously, her hair flopping around her face.

"Of course! We all matter! But ... sometimes ... we forget. We just forget."

We just forget.

Eclipse bumped against Jess' hand, which had come to rest along her flank. Jess resumed her movements. Deep and abiding as it seemed, Jess found her exhaustion wholly departed, leaving not even a whisper behind to cushion the throbbing of her eye.

"We do forget."

Love nodded, finally lowering and unlocking her hands. Her movements, crisply direct when Jess arrived, returned to her typical fluttering. It seemed like the reverse of Jess' current experience and made her think about what she'd learned a long time ago in science class, something about recycling? No, something about conserving energy.

Love made her exit long before Jess gave up on recalling whatever she thought she'd learned.

The hall stayed quiet for a long time until the sound of Zane exiting his room, beginning his measured daily pace down the hall reached Jess. She watched him pass through the open doorway. He did not look up, focused on his self-assigned mission with the obsessive drive he believed it warranted.

Jess stayed with Eclipse until Zane came back, listening until she heard his door's somber *click*, muting the sound of marked time. After one last scratch under the cat's chin, Jess left the room.

She stopped at Love's room and knocked. The door, caught loosely by accident or design, opened under the light contact of Jess' knuckles and Love looked up from where she sat on her bed. One hand extended, pointing, onto the quilt underneath her.

"I'm going downstairs for dinner." Love's face mirrored the surprise Jess felt on making the announcement. "Do you want to come?"

Love's eyes fell away, back to the patchwork that Jess was certain the woman knew by heart, and she resumed tracing the patterns there.

"I'm busy."

Jess nodded. It occurred to her that trailing one's fingers over fabric might be one of the better ways to spend eternity in Between.

"Okay. Well, Eclipse might want company while I'm away."

"She might?"

"Yes, and maybe ... maybe you'd like to follow the pattern on the quilt in her room while you visit her?"

"Her room?" Confusion converted into a small smile.

"She does seem like the boss," Jess said, and Love's fractioned smile rounded out. "And she likes us both. Remember?"

"Yes. Yes, okay."

Love got up and ducked past Jess in the hallway, but turned around in a flurry and wrapped Jess in her arms. Stunned, Jess returned the embrace.

The hug ended as quickly as it began, and Love slid into Jess' room with a flourish of skirt and a soft exclamation for Eclipse. The cat meowed pleasantly in reply.

Jess stood there, looking at the light slanting out of her room through the partially open door. The slight illumination cast a hazy trapezoid on the floor outside her room and presented a distinct contrast to the hall's gloomy end, where Zane's door stayed sealed tight.

There was something to learn here, Jess thought, navigating the short distance to the stairway. Something about how shutting yourself in a room might hold your darkness in check, but how it also stopped your light from reaching out.

Jess supposed Zane didn't believe he had any light to spare. Some people existed in a kind of dark dimension—people like Lucas—not seeming to care who they hurt, serving themselves to the exclusion of all others. Terrible as it was, at least Zane's mistake wasn't one he persisted in making over and over again.

The gloomy atmosphere Jess traversed upstairs brightened as she approached the first floor. Two strangers sat at the bar with Joe and Warren; to judge by the lingering laughter, the four of them had been sharing jokes. Jess sat at the table next to Sandman's and waved to the bartender, who glided over.

"I'd like a cheeseburger, please." The bartender gave a nod and turned briskly away. "For here," Jess added then, and earned an over-the-shoulder glance and slight tip of the head for her comic efforts.

"Dining in, eh?" Joe called, and Jess shrugged. She didn't feel entirely comfortable with Joe or Warren after the incident with her name song, and that wasn't going to change with or without apparently merry additions to the bar. The new people looked like a couple, and not just because of how close the woman stood next to the seated man—they also dressed similarly, in almost-matching outdoorsy gear.

The woman waved at Jess.

"Hey, there!"

Jess mustered a smile and lifted her hand in return.

"I'm Tracy, and this is Todd." The woman rubbed the man's back as she spoke.

"T-n-T," the man added, not quite turning. His voice, low and soft, seemed exceptionally so even in Between's often-extreme quietude. He hugged the woman close with an arm that Jess noticed shook slightly. The woman lifted her beaming face to his and hugged him back.

"Jess." Jess shook her head. "Don't mind me, I .... I just get a little quiet when I'm hungry."

She hoped the lie would be plausible, and to judge by the unfaded smile Tracy returned to her, it was.

"You sure do," Joe piped up, lending unwelcome support to Jess' story.

"Shut up, idiot. At least she doesn't get surly like you."

"Surly? I'll show you surly, dumbass."

The insults, dull and clearly for show, set the snuggling couple to unified chuckling.

"You sound like an old married couple," Tracy teased.

Warren laughed; Joe snorted.

"Gee, thanks."

"We've been married ... how many years, T?" Tracy tapped the tip of Todd's nose in what appeared to be a jibe of their own.

"Long enough," Todd responded. Tracy tapped his nose again. "Stop that. Twenty-one."

"Negative reinforcement," Tracy trilled, ruffling Todd's hair as he faux-grimaced with great dramatic effect.

Or perhaps with great effort?

"I don't like it on dogs or people, but sometimes I pretend with Todd."

"I should check on the boys," Todd said in his continuously quiet voice.

"No, hon, I'll do it. Just wait until I finish my drink. And smell that burger cooking? We should have dinner here and order one for the boys to share."

Todd nodded, seeming resigned. His lack of enthusiasm visibly drained Tracy, and Jess wondered at it.

"Two dogs, you said?" Warren asked.

Tracy beamed, energetic nature restored.

"Yes. Thunder Pike's Legend and Tomahawk Lightning."

"Fancy!" Joe said.

"Another T-n-T," Warren observed.

"No, that's ..." Todd began

"Not really ..." Tracy spoke in unison with Todd. Her voice carried a strength her husband's lacked, even though she didn't speak loudly. He nodded to her and she went on. "Those are their AKC names—formal names, if you will. Way too long of names to call them out in the field. When they're working, you need something short and clear so you can get each boy's attention quickly. We call them Pike and Tom."

"They're trained to respond to whistles and hand-signals." Warren shook his head and addressed his next remark over his shoulder. "Did you hear that, Jessamy?"

Jess fought the urge to look to the spot where her full name marred the wall. She kept her eyes on the people at the bar with effort.

"That's ... neat."

"Tracy says the dog will turn around to the right if she raises her right hand straight up, and to the left if she raises her left hand."

"Why would you want a dog to do that?" Jess asked, interested despite her determination not to be.

"For a blind retrieve." Tracy's enthusiasm suffused her now and she extracted her body from her husband's with an apologetic pat, turning to face Jess. "We run the dogs in field trials—competitions to find and retrieve birds, usually ducks and pheasants. Sometimes the dog gets to see where the bird falls and other times, a bird is planted without the dog seeing it; that's called a blind retrieve. The dog's handler has to help the dog navigate to the bird on blind retrieves."

Jess' interest held—a good thing, since Tracy showed no signs of slowing her narrative.

"You'd like your dog to run straight at his target, but he may have to swim a pond to get there, and it's harder to hold a line over a long distance, too. So sometimes you need to stop the dog—that's a single whistle command—and redirect him. Turning to the left or right on a redirect can make all the difference."

"I had no idea there were competitions like that," Jess said. "Do your dogs win?"

"Well, Pike's still in the Derby, which is a competition for dogs under two years old. He's got more energy than we know what to do with most days so it can be hard to get him to listen, even to a whistle; he was out in the second round yesterday in Fort Collins. But Tom is an old pro and he jammed at the Open competition!"

Todd touched Tracy's shoulder with a gently trembling hand and the slight contact registered with Tracy instantly, unlike the blank look Jess knew extended over her own face.

"Oh, I'm sorry. The Open is for all ages of dogs, and a 'JAM' is a Judge's Award of Merit. It's not as good as placing, but it's close."

"Tom's a good boy," Todd said. His warm words belied the serious face he turned to Jess.

"He sounds like it," Jess said. Todd nodded slowly in agreement.

Tracy shifted, reaching for her drink, and Jess caught a glimpse of Todd's water glass. Positioned close to his body, a straw extended from the glass to draw an even more direct line to refreshment for him. Jess tried to remember if she'd requested a water when she'd ordered her cheeseburger and decided she hadn't.

She wasn't thirsty, but like the cheeseburger for which she had no real appetite, Jess figured she might as well hold on to pretense.

And the cooking burger did smell delicious.

"All right then; I'll go check on the boys!" Tracy pushed her glass to the bar's inside edge and pressed another sideways hug onto Todd.

"Let me get the door for you," Warren said, leaping to the task.

"Why, Warren … how gentlemanly. Thank you."

"Still raining?" Todd asked, looking down at the bar.

Warren reached for the door, pulling it open in front of his body. It looked to Jess as if the shakiness she'd observed in Todd transferred to Warren, but she understood Warren's ailment.

Tracy peered outside, and Joe caught Jess' eye as they waited to hear what she saw.

"Oh, just a little drizzle." Tracy kept her voice merry, though she made a face at Jess. Jess barely noticed Tracy's playful expression … it was washed out by the brilliant white light that Jess saw pouring in through the door beyond Tracy. "Don't worry; I won't melt."

With that, Tracy dashed out into the world she'd left, her laughter shutting off like a switch even though Warren still held the door open, his face blank.

He closed the door as quickly as he could, but Todd turned just fast enough to see.

"That isn't … that's not right …" he said, apparently mesmerized.

The bartender nodded.

"Looks like we have another regular."

Shattered

In the frozen hush following Todd's pronouncement, Joe fumbled with his drink.

"Crap," he exclaimed, flicking whiskey off his fingertips.

"You got it, too?" Todd asked, diverted, or so it seemed.

"Got what?" Joe wiped his hand on his pants. "Barkeep, gimme the rag."

"The shakes. Should get them checked. Mine's Parkinson's."

"What?" Back at the bar, Warren took his drink and moved to Todd's other side—the side closest to the door.

Todd leaned in and sipped his water through the straw.

"Trace won't talk about it."

"I'm sorry."

Todd's long, quaking fingers flicked Warren's words away, discarding his sympathy like trash.

"Not as sorry as me."

The bartender handed Joe a cloth, having completed whatever pointless task she'd engaged in prior to Tracy's exit. Joe dabbed at the whiskey he'd spilled, his movements charged with half-hearted violence.

"What did you see?" Warren finally asked.

Todd shook his head.

"Nothing that wasn't there all along."

"You're not hallucinating, if that's what you think," Warren persisted.

"I haven't known what to think since the doc gave me my sentence." Jess gasped at Todd's choice of words. "But just wait until Trace gets back."

Jess jerked her eyes from Todd to Joe, who abandoned his cleaning efforts and stared at Todd like the other man was an oddity under a microscope.

"She ain't gonna come back," Joe said, deliberate and blunt. "She's stuck out there. You're stuck in here."

Todd's shoulders jerked up, falling back more gracefully as gravity assisted his shrug.

"She always comes back."

"Order up." Eli rang the bell. The sound was tinnier than Jess recalled, or perhaps it was the way the indefinite chime carried through the thickness of Todd's confidence.

The bartender glided through the bell's lingering ring to pick up Jess' order, indifference personified.

Jess envied her. From Jess' perspective as the most recent arrival in Between—prior to Todd—there was no way to understand his reaction ... or lack thereof.

"Don't you care?" The words charged out of Jess, trampling her determination and stampeding through the delicious aroma of the cheeseburger the bartender placed before her.

Again, the jerky shrug.

"No point in denying the obvious, I'd say. That wasn't natural, out that door."

"But Tracy ... don't you even care if she's okay?"

Todd directed the full weight of his gaze at Jess.

"She's better than okay. Always has been. Always will be, I know." How Todd's faith in his wife conveyed so fully in those soft-spoken words, Jess wasn't sure.

"How can you say that?"

Todd tipped his head, the motion significant and Warren started to stretch out his arm toward the man. But in spite of how it initially appeared, Todd's lean held.

"She's afraid. As it should be, I'd say. And I'm not."

Pronouncing it as gospel, Todd turned his head away from Jess. Warren shot Jess a look she could not interpret, even though it was sharp enough to part the steam from the burger and send a chill down her neck.

"Why don't you just go out in it?" Joe spat the words.

"Joe!"

"If you're not afraid, why don't you just go?" Joe plowed over Warren's next interjection before the other man could give voice to it. "I wanna know!"

Todd nudged his glass, looking down into it without any of the strain roiling off Joe and Warren, who glared at each other across the human barrier between them.

"Well, it's like this. I thought about it, you know, and I can't do most of the things I want anymore … not the way I want to do them, anyway. But there's Trace." His head drifted up, his movement as easy as any Jess had seen him make yet. He looked at Joe, holding the other man's gaze with a force of will Jess didn't think she'd ever possess. "There's Trace, and I can't leave her. Not yet, not like this. Not while I can still feel as good as a sunrise every time she smiles. Not while I can still smell her hair while she's asleep next to me."

Todd's voice wavered, but it didn't break. And in the silence that descended across the bar, heavy with emotion, Jess could hear him breathing.

Jess could hear him breathing.

"He's breathing!" Warren looked as stunned as Jess felt. "He's alive!"

Joe reacted perhaps more predictably to the abrupt end of Todd's tenure in Between than the others.

"For the love of Pete ... that's got to be the shortest regular ever. Calls for a drink." He signaled the bartender even as Warren shook his head.

"No, wait. He probably just hasn't realized he doesn't need to ... Todd, do you have a pulse?"

Todd looked at each of them directly, even Jess, and then settled his gaze on Warren.

"Sitting here talking, why wouldn't I?"

"Can you check?"

Todd laughed and extended his arm to Warren.

"Don't think I could hold steady on the spot if I could find it, but you go ahead."

While Warren bent to the task, Joe drank deeply from his replenished whiskey. Jess found herself taking a bite of her cheeseburger and chewed as a matter of course, but the experience of eating was lost on her as she waited for Warren to find Todd's pulse.

Or not.

"It's there," Warren said, finally. "I think."

"What in the hell do you mean?" Joe growled over his glass, nearly empty already. "It's there or it ain't."

Warren straightened, shooting Joe a baleful glance over Todd's head.

"It's there, but only once a minute or so."

"You're nuts," Todd said. "How could I be alive if ... " Jess took another bite of her burger and felt strange even under the circumstances. She wondered, as Todd put the pieces of the puzzle together, if the reason why Warren and Joe drank and ate so regularly was so it wouldn't seem so odd to do so, should they ever escape Between.

"How could I be … " Todd repeated himself, glancing toward the door and back at Warren. "You mean to tell me you don't even have heartbeats?"

"Hold your breath for him, Warren. Show the man."

Jess pushed away from the table and pulled up her sleeve just past the elbow, holding her arm out toward Todd. The three men turned at the sound of her chair scraping across the floor and Todd raised his eyebrows as she approached.

"Look. Right here." Jess tapped the crook of her elbow where the bluish-green vein she'd etched on her kindergarten self-portrait—and had been accordingly and promptly teased by her classmates for her pale skin and prominent blood vessels—lay dormant. "Look. No pulse. No movement. No nothing."

Todd looked but his face remained calm, and so Jess snatched his water glass and slammed it against the floor.

"Hey!"

If her heart could have beat, it would have pounded as Jess bent, straightening with a significant and jagged fragment from Todd's glass clenched in one hand. She hesitated just a moment and then pulled the wicked point of the thing along the line marked by her vein.

As pain shot through her, Todd reached for her hand—the one gripping the glass—but Jess stepped backward, driven. She pressed the glass harder into the gash she'd created, twisting, and then released her grip.

With the hand that held the glass now bloodied, too, Jess extended both wounds toward Todd. Her hand healed first, so she raised her gaze to Todd's face and watched him as the tear in her arm finished repairing, ejecting the glass shard.

It dropped to the floor with a gentle yet deafening noise.

"Well, I'll be a monkey's uncle. Bourbon, straight up." Todd raised his voice with his order, his eyes still on Jess. "You want one?"

"N-n-no. I ..." Jess realized her arms remained outstretched and lowered them. "Thanks, but no. I need to clean up this mess and get back to my dinner."

"That's all," Joe said. "Jessamy's doing the demos now."

"She certainly is." Warren sounded as breathy as a schoolgirl with a first crush.

"Can I please have the broom and dustpan?" Jess felt her stomach drop down from her throat as she forced the last word of her request.

The bartender blinked, the movement briefly obscuring her intense eyes. It was like a cloud passing over the sun on a sweltering summer day and Jess savored the minute reprieve. Then the bartender moved away without comment or empty reassurances.

"I can pay for the glass!" Jess called after the bartender, who arrested her motion with something remarkably like surprise. But then Joe laughed and the bartender resumed her rote movement, exiting the bar and heading down the hallway.

"'Please' and 'thank you' won't get you outta this, girl."

"What will?" Jess fired back.

"If I knew, would I be here to tell you?" Joe raised his voice, looking past Jess to Todd and Warren. "Tell any of your sorry asses?"

"Relax, idiot."

"Screw yourself, dumbass."

"Is that how you talk in front of a lady?" Todd interjected, managing to embed amusement within severity, adding a sweet center into his tone.

Joe glared at Todd and then shrugged.

"You shouldn't do this again, Jessamy, really," Warren said. "It leaves scars."

Jess raised the arm she'd sliced, examining the knot she'd created. Except for the fact that it healed, the mark looked almost exactly like she'd imagined it would, back when she'd daydreamed about hurting herself.

The hazy memory underlying the harsh sight before her spread like ice through her veins. But when the bartender stepped onto the glass splinters behind her, Jess pulled the frozen, scattered bits of her being back together in an instant. She took the broom and dustpan the bartender extended with a slight nod and whisper of thanks.

"You are welcome," the bartender replied, drawing a gasp from Warren and stunned silence from Joe.

'Let me ..." Warren began, but Jess stopped his words with a glance.

"No. It's my mess and I'll clean it up."

"Your burger will get cold."

Jess laughed, and it sounded remarkably like the glass she'd just shattered.

"No, it won't. I'm a waitress. I'll have this cleaned up before you know it."

And she did, too, collecting the broken, blood-spattered pieces of her impromptu demonstration with practiced efficiency.

"You should of took notes, dumbass."

Warren shook his head and stood, motioning to Jess.

"I'll show you where it goes. This way."

Just past the bathrooms, Warren paused and pointed to a metal monstrosity dominating the end of the hall.

"The back door is there. It doesn't open for anybody except the guy who makes deliveries. This," and Warren patted the narrow door next to the men's room, "this is the storage closet."

Warren opened the closet and pulled a dirty string that lead upwards to a single, bare bulb. Harsh and limited light revealed a cramped world of utilitarian cleaning supplies, shelves laden with toilet paper and folded bar rags, and other practical items.

Several bins squatted under the lowest shelves, one of which was hand-labeled "GLASS." Jess added the detritus from her dustpan to the appropriate bin and the resulting noise jarred her, resounding throughout the small space.

Jess looked at Warren, who took the broom and dustpan from her and hung them on hooks near the closet door.

"There was a bar fight a while ago. We don't usually break that many glasses ... or work so hard to jam them into our skin when we do."

Jess held her ground against the chastisement in Warren's voice as he picked a well-used rag out of another bin.

"I'll just give a swipe over the floor with this, in case there's any blood," Warren said.

Then Jess dared to say it.

"It wasn't anything I hadn't already thought of doing, you know. With the glass. The scar doesn't matter to me."

"It should."

"Well, it doesn't. And I'm not going to be sorry about it. I chose, you know? I did. It ... it'll remind me ... I can be brave, too."

Warren didn't say anything to that. He stared at Jess a long time, his eyes flashing signals she couldn't interpret. She supposed the mysterious messages carried great import—like what she'd tried to convey when she'd spoken—but expressions were even murkier things than words.

Jess wasn't even sure her speech made sense, but she was sure of one thing.

"My burger's getting cold."

She walked away, leaving Warren behind.

Storm

J ess nibbled at her cheeseburger. While not precisely "cold," it had lost its steamy excess. She felt that way herself.

Todd and Joe engaged in animated—if stilted—conversation long past the time when Jess consumed her last bite.

"No sleep, either?" Todd's shoulders jerked upward in incredulity and shuddered on their way back down. "What about ...?"

"Sandman's special," Joe interjected. "Far's we know, he fell asleep when he come in so that's how he'll stay."

Todd seemed to be mulling it over.

"What's the point of forever without some creature comfort?"

"You can eat," Warren offered, tipping his head toward Jess.

Joe raised his glass.

"And drink!"

"That's something," Todd allowed. "But it's not enough."

Joe snorted.

"Nobody never decides for themselves what's enough." He ladled derision over the last word like gravy, hot and thick. "Goldilocks' just a story. Real life ain't too much, too little, or juuuuust right. It's what it is, and that's all."

"And you call this 'real' life?"

"What would you call it, then?" Warren said, giving voice to the curiosity Jess held back.

Todd considered the question before making his pronouncement.

"Surreal half-life."

"And what's that mean?" Joe demanded.

"It's the best I can do." Todd's voice contained his shrug this time.

"It's better than you can do, idiot," Warren needled Joe.

Jess wanted to plug her ears to obscure Joe's habitual reply, but she couldn't muster the energy. Besides, the words never came. Instead, the door to the bar opened and Jess watched, stunned, as Tracy hurried back inside, drenched and frantic to close the door behind her.

"I couldn't wait out that downpour a minute longer," she exclaimed, flicking droplets of water off her head as she shook it. "I've never seen such rain! It wasn't anything much when I stepped out, but the minute I let the boys out to air, it ... Todd, what are you drinking?"

"Now, Trace, it's just a nip of bourbon."

"Todd, really? You'll be too sleepy to stay awake and help me get back home!" Tracy cocked her head, listening to a storm Jess couldn't hear. "Although, if we have to wait much longer, I might not be able to drive all the way back tonight."

Jess shot a glance at Joe, but he'd gone back to his drink. Warren shook himself out of his apparent trance enough to offer Tracy a seat next to Todd.

"Thank you. Where can I hang my coat?"

Warren extended his hand while Jess stared, dumbfounded.

"Give it to me; I'll put it over a chair."

As Warren moved away with Tracy's coat, the woman arrested her movements with a start, hands flying up to cover her heart.

"Goodness, that strike must have been almost on top of us!" She glanced around the bar. "Didn't any of you hear that?"

"Hear what?" Joe said, and Warren, draping the saturated coat over the back of the chair across from Jess, sighed.

"Joe's hard of hearing."

"Nuh-uh, dumbass."

"What about ..." Tracy began to point but again, Joe jumped in to explain Sandman, sparing Warren.

"Him? He sleeps like the dead."

Tracy was not entirely diverted, and directed her accusatory finger at Jess and Warren.

"And you two?"

"I like storms," Jess offered. It was true, or used to be. She found the idea of a storm right over her head that she couldn't see or hear to be unsettling and sad.

"I don't scare easily," Warren said.

Joe faked a cough that clearly contained the word, "Bull."

"Well, I do." Tracy maneuvered Warren's abandoned stool as close to Todd as she could and climbed onto it.

"Gets cold easy too, she does," Todd said, lifting one arm and wrapping it around his wife.

"Try whiskey," Joe suggested.

Warren, rejoining the group at the bar, rolled his eyes.

"Oh, thank you, no. But what I wouldn't say 'no' to is an Irish coffee," Tracy said. The bartender nodded. Tracy glanced over her shoulder at Jess. "Would you like something? Maybe they have hot chocolate?"

Jess shook her head.

"No. But thanks."

"Where are you all from?" Tracy asked. "I didn't ask that already, did I? My memory's not what it used to be and every one of you must have parked behind the bar, because we didn't see any cars when we drove up."

She paused, looking at Joe expectantly.

"Vegas," Joe said, just when Jess thought he would refuse to speak.

Warren chimed in next.

"Sacramento."

Then they all turned to Jess.

"Jessamy?" Warren prompted.

"Montana," she finally bit out. "Butte."

"We're from Colorado Springs," Tracy said. "And we all wound up in this little bar out on the prairie in South Dakota. Fancy that!"

"Yes. Fancy that." Warren elbowed Joe, who glared at him.

"Where are you heading?"

Tracy asked that question with a sweet inquisitiveness Jess supposed she'd once possessed, too. But now that she was trapped in Between, questions bared previously hidden fangs at every opportunity, even those she saw coming.

Jess found the repeated bites excruciating. Though smarting, she forced herself to respond first.

"I don't really have a plan. I'm ... between jobs."

Joe, who had been attempting to drain his glass of all its whiskey—a substantial amount—blew the residuals back out. Warren pounded his back, and Joe quickly slapped him away.

"'Between jobs,'" Joe laughed, and it snagged on the uneven edges of the conversation's underlayment. "That's ..."

"An accurate description for all of us, I'm afraid," Warren finished.

Tracy shook her head.

"The economy is just awful, isn't it?"

"Never been the same since 9-11," Todd said. "Never will be again."

The atmosphere at the bar became uniformly somber then, and Jess surmised Joe and Warren must know about the events of September 11, 2001 from other occasional patrons. She supposed talking to people who came into the bar was a reasonably good way to keep up with current events.

Future events.

"I'll find something soon," she dared to say, trying to break the gloomy spell cast by Todd's observation. "I'm a waitress, and a good one. Something will open up."

"Can't live on tips alone," Todd said. "And tips is about all you make in food services."

"Todd, you know a strong young person can work her way up. And Jessamy is strong."

"Jess," Jess said, meeting Tracy's eyes and wondering what on earth would compel the woman to make a statement about her strength, with red and swollen evidence to the contrary staring her in the face.

"You're strong, no matter what you call yourself," Tracy said, intensity in every word. "I can tell."

How? Jess wondered, but could not ask. She dropped her eyes.

Warren redirected the conversation back to its previous, more structured track.

"I'm not sure I'll find any work. My skills are ... outdated."

"You got skills?" Joe derided. "News to me!"

"And how long have you gentlemen known each other?" Tracy said, diverted.

"Too long," Warren said, raising his voice over Joe's, "Long enough."

"Familiarity breeds contempt," Todd said, and Tracy wrapped her arms around him.

"Familiarity breeds comfort," she returned. Their heads dipped, meeting in a gentle bump that illustrated Tracy's assertion to perfection.

"Well. There will be no breeding in here." Warren's eyes fluttered to Jess just as he finished interjecting the play on words, and she winced at his dismay. She looked away, hoping he wouldn't compound her own discomfort by apologizing.

At least the evidence of the child she carried wasn't as obvious as her inability to rescue herself. And Tracy called her strong! The compliment, Jess found, stung worse than Tracy's questions.

"Oh, that's divine."

Jess looked up to see Tracy sipping from a coffee cup. The bartender must have just delivered the spiked drink, for she nodded at Tracy's approval and turned away, taking the bottle of Irish cream with her.

"All it needs is a touch," Tracy went on with a sip and a happy sigh. "Most places add too much, but here ... well, it's like you read my mind. Thank you!"

It was another comment whose meaning multiplied in Between and it made Jess shiver. When the bartender looked directly at Jess, her shiver morphed into a shudder.

"You are welcome," the bartender said, her eyes shifting smoothly from Jess to rest on Tracy.

"What a lovely voice you have. Isn't her voice amazing, Todd? It's almost musical."

"It is," Todd responded, squeezing Tracy with the arm curling around her body. As she curved into him, Todd crooked his other arm, bringing it up from its rest on the bar toward his head. From where Jess sat, it seemed clear that Todd wasn't trying to support or balance himself.

He was trying to feel his pulse.

Pointlessly, Jess held her breath as Todd pressed and paused. He tried several times before he gave up, lowering his arm to the bar more quickly than he'd raised it, as if its weight had become unendurable.

"Ugh, that rain!" Tracy cradled her cup with ferocity. "We might need an ark instead of a truck."

Joe rapped the base of his glass against the bar, signaling the bartender for a refill.

"You don't believe that crap, do you?"

Tracy and Todd turned as if one indivisible being. And in spite of not wanting to care, the knowledge of just how divided Tracy and Todd currently were compelled Jess' interest.

In that instant, it hurt not being able to breathe as a matter of course—Jess wanted to be able to suck strength from the atmosphere with a deep draw of air, a true breath of necessity for the struggle of "simply" living. She made an effort but Between's stagnant air might as well have been a vacuum; it left her as breathless as she'd been since her transition.

"Well, I was raised LDS—Mormon, you know—but I left the church years ago, so ..." Tracy shrugged. "I don't really know, to tell you the truth. But I can see the appeal of an ark with this kind of downpour."

Joe, who Tracy did not know couldn't hear a downpour in the world outside Between any more than he could hear a nuclear blast, shrugged.

"You've got the dogs for it," Jess said, and then giggled. "Sort of."

Tracy, craning her neck to look at Jess, looked blank, and then burst out laughing.

"They are a pair, those two, but they won't be able to repopulate the world!"

"Not that they don't try sometimes. Dogs will be dogs, and male dogs will be horny."

"Todd! Stop!" Tracy broke from their loose embrace, swatting Todd's shoulder. "You don't always have to find a way to say that, especially in public."

Jess wondered if every couple of long standing had their own banter, and if they did, why she'd not noticed its charm in the past? For all the tired, easy contempt familiarity could have produced here, it was plain to anyone—even those without a pulse—that for Todd and Tracy, indomitable love flourished instead, tempered by time's conviction.

It hurt Jess to think what she'd found with Lucas was so far removed from what Todd and Tracy shared that it required capital letters to emphasis its OPPOSITE nature.

The exhaustion of being present without living fell over Jess like a veil and she failed to follow the conversation as it meandered along. Words rang hollow and meaningless through her wooden efforts to ingest the remainder of her pointless meal; laughter resounded tinny and distant even as Jess pushed her unfinished food away.

She sat there ... just sat there. She was a side-note, a tangent. Peripheral, negligible, worthless ... and she felt it all as intensely as if stabbed by knives—no, as if run through by javelins.

Was this the sort of thing that eventually drove people out the door in spite of death lingering there? Did the proverbial last hope finally abandon them as definitively as their breath had done?

Jess jumped, startled by the intensity of her despair, and registered Tracy making a similar motion.

"This is insane," Tracy exclaimed, meeting Jess' glazed gaze and puncturing it with those words.

"It sure is," Jess managed to reply, even though she knew that entirely different situations inspired their similar sentiments.

112

"It's too bad you don't have rooms here. I'd take one in a …" Tracy continued, now speaking to the bartender. Her words broke off as the bartender cocked her head, smiled, and pointed upwards. "Oh, you do not. Really? But would you let us bring the dogs … you would?" Tracy clasped her hands together as the bartender nodded. "If this isn't a miracle, I don't know what is."

Jess wondered why she listened when it didn't really matter. Nothing really mattered, especially Jess herself, and then she remembered one thing that did.

"Eclipse!"

Jess said it without thinking and because of that, without modulating her tone. Four torsos pivoted, bringing four pairs of eyes onto her and making instant mockery of the notion dominating Jess' thoughts. The bartender, already facing her direction, merely shifted her eyes, upping the total regard upon Jess to an even total of ten orbs.

The speculation shattered Jess' preoccupation.

"My cat." Jess pushed back her chair and stood, horror gripping her as she remembered the static life of her child, also hanging in Between's makeshift balance. "I … I should make sure she's in my room before you bring your dogs."

Jess fled as fast as her benumbed body and spirit could take her, hurrying to make wholly honest the half-truths she'd spoken.

Riddles

Jess found the cat in her room with Love, curled in a ball on the bed while Love traced the quilt's patterns around her.

"Eclipse likes to pretend she can still sleep," Love said, looking up at Jess' entrance. The lines of her face shifted from tranquility to concern. "What's wrong?"

Jess paused, wondering how to summarize this, the latest in the daisy chain of wrongness blossoming in Between. She decided to skip to the specific concern she'd expressed at the bar.

"There's a couple staying the night. They have two dogs they'll be bringing upstairs ..."

"Oh! Let's shut the door."

Love rose to complete the task and Eclipse raised her head, startled from her assumed somnolence. Jess beat Love to the door and pressed it shut behind her, leaning against it. Love sank back onto the bed.

Eclipse regarded Jess with a wide stare and a slow blink and then resettled herself. Love offered the cat a lengthy, comforting stroke from head to tail.

"What else?" Love asked, her voice back in its usual range with its typical timbre. She bent her head and began running a finger over the quilt again.

"Tracy, the woman, isn't a regular. But Todd, Tracy's husband, he is ... except he isn't. He has a heartbeat, just barely."

Love's hand didn't pause in its delicate motion and she didn't look up, but she sounded surprised.

"That's different."

"It hasn't happened before?"

"What part?"

Jess paused, considering.

"All of it, I guess."

"Well, maybe it happened before I came. But it hasn't happened since. Regulars come in alone, except Warren and Sandman, I guess—and that's different another way. Even me and Joe came in alone. And your heart ... it just stops. It doesn't pretend, like Eclipse pretends to sleep."

"Then why ..." Love did raise her head then, frowning sternly. Jess understood the rebuke and rephrased. "Then what is different about Todd?"

Love shrugged, going back to her task with maddening calm.

"I don't know. Ask him."

Jess rejected that all-too-reasonable suggestion, her mind already jumping through hoops in hopes of solving the puzzle on its own.

"He's sick," she said. "He has a shaking disease. Parkinson's?"

"I don't know that sickness. But I know whether sickness comes first to your body or to your mind, it can make you sad. Real sad—the kind that runs through every part of you. The kind that makes you look forward to your death even if you don't go looking for it."

Love's description made Jess think harder, pause longer. Love's words—Love's instantly relatable words—plucked understandable fear and terrifying comfort out of the raw emptiness enmeshed in Jess' experience for so long she scarcely remembered being without it.

"Is that what brings us to Between? Looking forward to death, even if we don't search for it?"

"I don't think we come to Between. I think it comes to us. I think it wants us to make a choice."

"But I made a choice—we all did. We didn't go out!"

Love brought her tracing finger up, redirecting it toward Jess.

"If you chose to live, your heart would beat."

"That's not something I can control. You don't 'think' your heart to beat, it just does."

"Not here, it doesn't," Love said, and wagged her finger. "Quiet. I hear the dogs coming."

Jess heard them, too. Their claws, seeking stability on the stairs, resounded as if representing twice the number of animals they actually bore. As they drew closer, she heard them panting as well, making a living, raucous racket—alarming Eclipse so much that she jumped up and then down, slipping underneath the bed before Love or Jess could reach for her.

"Easy, boys ... easy." It was Tracy's voice, followed immediately by a stuttering cascade of sound. "Pike, stop that! Oh, next time I'm bringing extra towels to dry you off so you don't paint the inside spaces as wet as Mother Nature's doing outside. I should know better, I really should ..."

Tracy passed Love's door and ushered the dogs into the room next to Jess'. The muting of the dogs' abundant noises when Tracy closed the door was a relief approaching a blessing.

"Eclipse ... Eclipse, it's okay. They're gone. They won't come in here." Love knelt next to the bed, lowering her head to direct her words to the cat, who remained deep in her makeshift burrow.

"I'll get out of here so you can make Eclipse comfortable ... although as loud as those dogs are, you might want to take her into your room," Jess said, scrambling to her feet as quietly as she could. She exited the room without waiting for Love's acknowledgment or reply.

And almost ran into Tracy in the hallway.

"Whoops!" Tracy reached out a hand to steady Jess, but Jess stepped out of reach. Tracy almost frowned at Jess' rapid reversion, catching the expression and modulating her face into a small smile that bespoke a perception Jess loathed seeing ... yet again.

"I got the boys settled," Tracy said, jerking her thumb back toward the door behind her and then rolling her eyes as a "thud" and popping noise ricocheted through the walls. "Excuse me." She walked back to the door and rapped sharply against it, silencing the sounds in a split second. "Tom! Pike! You settle down and go to bed now, you hear me?"

"Dogs," Tracy said, shaking her head as she came back to where Jess remained, frozen. "Your poor cat must be beside himself ... herself? ... yes, herself." Tracy slid an arm around Jess' shoulders before Jess could react and gently steered them both to the stairwell. "So, do you recommend the burgers here? I saw you didn't finish yours."

"I'm ... they're very good. I'm just not that hungry." Jess found the light weight of Tracy's arm oddly comforting; she let herself be escorted down the stairs wrapped in the half-hug.

"It comes and goes, doesn't it? The way I remember, anyway. Morning sickness, all-day sickness ..."

"I ..."

Tracy released Jess' shoulders and stepped slightly in front of her as they reached the bottom of the stairway.

"I can't help but envy you. I was never able to carry one to term." Pain moved over Tracy's face in a solid cloud. It blotted out the light Jess now understood to radiate from determination rather than natural tendency.

"You'll take care of this baby, protect her from anything that might hurt her. You'll take care of this baby all her life, won't you."

It didn't sound like a question but Jess nodded, her paltry assurance making her temple flare as brilliantly as a star going nova.

"That's why you're strong. But you must believe it ... every minute, every day. You can't forget it for a second! You can't let anyone harm the life you nurture inside you. No matter who they are or what they say or how many times they say it won't happen again. You hear me?"

As intensely as she wanted to proclaim for her own the dedication Tracy exemplified, it was, instead, a tired refrain that emerged when Jess opened her mouth.

"You don't understand ..."

Tracy grabbed both of Jess' shoulders then—as tightly as Lucas might have done but without the desire for control in her grasp, only desperation birthed by loss.

"But I do. My best friend, Serena, she told me I didn't understand, too. But I did. And Serena kept going back to the man who hit her until one day, he did more than use his hands ... he took a gun and he shot her. He shot their four-year old son, he shot their newborn daughter, and then he shot the mother of his children. The last thing he did was shoot himself and I wish to God almighty that was the first thing, but it wasn't. It wasn't."

Tracy shook her head as if in physical pain.

"I do understand, you see? And so do you, so stop pretending you don't."

Tears drained Tracy's eyes, reminding Jess of what bled from the wall when she carved her name. The comparison chilled her, inspiring her to stay and absorb Tracy's every word, to witness each emotion driving her. Jess grew numb as Tracy's agony coalesced, changing into confusion and sadness, hope draining her as fluid leached her eyes.

"You don't believe I'm strong enough to l-l-leave," Jess whispered.

Tracy blinked, and to Jess' shock, laughed.

"Oh, hon. Of course I believe you're strong enough to leave."

Tracy dragged one forearm across her eyes, smearing the evidence of her outburst into the fabric of her sleeve. She faced Jess' disbelief, meeting it with a challenge.

"Of course I believe you're strong enough to leave," she repeated. "Any woman strong enough to stay is more than strong enough to leave. That's what I understand ... and what you don't."

Instead of confronting the import of those words, Jess whirled away from the first floor's light and fled up the stairs to her room's dim isolation. There, she shut the door hard, remembering Eclipse only after the violence of the sound penetrated the remnant threads of the spell Tracy wove.

Fortunately, Love had followed Jess' suggestion, leaving the room blissfully empty.

Any woman strong enough to stay is more than strong enough to leave.

Nonsense!

Jess looked down at the small, clenched ball of her hand, white-knuckled and lifeless, curled around the doorknob. She could never fight Lucas, never get away from him ... he'd follow her, he'd hurt her worse than he ever had. Maybe he'd even kill her ...

What kind of strength did Tracy think she had to stay, to keep getting hurt? It wasn't a question of being tough. It wasn't a question at all, Jess fumed, ripping her hand from the door and shaking the bloodless knot in a futile attempt to release some of the tension holding her together.

Jess couldn't answer unposed questions, couldn't solve impossible riddles, couldn't make hopeless choices.

Any woman strong enough to stay is more than strong enough to leave.

Ridiculous. Maddening. Wrong.

A soft sound arrested Jess' mental turmoil, and she recognized it as Zane's door before the additional tempo of his time-keeping efforts reached her as he passed. In an instant, Jess' anger at the trap her own life had become transferred to Zane, and she wanted to rattle him just as Tracy had shaken her—to urge him to do things differently and break free from the holding pattern to which he committed himself.

But Between held them all, even Tracy, though she remained ignorant of her auxiliary entrapment. Between's prison remained immutable for its regulars, its supernaturally assigned sentences of unknown duration fixed, with death the singular promise of liberation.

That idea gave Jess a pause so intense she felt its coldness as physical sensation. If Between, unreal though it seemed, represented the true impediment, could it ... could it be that Lucas, real as he was, also possessed less power than Jess assigned him?

The notion passed almost as quickly as it came.

But tendrils tickled Jess' mind when Zane trudged back to his room. And ghosts haunted her when Tracy and Todd ambled by much later. When quiet settled on Between's second floor with all the dignity of Eclipse arranging her lithe body for one of her faux naps, Jess stood exactly where she had been standing earlier, thinking about whether what Tracy said could somehow, some way, be true.

Any woman strong enough to stay is more than strong enough to leave.

Whether she, Jessamy, could somehow, some way, be just ... strong ...enough.

It was Jess' longest night yet in Between. She wondered if she'd transformed into a statue, converting the impossibility of her life into functional immobility. She fancied, without appropriate terror for the prospect, she would eventually crumble, bit by bit, until nothing but rubble remained.

Only remembrance of the life within her—on hold with her—reminded Jess of how it felt to want to live. She frowned then, thinking about Love's idea that she had to will her heart to beat in Between. This didn't explain the inert "life" of her baby ... unless the tiny fetus within her was too tied to Jess to do anything beyond following her lead?

Jess found her hands cradling her barely-there belly, one clasped over the other in a doubly protective layer. She tried—oh, how she tried—to force her heart to beat, her lungs to inhale with the effortless reflex they'd once possessed, and her mind to seek the temporary stasis of sleep rather than the eternal stagnancy Between offered ... one way or another.

She labored all night to bring herself back to the fullness of her own life so she might truly mother the barest beginnings of the life inside her.

By the time Tracy rose to take the dogs downstairs, Jess conceded failure. She mourned where she stood—neither alive nor dead—crying without sound or tears, suffused with abundant desire to fill the pervasive emptiness.

But without the knowledge or means to do so.

Morning

J ess roused from mourning after Tracy's return, sans dogs. She and Todd spoke loudly in their room and while it seemed an even-tempered dispute as far as Jess could tell, it carried clear tones of disagreement. Jess finally determined to escape from her room but just as she began the process, Tracy exited hers as well.

"I'll be back in an hour, then. No more!" Tracy pulled the door shut with excessive force and sighed, letting her hand fall from the doorknob with a heaviness that spoke to something beyond mere gravity.

She jumped when she looked up and saw Jess frozen in her own doorway.

"I'm so sorry; I hope we didn't wake you."

Though she'd just spent the better part of a night yearning for the simple ability to sleep, Jess felt pleased to be able to answer honestly.

"No, you didn't."

"Well, you look like you haven't slept a wink ... I'm sorry. I shouldn't have said that, either. Let me buy you breakfast; Warren tells me Eli makes an amazing omelet."

Jess, who had no idea Eli cooked anything other than burgers and the occasional deep-fried appetizer, found herself suddenly curious to determine the extent of his cooking repertoire.

"That sounds really good, actually."

"Wonderful! Todd won't ... well, he won't be up for a while, and I don't like to have breakfast alone." Tracy moved briskly toward the stairs and Jess hurried to follow. "You know, this will be nice. I'm surrounded by boys at home, so female company is a treat."

Tracy lapsed into silence for a few steps, but faced Jess once more on the landing.

"Don't get me wrong. I love Todd and the dogs to dea- ... to pieces, but I ..."

"I understand." Jess rushed the words out in an attempt to smooth the worry lines deepening over Tracy's face.

The incongruity of Jess' understanding today overlaid Tracy's from last night, flopping down uncomfortably like a sack of dirty laundry.

"What kind of omelets does Eli make?" Jess asked, striving to sound casual and knowing she wasn't succeeding.

Tracy's smile started out lopsided but it evened so quickly Jess nearly missed its forced beginning.

"Let's find out, shall we?"

Joe and Warren were, of course, at the bar, but Jess wouldn't have expected otherwise. Someone had laid a blanket over Sandman's shoulders and Jess knew that if Tracy hadn't personally done so, it must have happened per her request. While she might not have borne a child herself, Jess recognized in Tracy an innate mother—one who cared for others out of genuine concern.

It tore at Jess to recognize such kindness, particularly here and now.

"So what's for breakfast?" Tracy seemed to be asking the room at large as she and Jess seated themselves.

Warren answered for the incongruent group as the bartender readied her pad and pencil.

"Eli can make pretty much anything, but most people seem to like his Denver omelet best."

"That's what I'll have, then," Tracy declared. "Todd and I always go with the house specialty. How about you, Jessamy?"

"The same," Jess said. And wondered anew at the sound of her full name, which she'd eschewed in Lucas' presence.

As the bartender delivered their orders to the window and sounded the bell, Jess considered how "Jessamy" rang less false in her ears today. "Jessamy", in fact, sounded more like her name now than "Jess."

Her eyes shot to the wall, finding her etching like a dart flying true to the precise center of a bull's eye target. Warren's name and Sandman's, she found with slightly more effort.

Then she had to ask.

"Joe?"

"What?"

"Where's your name?"

Joe turned, regarding her with a blank expression. After a long pause, he lifted his hand—curled around his omnipresent whiskey—and extended his arm, pointing with the drink.

Jess followed the downward slant and strained her vision to find "JOE DRABYAK" carved in block lettering behind Sandman's table.

"Should of made it bigger," Joe observed, taking a perfunctory slug of whiskey before shifting back to face the bar. "Least I used the cap letters."

"What an interesting tradition! Do you all have your names on the wall here?" Tracy kept talking, giving no one the opportunity to answer. "Joe Dra ... Joe, how do you pronounce your last name?"

"Just like how it's spelled," Joe said, and Warren laughed. Joe glanced expectantly at his drinking partner, but when Warren declined to speak, Joe continued.

"Just a thing for us regulars. Stick around long enough and you can add your name, too."

124

Tracy shook her head.

"Oh, I don't know about that." Her smile slipped again, Jess saw. When Tracy noticed Jess regarding her, she looked away, glancing all about her. "Odd there's no jukebox here ..."

It wasn't the oddest thing about Between, but Jess didn't say that.

"Between's unique, alright," Warren said, speaking into his glass.

"It is that," Tracy agreed, too quickly. "So, Jessamy, when is your baby due?"

Warren lowered his glass without drinking.

"I'm only about eight weeks along," Jess answered.

Tracy tipped her head back, thinking about it.

"So, a Christmastime baby? Or close to that ... goodness. That's wonderful."

Jess considered how this pregnancy was less than 'wonderful' for so many reasons and her eye began to throb. Then it occurred to her to think how very long she could be pregnant, and while caught up in the horror of that contemplation, realized Tracy still waited for her response.

"I hadn't really thought about it!" She forced the words as an exclamation. She struggled to do the math, using her fingers to count for she'd never been able to figure time's passing otherwise. She could calculate tips in her head, but any time she tried to sort out days, months, or years, she'd wind up one short or one long.

"I think you're right. But it's hard to say exactly. I ... I haven't been to a doctor yet."

"Oh, but you need your vitamins and ..."

"It's okay, really. When I get out of here ..." Tracy's eyes widened, and Jess stopped. "Well, when ... I'm just waiting ... I'm going to get a new job and find a free clinic."

Tracy nodded, and relief washed over Jess at the affirmation.

"I'll give you our home number, Jessamy. If you can't find something near here—or wherever you end up—you call me and I'll help you. I'll search online for you, make some calls if you'd like."

That caught Jess off guard, yanking her from the vague dreams she had of being "Jessamy" and thrusting her back into the chaos of being "Jess." *Help.* Lucas told her he'd "help" her, too. Remembering how far Lucas' help degenerated from the first time he smiled at her injected a horse-sized dose of fear directly into Jess' veins.

But Tracy wasn't Lucas. Tracy waved to the bartender, oblivious to Jess' stunned state, and asked for a piece of paper and loan of the bartender's pencil. She wrote neatly and passed the paper to Jess while murmuring gentle "thanks" to the bartender.

Tracy offered help, and it was Jess' option to accept it.

"Thank you," Jess managed, studying the number noted prominently on the back of the order sheet. She even smiled at the "T-n-T" written underneath it.

"Just if you can't find a doctor yourself. I always think it's better to find your own physician, especially with something so personal as a baby on the way." Tracy spoke softly, inclining her head toward Jess and away from the disinterested men.

"I appreciate it," Jess said, and found that it was true. At least, it was true for the person she wanted to be ... for the Jessamy Mama raised.

Tracy patted Jess' hand and sighed, looking around the bar. Her eyes rested lightly on the wall with its burden of names and then she brought her gaze back to Jess.

"I cannot see scratching my name on the wall there." She forced a laugh. "I'd just as likely cut myself doing it, and get blood all over the place."

Jess' return smile tightened under the force of memory.

At the bar, Warren coughed.

"You ladies are in for a treat," he said. "Eli is his best with breakfast."

"It is the most important meal of the day," Eli's voice boomed from the kitchen. Jess peered around the barricade of Joe's body and saw Eli's face in the window just before he straightened. He set two plates into the space his great head just occupied and rang the bell.

"Order up!"

"That smells heavenly," Tracy declared, leaning over the food when the bartender set it down. "And what a generous portion—I may need to share with the boys ..." She took a careful bite from the edge, and closed her eyes as she chewed. "No ... no, this is far too good to share, even if poor Todd has to roll me out to the truck after I eat it all."

Tracy dug in as if famished—and since she was alive, Jess supposed she must be quite hungry. While the aroma seeping through the air took "delicious" to an extreme, Jess struggled to eat. It did not escape her that while she'd received the gift of being able to eat anything without gaining an ounce, she failed to properly appreciate even a beneficial aspect of her luck.

Because this "good" fortune blended inextricably with the worst of tidings absolved Jess from feeling too much guilt.

She smiled at Tracy and made an effort to eat enthusiastically. The omelet was exceptional, as advertised, and that helped.

Of greater aid and import was Tracy's conversation.

"I love wildflowers this time of year," she began. "Forget-me-nots are my favorite; have you ever seen them blooming in the mountains, Jessamy?"

Jess had, and nodded an affirmative.

"They remind me of hand-stitching on quilts, like the ones upstairs—there's a delicate nature to Forget-me-nots. What do they make you think of?"

Stymied by the deceptively simple question, Jess said the first thing that came to mind.

"The sun in a summer sky."

"Those are the exact colors, aren't they? The perfect sky-blue and the bright yellow star in the center. A forever summer, that's what Forget-me-nots look like."

From flowers, Tracy asked Jess about Eclipse. Not how long she'd had the cat, but what Jess liked most about her.

"She's very soft, but her purr is the best. A cat won't purr if she isn't comfortable with you."

Tracy laughed, and then scurried to hide her open mouth behind her napkin.

"Excuse me, but that's one thing my boys can't do... purr. And they're too active, I think, for a cat to be comfortable around them. Pike is more of a snuggler than Tom—once he's good and tired out, that is—but he can't purr, and that's a fact."

In contrast with what she'd said to Jess last night, Tracy chose only easy topics this morning. And Jess delighted in breakfasting with the other woman despite the strain of the previous evening.

Joy in a timeless state bore a striking resemblance to joy in the "real" world, and Jess knew it by the rapidity with which the meal ended ... seemingly right after it started.

"Incredible," Tracy proclaimed, tucking a generous selection of bills alongside her empty plate. "I'll just pop outside to check the weather—it was fine when I took the boys out earlier—and then go up and see if Todd's ready yet."

She stood, prepared to match words with action, although she did place one hand over her midriff as she straightened.

"Goodness, I'm full. But it was lovely ... thank you," she called in the direction of the kitchen, raising her voice. She lowered it again as she turned back to Jess, eyes sparkling as if to defy ever-knowing darkness. "Thanks for joining me, Jessamy. I enjoyed talking with you."

Then Tracy did exit Between, with an ease and comfort Jess envied. She walked right out into the searing brightness Jess saw, into the demonic chaos Warren feared, into the flat darkness Joe knew. Because Tracy didn't see any of it ... she saw the rest of her life, starting with an ordinary day outside the extraordinary oddity that was Between.

"What's Todd going to do if she can't get back in? What's she going to do? How many times can she just come and go and why just her?" Jess demanded after the door closed behind Tracy.

Joe cast a cantankerous glance over his shoulder; Warren shrugged, not bothering to face Jess.

"Who knows? Wait and see. Hey." Joe nudged Warren's elbow with his own. "Hey, that'd be another name for this place."

"Not really," Warren retorted. "You forget about Don." He pointed to the wall, closer to the door. Jess and Joe both squinted in that direction. "He did his name in Braille—well, that's what he said. Doesn't look like anything to me."

Joe snorted. "Didn't know that was a name. Anyways, before my time."

"Not before mine," Warren bit out the words with sharpness bolstered by torment.

"But ... " Before Jess could redirect the conversation, the door reopened, showing Jess, Warren, and Joe everything they didn't want to acknowledge.

Out of their individual visions stepped Tracy, once again.

"Beautiful day, isn't it?" She beamed, shoving the door shut. "It always is, after a rain."

Shadows

"If it's a beautiful day out there, it's only because of you," Todd called from the stairwell.

Tracy dashed across the bar and met her husband, wrapping her arm around his waist. "Todd, why didn't you wait for me?"

"Now, Trace, you know I still get around fine, long as I go slow." They strode across the floor together in a singular motion that might have seemed awkward if it hadn't been so seamless. "You had breakfast?"

Jess looked across the evidence of her repast with Tracy and then up, meeting Todd's eyes. His formerly hooded gaze seemed to have unveiled overnight.

"I did, with Jessamy." Tracy smiled when she said it, squeezing Todd against her. "Sit, sit!" She directed Todd to the chair she'd occupied earlier as the bartender emerged on the scene to collect the used dishes. "I don't need any change, but can we get a couple of coffees? To go?"

The bartender paused, giving Tracy both a sharp look and a slight nod, and then continued on to clear the table.

"No point in sitting when we're about to leave," Todd commented, though he was already seated when he said it.

"I was thinking we should have a cuppa first and then refill if it's good and strong," Tracy said, patting his arm. "You let me know if you like the coffee when it comes; I've got to visit the restroom."

Since the bartender's hands were occupied, Jess numbly pointed down the hall.

"Yes, I know, but thank you," Tracy acknowledged with a wink.

When the bathroom door shut behind Tracy, Jess leaned forward. Her voice, when it emerged, sounded strident even to her.

"You can't leave; you'll die."

Todd leveled the fullness of his vision at Jess, and raised a trembling hand to his throat.

"It's back up to speed," he said, pressing his fingers against his neck.

"What?" Jess grabbed Todd's other hand, flipping it over and searching until she found the pulse point there.

And felt his sure, steady heartbeat.

Jess let go of Todd as if he was an ember fresh from the fire. "How?"

Todd shrugged, letting his raised hand join its partner on the table. He tapped the plain gold band encircling the third finger of his left hand.

"I held that woman all night while she slept and I didn't. I felt her breathing while I didn't. I heard the dogs when they came over to check on me, to nuzzle her. She slept, I didn't. She breathed, I didn't.

When I was diagnosed, we both didn't sleep. It's like I've been holding my breath ever since. And she ..."

Todd paused, looking down the hall and back to Jess.

"She made peace with it. She's scared, but she's at peace. I used to think about how much it was hurting her to see me start ... going. It was all I could think about. How much she has to do, how much more she'll have to do. But she ... she just wants to be together, as long as we can. That's what she always wanted. She doesn't mind if she has to take care of me ... and I thought about it.

I decided I don't mind if she takes more care than she needs. It's how she loves, that's all."

Jess heard the door open down the hall and knew Tracy was returning. Todd must have heard, too, because he lowered his voice as the bartender placed a cup in front of him, and one to his side. Steam slithered out the tiny opening in the lid, dancing like a snake for its charmer.

"I won't take her chance to love away from her. If I did, I wouldn't be loving her as much as she loves me."

"Todd, you'd better not be giving away my coffee." Tracy bent to kiss Todd's cheek before occupying the chair next to him. She carefully opened the lid of her cup, freeing the trapped heat and inhaling the scent.

"It's strong, alright," Todd proclaimed. "Can tell by the smell."

"I knew it was strong last night when I had it Irish but you never quite know how coffee will stand alone. So let's see if it's good?" Tracy's eyes smiled over the cup she raised and the corresponding expression on her lips broadened after she sampled the coffee. "Oh, is it ever."

"Too hot for me." Todd's words broke through Jess' numbness. Her eyes fell to the paper slip on which Tracy had written her phone number, still lying on the table.

Tracy swapped her open cup with Todd's still-sealed one. "It'll cool faster this way. You're sure to want a second cup."

"I do," Todd agreed.

He was looking at Tracy, not his coffee.

Jess regarded the couple, their eyes locked in a way that excluded everything around them. Though "only" having coffee in a run-down bar, by the love woven tight between them they could have been dining on delicacies in the private alcove of a world-class restaurant.

It burned to look directly at something so brilliant.

Jess reached for the paper, tucking it into her pocket before Todd looked away from Tracy, breaking the spell.

"Saw that cat of yours," he said. "Unless there's two living here?"

"There's just Eclipse." Jess' voice sounded flat in her ears, but she supposed it would seem normal to anyone else.

"Pretty thing. Shy, though."

"Yes. She hissed at me when I found her in the entryway."

"Oh, poor dear, she was probably abandoned," Tracy offered. "That or she saw ..."

"Trace." Todd said it gently, but his single utterance halted Tracy's flow of words as effectively as a switch.

"Well. It's good she has you now. And the rest of you." Tracy threw her last comment over her shoulder.

"We got a cat?" Joe drawled, though he did not deign to turn around.

"We do, idiot." Warren slapped Joe's shoulder. "Black cat, too."

"Sounds about right." Joe raised his glass with exaggerated slowness. "Dumbass."

Tracy shook her head and sipped her coffee.

"They're as bad as us, Todd."

"Worse, I'd say," Todd replied. The couple went back to gazing at each other and Jess felt superfluous all over again.

She wanted to leave but felt ill-prepared to excuse herself. The bartender caught her eye, and Jess raised one hand in a feeble wave.

"Ice water, please?"

The bartender nodded in a short, flat motion. The absent undertone of the gesture both comforted and unsettled—a hallmark incongruity of Between.

Jess' water arrived shortly and Tracy asked if it was as crisp as the coffee.

"Coffee can't be good without good water," Todd said, when Jess didn't answer right away.

Jess thought about the water that had run through the old house she'd grown up in with her mother. Though she'd never considered that water as good or bad—had never pondered it at all, really—just thinking of it now made her mouth feel as if it were about to pucker.

"Maybe that explains why I never liked coffee?" She forced a smile for the couple in front of her and then took a sip from her glass, reflecting on the minute sample with unfamiliar care.

"You know, you're right. This is very good."

"Water don't taste like nothing," Joe snorted.

"Oh, but it does," Tracy argued, eyes sparkling. "It tastes like purity or it tastes like it picked up something vile on its way from wherever it came through the pipes to get here."

"Pipes, hell." Joe rattled the cubes in his glass. "The way the whiskey tastes here, the water's angel pee!"

"Excuse Joe," Warren said, and Joe directed a daunting frown at him.

"Excuse *me?*"

"You've had a few too many. A few too many barrels," Warren went on, undeterred. Then he laughed in the face of Joe's wrath until Joe's facade broke with a smirk.

"You shouldn't talk. But you do. And too much, too."

"But we all agree—it's good water." Tracy raised her cup. "To good water and good company."

"I'll drink to that." Warren looked at Joe. "And when do you suppose we might get some good company?"

"These folks," Joe waved his glass in Tracy and Todd's general direction, "are plenty good. You're the problem."

"Of course, of course," Warren said, slapping Joe on the back. "How about you buy the next round?"

That jibe raised Joe's ire again, but Tracy laughingly intervened.

"Here, let us buy you one for the ... entertainment we've enjoyed here. Between is a bar unlike any other and all of its regulars are special, too."

"What do you suppose she means by that?" Warren asked Joe.

"She's talking about you, Warren, not about me."

They spent the next half hour or so in casual and joking conversation, trading dull jests and shallow questions with no particular agenda—unless lightheartedness itself was the plan. It irked Jess, and yet, the time passed in relative painlessness apart from the intense glances between Todd and Tracy ... those made Jess feel as if she were treading a tight-wire between awe and envy.

Like her thoughts regarding water's flavor, Jess couldn't recall a previous awareness of her feelings about abiding love. Perhaps her former ambivalence contributed to the present import—that, and the singularly oppositional nature between Todd and Tracy's united bond and what Jess shared with Lucas.

No, "shared" wasn't even correct. Jess' and Lucas' relationship stood on the treacherous foundation of taking: what Lucas took from Jess, and what she let him take ... because she'd rather let him take than be alone.

Where did that come from?

The thought was icy, colder by far than the water in her glass. Jess felt for so long—without putting it into words—that she couldn't break away from Lucas. Now she bore the burden of the anathematic notion that she played a role in choosing to remain with him.

Jess traced the path of a drop of condensation down her glass with her finger and then angled it sharply away to one side. Conversation continued to flow around her without her participation and water continued to condense on Jess' frigid glass. The next water droplet began its decent but hesitated when it caught in the line Jess had created, clearly beginning to follow this intercepting course before gravity overwhelmed its detour.

The drop's momentary deviation startled Jess, or perhaps it was Tracy's words that yanked her out of her musings back into the main-stage happenings in Between.

"Ready for your second cup?" Tracy asked Todd. "We really should be going."

She waved to the bartender.

"Refills, please?"

Todd inhaled deeply and Jess dropped her eyes back to her glass, preferring its stoic stance to watching Todd's pleasure in his again-automatic intake of breath. He breathed because he needed to do so and enjoyed the fact. Jess rode a wave of invisible jealousy.

"I'll just make a pit stop and then we can head out," Todd said, rising.

Jess watched another drop on her glass start to move and this time, she etched a more gradual path below it. Scarcely satisfying, this activity was nevertheless something to do ... something she could affect, at least for a time.

"Jessamy." Tracy stretched her hand toward Jess after Todd moved away, drawing Jess' focus from her glass. She looked up, meeting Tracy's compassionate gaze with unease.

"Jessamy, whatever happens, you are strong enough. More than strong enough—I know you are. You try to believe it, too, and keep trying until you do. Please."

The words were barely a whisper, but their intensity belied the volume with which Tracy delivered them. In that instant, Jess almost believed in her own strength again.

Almost.

When Jess tore her eyes from the warmth of Tracy's back to the sodden, cold surface of her glass, she saw that her latest endeavor resulted in a longer digression than the previous one. The slower rate of change had led to a more significant and successful alteration in course.

Jess was no water droplet and Lucas certainly wasn't gravity. But if even a minim could—with a little help—avert succumbing to a straight line descent, maybe ... maybe Jess could, too.

Todd returned and Tracy rose from the table.

"Thank you for visiting Between," the bartender said, her musical voice sounding slightly off to Jess' ears. Still, the phrase galvanized her into action.

Jess jumped to her feet, interrupting Tracy's reply to the bartender before she spoke a single word.

"I'll get the door." She dismissed Tracy's protestations with a gentle wave. "It's fine. You've got hot coffee."

"Well, thank you, then." Tracy picked up both her cup and Todd's, surveying his progress. "Nice meeting you all." Her gaze touched Joe, Warren, and the watchful bartender ... then she brought her eyes back to Jess. "Good luck getting ... finding ..."

As Tracy floundered, Jess opened the door, hiding most of her body behind it and sheltering herself from the whiteness lurking outside. The eerie brilliance cast dark shadows from Tracy and Todd onto the bar's floor.

"Go on, Trace," Todd urged. "We'll be airing the boys again before we leave the lot if you don't go on." He stepped outside, his shadow nothing but the disembodied arm he stretched back toward Tracy.

Tracy nodded sharply then, a motion Jess saw peripherally as well as reflected in the odd, partial silhouette on the floor as Tracy followed Todd.

"You're strong. Don't forget, Jessa ..."

Her voice vanished as she crossed the threshold, breaking Jess' name nearly as far as Lucas did.

Jess closed the door, blocking her death's light as quickly as she could. The idea of losing herself cast a shadow that excluded all else, save terror.

Blame

"Has anyone ever come back?"

Warren raised his stare from his glass and directed it at Jess.

"Come back?" he repeated.

"To Between. Has anyone ever got out and come back later?"

Joe looked up next and scowled but Jess refused to back down. In the interminable expanse of time since Tracy and Todd left, no one else had entered the bar—not even one random patron.

And Jess was bored.

"How's a body gonna find it again?" Joe demanded.

"People win the lottery twice," Jess retorted, remembering a television show featuring such a person. "People get struck by lightning more than once, too." Though she'd only heard that story peripherally, bandied about by two older gentlemen who came in daily for coffee at the first restaurant she'd worked, she found herself saying it now as if it were gospel truth.

Joe appeared unconvinced, and his face stayed drawn down in the imposing frown he affected so well

"Maybe they do, maybe they don't. How'd we know? Not gonna get to carve your name twice."

"Sure, you could." Warren seemed interested, and straightened up as he spoke. "The wall only sings once, but even so, you could carve your name as many times as you wanted."

Joe lengthened his spine as well, rising like a dragon about to do battle.

"If you're going there, maybe they carved it twice while they was here once because there wasn't nothing else to do. Even if the wall sung twice for two stays, seems like you can write anything up there long as you think it's your 'true name' when you write it."

Joe spat his last sentence with such vehemence that Jess imagined she could see the residue of his words physically impacting the bar.

"Did you ever look? I mean, really look, up close?"

Joe managed to import an even greater grimness into his expression.

"Girl, we talk and we drink and we look around this bar all the time. What else we got going on?"

Warren shook his head.

"A few names might be similar, now that you mention it," he said.

Joe laughed.

"Of course, because I ain't the only Joe out there, and ... Warren. Warren, you dumbass ... you ain't serious ..."

But Warren did seem serious; he moved halfway across the bar by the time Joe gave up on him. Jess dared to gently punch Joe's shoulder as she rose to follow Warren and when she did, finally saw something other than a scowl cross his face. She couldn't discern quite what that other expression meant, but they'd been a gloomy group since Todd and Tracy departed—she preferred almost any emotion to sorrow.

Warren turned from his early perusal at the wall.

"This would be easier with a piece of paper."

"I'll ask the bartender," Jess replied, and reversed her path. "Oh!"

She almost bumped into the ethereal woman, who apparently glided up behind her. From his perch at the bar where he now faced them, Joe chuckled, drawing Jess' eye even as the bartender extended an old spiral notebook and pencil.

Jess took the proffered materials and the bartender, her errand completed, moved to the nearest table and began polishing its glossy surface.

"What ..." Jess began.

"Tic-tac-toe," Joe said, smirking. "Warren, you remember?"

"We used to play tic-tac-toe, yes. You mean to tell me there's a page in the old book we missed?"

"Of course, dumbass. Because you got sick of losing."

"Your memory leaves much to be desired," Warren said, his words as dry as Utah on Sunday morning.

Flipping through the pages as the two men spoke, Jess found most of them crammed with crosshatches, Xs, and Os. The shapes were larger in stature and irregularly placed near the front of the book and became more diminutive and carefully planned toward the back.

She found only a few unmarked pages.

"I can write small," she said. She bent the cover and intervening, full pages around, and rested the notebook on her forearm, pencil ready in her other hand.

"I'll read them off for you?" Warren suggested.

"Sounds good. Go."

"Roy Donovan, Terence Ruser ... wait, maybe I should spell them. I'll start over. Roy Donovan, R-O-Y D-O-N-O-V-A-N. Terence Ruser, T-E-R-E-N-C-E R-U-S-E-R ..."

Jess made hasty corrections.

"That works. Keep going."

The process would have been slow by normal standards, Jess supposed. Warren struggled to read a few of the inscriptions and Joe joined him to frown and puzzle over a particular name near the floor with the appearance of a raised scar instead of an indented engraving.

Engrossed in the unusual, illegible name with Warren and Joe, Jess scarcely registered Zane's routine arrival.

Warren was the first to be completely distracted from the perplexing "scab" of a name.

"Zane, shut the door already!"

Jess looked up from the notebook then and beyond the brightness she saw flaring out around Zane's body, she saw something else ... something she should have noticed immediately, for its lack enhanced the unusual quiet of Zane's pilgrimage.

"Zane!"

Jess dropped the pencil and notebook and ran forward, wrenching the door from the motionless hand holding it, all the while staring at Zane's other hand ... the one he always used to keep time. Because he stopped tracking time, that hand was free to raise and fight Jess for control of the door. Although skinny to the point of caricature, Zane was strong, too.

Zane's wiry power could not beat Joe and Jess together, however; the two of them finally prevailed.

"What're you doing?" Joe shouted, leaning back against the disputed door.

"He stopped!" Since she held Zane by his upper arms, her body between his and the portal Joe continued to guard, Jess couldn't point at the stillness of Zane's hand. "He stopped keeping time!"

Warren moved, placing a leaden arm around Zane's shoulders, his manicured nails clean and smooth, distracting Jess' gaze from the blankness of Zane's face as they moved together past her. The tension Jess had felt in Zane's body remained visible, but the urgency underlying it seemed to have disappeared.

"Come on, Zane ... sit down and take a load off."

Warren steered Zane to the nearest table. Zane sat on the chair Warren pulled out for him, hands dangling at his sides. The rigidity of the rest of Zane's body kept him from mimicking Sandman's full collapse nearby, hunched in perpetual sleep at the table he might never leave.

But the lines of Zane's face sagged in misery along with his arms and broadcast as certainly as a scream the despair through which Sandman slept.

"There isn't any more space," Zane said then. "In my room. The walls are full—they're full of time. Why can't I leave?"

Jess looked at Warren but his face was a reflection of the puzzlement she knew scrawled across her own: furrowed brow and thin-lined lips.

"Poor dumbass Zane." Joe abandoned his post by the door and moved around Jess, dragging out the chair next to Zane and easing his body onto it. "He thinks just because he filled up the walls with more marks than we got in the tic-tac-toe book, he done served his time. It ain't over 'til the fat lady sings, Zane."

He ruffled Zane's hair and glanced up at Jess.

"Get us some of them ice waters you like, Jessamy, and we'll sit with Zane."

Jess stood still, not convinced the danger had truly passed.

"He wasn't trying to go to his death. He just thought he was done." His assessment imparted, Warren took the seat on Zane's other side.

"Are you sure?"

"Sure, we're sure. Don't we look like we're sure?" Joe sounded like the same, irascible grump Jess assumed he truly was, but when he caught her eye over Zane's head, he winked.

"Okay." Jess continued to wrestle with the notion that Zane's lack of timekeeping didn't mean he'd given up on outlasting his waiting death but she had to admit he didn't look like he intended to fling his body out the door.

Jess turned to the bar to place the order for ice water and found the bartender already filling a second glass.

"None for me," Jess said, leaning in as she said it. She glanced at the table and saw Joe waving his hand in front of Zane's face.

"Don't do that, idiot." Warren slapped Joe's hand away; he didn't seem to have much energy to put to the task.

Three glasses were now ready and Jess murmured thanks without meeting the bartender's piercing eyes. She carried the glasses to the table in a little pyramid, fingers stretching around their perimeter and thumbs curving in along the edges of the two nearest her body.

"Here," she said, sliding one each to Zane, Joe, and Warren.

Joe pushed his glass away in disgust.

"He's back to not paying attention to nobody. I'm never gonna get to play poker."

Jess felt a surge of pain in her eye and its intensity made her gasp, drawing her hand to the sensitive spot without conscious effort.

"Take Joe's glass," Warren said. "He won't drink it without any whiskey to 'balance' it."

"Just for a minute." Jess scooped up the glass and moved to the fourth chair, the one opposite Zane. Because Warren and Joe pulled their chairs closer to Zane's, she felt like an outsider and the resumed throbbing at her temple only emphasized that impression.

Jess pressed the glass against the side of her head. And the four of them sat in a silence that swelled like an inflamed boil.

"This' dumb," Joe finally grunted, scratching his chair back and stomping over to the bar. "Whiskey!"

"You don't notice it much anymore, do you," Warren said to Jess then, nodding at her. Jess decided Warren wasn't seeking an answer as much as making a statement.

She just looked at him. Eventually, her staring felt rude.

"No. It's still there, though."

Warren sighed.

"They say you can get used to anything." He started by directing his words to Jess, but he glanced at Zane as he finished. "It just takes time."

"Time!" Zane's voice came out high-pitched, and the laugh following his near-shriek emerged solidly hysterical. Jess lowered the glass that now felt clammy in her hand.

"It feels like time is going on in here, Zane, but it's stopped." Warren jerked his thumb over his shoulder toward the door. "Someday it'll start again, and then you'll go back."

"Go back!" The words came out in the same, unnerving pitch.

"Like we got our very own parrot." Joe's disdain dripped, saturating and slimy.

"Shut up, idiot!" Warren's voice cut crisply through Joe's, daring the other man to speak again.

At the bar, Joe shrugged, turning his back.

Jess probed her temple with her fingertips. It felt as it had since she entered Between, slightly squishy with the beginnings of the bruise that might never have a chance to fully develop.

Or to heal.

"Look, Zane," she said, pointing. "It's been like this since I came in. Someday it'll heal," and Jess fought to believe her own words, "but not here. Same as you, Zane. Here you have to wait ... like you would in jail."

Zane's eyes ripped from the abyss between them and latched onto Jess'.

"In jail you know how long it'll be," he said. "In jail you might even get time off, if you're good."

"Not always." Warren spoke up before Jess could think of anything to say. "Some sentences are mandatory ... I've heard."

Zane transferred his stare to Warren.

"Mandatory?"

"Parrot's back," Joe said, but he kept his voice low—Jess barely heard him.

"Yes. Mandatory—no time off. Because sometimes even the judge doesn't have a choice on how long a sentence will last."

"Who's our judge?" Zane asked.

"Between," Jess offered. "I guess?"

They fell silent, and then Eli's voice boomed out.

"The harshest judge lies not outside, but within."

"Oh, here we go!" Joe slapped the bar hard.

"What do you mean, Eli?" Warren asked, and Jess and Zane looked to the kitchen window where Eli peeked out. Only one of Eli's eyes was visible, sharp and shining, blazing intensely like Jess' memory of the Sun.

"You know what it is that I mean." The corner of Eli's singular eye crinkled with a smile they could not quite see. He withdrew his face from the opening.

"Jim Beam on the rocks forever for $3.99 ... and your soul. Fortune cookie crap for free." So saying, Joe toasted the empty window and drank deep from his glass.

Zane rose like a fire fueled by white gas.

"It's my fault." Jess stood, too, ready to lunge at the door but Zane rocketed to the stairs instead, repeating the same words until they merged and shortened. Their volume decreased with distance, though their accusation lingered.

"It's my fault, it'smy fault, it'smyfault, myfault, myf ..."

146

"Ugh," Joe said succinctly when Zane's door slammed shut.

Warren sighed and shook his head.

"Do you want to get back to those names, Jessamy?"

It took Jess some time to remember what Warren was talking about, and longer to recall she'd dropped the notebook and pencil.

"I guess." She navigated to the notebook easily, but it took a bit longer to find the pencil, which had rolled and lodged in a crack in the floorboards.

Warren met her at the wall.

"Where were we?"

"Ahh ..." Jess scanned the notebook. "Arthur Woonsocket."

"And I thought Drabyak was bad." Joe materialized next to Warren, glass in hand.

"It is. What? You said it, idiot."

"Don't mean you got to agree, dumbass."

"Are you here to help, or just to make trouble?"

"Trouble."

"I figured."

"Who's next?" Jess prompted.

"Mae Pert ... Persich?" Joe's frown encompassed the name he struggled to pronounce.

"Spell it out, troublemaker." Warren jostled Joe with an elbow.

"Watch the drink. M-A-E P-E-R-T-Z-S-C-H. Look at that—that ain't right."

"Got that?" Warren waited for Jess' affirmative, and then read the next name, "Andy Interesting, A-N-D-Y I-N-T-E-R-E ..."

"Just like it sounds," Joe interjected. "Another made-up dumbass name. Next one's Mickey Kay, M-I-C-K-E-Y K-A-Y, not M-O-U-S-E."

Jess scribbled as fast as she could and the list grew.

They didn't find a match, but it wasn't for lack of trying.

Cocoon

"Nothing matches."

Jess had been over and over the notebook. Even though she'd posed the question about possible return visits to Between out of boredom, she found herself disappointed at her negative findings.

"Wasn't no game of poker, but it wasn't all bad," Joe said.

Jess looked up, wondering if he meant the words to be consoling, but found no clue in Joe's perpetually dour expression.

Jess' eyes fell back to the paper before her. She'd drawn lines to connect similar names and the result looked nothing like a spider web ... unless, perhaps, there existed an intoxicated arachnid architect who had failed web design.

"There's a few with the same first names, or names and nicknames. But that doesn't really matter, does it."

Jess shoved the notebook away from her body and asked the bartender for water and the ice bag.

"Thought you weren't feeling that as much?" Warren asked.

"I'm feeling it now." Between taught Jess that not only could awareness of omnipresent pain come and go, but even a lifeless person could become exhausted by thinking alone.

In due time, the ice bag arrived and with it, a glass of water. Jess pressed the bag against her head and watched condensation roll down the glass.

She did not reach out to interrupt the paths of the droplets.

Eventually, the ice melted, leaving insufficient coolness to provide a semblance of relief to Jess' skin or further condensing to her glass. She lowered the warming ice bag to the bar and realized, without shock, that she could probably watch the entire evaporation process.

Eternity, at least within Between's confines, was not all it was cracked up to be. Whatever else the strange stagnation of time could accomplish, elevating indifference beyond any previously known heights was not one of the bar's more shining achievements.

The bartender appeared, unsummoned, to refresh Jess' ice water, and the slight change in scenery inspired Jess to impart a single mumbled word.

"Thanks."

"Hey," Joe said suddenly, catching Jess' attention with the sharpness of his tone. "Hey, how long since Zane's been down?"

"He hasn't come back since he decided it was 'all his fault,'" Warren answered.

"How long's that?" Joe demanded.

"Days?" Jess guessed.

"Weeks." Warren sounded more certain.

"How can you even tell?" Jess asked, striving for curiosity through a lethargy of enveloping dullness.

Warren shrugged, his movement abbreviated by ethereal and inescapable pain. He cleared his throat, tried to smile.

"I feel it. I've been here long enough; I should be able to know something useful."

Joe snorted.

"Yeah. With all that detail, won't none of us miss no appointments. Meetings and crap."

"Idiot."

"Dumbass."

Their words were as lifeless as anything else in the bar.

That thought prickled Jess, nagging like a thorn just barely prodding flesh. She turned toward Sandman's table and the feeling intensified.

"How do you know Sandman's sleeping?"

Joe glanced over his shoulder.

"We. Look. At him." He spaced the words carefully.

"But he's not breathing. He hasn't got a pulse!" Jess slid off her barstool and took one step, pointing. "How do you know he's ... how do you know ..."

"How do we know he's not dead?" Warren's voice burned, icy and hot. "How do we know *we're* not dead?"

"Sit down, Jessamy," Joe directed. "I don't got energy to deal with you losing it so soon after Zane."

"But ..." Jess tore her gaze from Sandman to Joe and back. Panic erupted inside her, hatching from anxiety's egg into a full grown, many-headed hydra. It was a foreign, massive sensation for one who had become accustomed to being dead inside ... long before she'd entered Between.

Warren added his urging to Joe's, and patted the bar seat Jess had abandoned.

"It's okay, Jessamy. Sit."

Though she had no need for air, Jess found herself inhaling and exhaling in little gasps. A time-honored and utterly contraindicated prescription for panic, this behavior would— outside Between—lend itself to an intensification of all the unpleasant sensations that accompanied an attack.

Jess remembered some distant relative urging another to breathe slowly, recalled the complaints of the terror-stricken man about how shaky and weak he felt, how he couldn't breathe, how his heart was racing and skipping beats and ...

This specific recollection, a symptom of fear that could not possibly touch her, crushed Jess' monstrous fright, reducing it back to an empty shell in an instant.

"Gonna make it, girl?" Joe's heavy hand tugged lightly on a lock of Jess' hair as she stood there, residual tremors easing.

Jess looked at him and found his sharp eyes absurdly gentle.

The moment passed quickly.

"I want another whiskey." Joe winked and shook his glass. "You buying? Or do I got to stick with old Jim Beam?"

Jess negotiated the slight distance to her bar stool and sat without replying.

"Jim Beam it is. Barkeep, set me up."

Peripherally, Jess saw the bartender nod and advance to refill Joe's glass. She picked up her glass slowly ... and then set it down with a smack, splattering droplets across the bar's horrible, glistening shine.

Anger suffused Jess now, filling her hollow core. It enraged her that she couldn't have the fullness of the experience her emotions demanded because of the absurdity of circumstances that detached her body from life.

As if anybody trapped in Between could possibly have a "life" anyway!

Jess studied the watery mess she'd made, reflecting on how easy it would be to clean. How readily the quiet bartender would restore the scarred wood's glow. Underneath her wrath, Jess felt her old, apologetic nature tickling ... but her resentment insisted on dismissing this.

She gave in to temper and stood, abandoning her post at the bar without comment.

"Let her go, Joe," she heard Warren say behind her. She hoped Joe took the advice.

Upstairs, Jess surged into Zane's room, barging in without even a knock to announce herself. Her personal storm abated the instant she saw the room's interior, the wallpaper peeled and littering the floor. And on every wall, across the surface of the desk, even on the ceiling, the marks ... so many marks, all neatly inscribed, four straight up and one slashed across the rest of the set.

Jess stood there, staring, the imprints of time surrounding her. She kicked a clustered mass of wallpaper on the floor and found no unmarred space there, either.

"Go away." Zane sat on the floor and spoke without force, not raising his head from its resting place, sagging against his thin chest.

"Why?" Jess asked, emboldened by the slurry of residual anger and lingering anxiety trapped inside her. "Not like you're busy or anything."

Zane lifted his head and met her eyes from his position against the far wall, then lowered his head once more. He moved like a puppet on a roughened string.

"Go away." The repeated words carried even less power than their first, feeble utterance.

"No."

"Why not." Zane's weak voice included no inflection, but Jess took his words as a serious question.

Eventually, an answer came to her.

"I don't have anything to do. Can't I do nothing here for a while?"

Now Zane's head rose more readily, as if he found some reason to consider Jess' request. And because she had clearly voiced it as such, Jess waited for Zane's reply. He took his time but finally, he spoke again.

"I guess."

Jess felt instant relief pour into her emotional stew. She gave no voice to her gratitude for Zane's grudging acquiescence but simply crossed the room to join him. Slips and curls of wallpaper rustled as she moved, whispering like entrapped ghosts—malevolent because Jess disturbed them, benign because they had no recourse against her.

She positioned herself a few feet away from Zane and sat on the floor there, landing half on and half off a particularly large piece of wallpaper that crackled as it flattened. Jess pulled her knees up, leaned forward, and clasped her arms around her legs.

Silence descended then, a thorough quiet thickened by the absence of breath and heartbeat. Jess thought about that as her emotional slop settled. Even in the quietest place she'd been before Between, she'd heard the draw of her own breath, the throb of her own heart. Here, if she sat perfectly still, she heard nothing ... not the softness of air entering or leaving her lungs, not the *whoosh* of blood moving through her veins at her heart's tempered demands, not anything.

As the silence stretched, Jess noticed remnant sounds, distant and muted. She heard a murmur as Love spoke to Eclipse, heard a clinking glass from the bar below. She wondered briefly if someone new entered the bar but when the stillness returned and grew, wrapping itself around Between, she knew no one had.

When her mother died, Jess thought about heavenly places she would like Mama to be. As desperately as she wanted to believe her mother safely ensconced in some perpetually joyous afterlife, it was painful to be alive without her. So Jess had finally pushed away all thoughts of supernatural maternal adoration—she'd traded the memory of a true and deep love for the reality of the hollow echo Lucas provided.

In all the thoughts she'd ever had, Jess never managed to contemplate a place like Between: not life, not afterlife, not joy, not sorrow ... Lucas' last strike began to throb soundlessly alongside her eye as she wondered whether the mixed blessings of finite life surpassed the absence of either goodness or cruelty in ageless limbo.

She had to get out sometime, didn't she? One way or the other? And what about her baby? Whatever else this situation could be to Jess, it was utterly unfair that all the potential and possibility of the life caught inside her lay trapped, sentenced to oblivion with her.

Jess glanced at Zane, who hadn't moved, and then around at the various surfaces where he'd tracked his "sentence" in tick-marks when clocks had been denied. In that moment, Jess saw no appeal in Between, literally or figuratively. She lowered her chin to her knees and stared out across the waves of wallpaper, wishing the quiet around her could permeate her brain.

Footsteps sounded, growing louder as they moved up the stairs. Jess didn't want to care who ascended the steps and felt an absurd, small shot of pleasure when she succeeded.

Because her empty gaze aligned with the door, still ajar, Jess saw Joe as he pushed into the room. She registered the disgust on his grizzled face and understood its change when his eyes met hers over the disarray—an interjection of pity.

He shook his head, the vehement motion sending ice cubes in the glass he carried into jingling their agreement.

"Dumbass." Joe's tone included no gentleness; he gazed at Zane as he spoke, but he might as well have been looking at a statue for the response he received.

When Joe's eyes came to rest on Jess, she knew he wanted her to speak.

Jess found a new depth of not caring, there on the edge of the wallpaper ocean between herself and Joe. Silence reigned again, but for the occasional impact of ice against its constraining boundaries. Zane sat, Jess stared, and Joe watched until even ice stopped punctuating the absent conversation with its frozen, erratic ellipses.

"Two dumbasses, then," Joe said at last. He tossed back the remains of his drink and left. The door gaped open as if dumbfounded by his pronouncement; Jess didn't feel surprised.

She didn't feel much of anything, but even if she could have cared about that, she wouldn't.

That was the story Jess reiterated in her mind's isolation. She told herself the tale over and over, as if doing so would manifest it into reality, not unlike the time Zane recorded. Joe's footsteps faded, Love's unintelligible comments ebbed and flowed, Zane hunched motionless, and Jess kept on thinking it was perfectly okay not to care about this ridiculous, extraordinary, lingering death she experienced because she couldn't face stepping outside and having it over in an instant.

The devil of Between, with which Jess found familiarity even if she didn't know it in the sense of the "whys" and "hows" Love maligned, still felt preferable to the white death-devil outside ... the one Eli once shook hands with, the one Jess could not see through or past.

When the irony of her persistent hope in the face of Between's embodied hopelessness breached Jess' feeble tale of ambivalence, she lowered her head to her knees and tried desperately to cry. But she couldn't, any more than she could refute Joe's assessment of her inactive reaction.

And so Jess sat: absently present, fixedly displaced, and let Between's bleak sanctuary saturate the entirety of her being.

Emergence

It was Eclipse who finally broke through the barricade of despair in which Jess cocooned herself. Jess became aware of times when the cat crossed the room, her footfalls alternately cushioned by wallpaper and quietly tapping against the marks on the floor, her claws stretching out to secure her progress.

Now and then, Eclipse bumped up against one of Jess' hands, breaching her wall of self-isolation, though Jess pretended it didn't happen and refused to move in response. Once, the cat even licked Jess' wrist, dragging her sandpaper tongue across Jess' skin, harshly replacing the caress of stale air.

These tickles of contact brought Jess intermittent respite from the yawning abyss of her personal quarantine—an extended expanse of time that had no name, but if it did, might have been dubbed "emptiness immemorial." After tender nuzzling and attempted washing failed to inspire Jess' exodus from her determined exile, Eclipse did the one thing Jess could not ignore, even with her most profound resolve or in her most devout despair.

Eclipse peed.

The stench raised Jess' head as if the gravity that held it on her knees so long vanished outright. The meaning penetrated Jess' being as if she had never been trapped in mental quicksand.

"She's alive?" Jess found her voice and it sounded shocking in a room long accustomed to quiet. She searched the room, gaze alighting on Eclipse in the corner near the door, pawing at wallpaper scraps there. "You're alive!"

"What's that?" Zane, too, roused from his resigned stupor, but Jess could only stare at the cat. Eclipse took a few steps away from her make-shift toilet and sat, looking quite pleased.

"Mrrrow," Eclipse drawled. Then, having finished her mission and commentary, she exited the room.

"What's that?" Zane repeated.

Uncharitably, Jess recalled Joe's branding Zane as a parrot.

"It's cat pee. Eclipse is alive!"

Jess scrambled out of the position she'd held through who knew what else or how long and followed the cat.

"Wait! Who's gonna clean this up?" Zane called after her.

Jess overtook Eclipse near Love's door and scooped the cat into her arms. Eclipse protested this indecorous treatment, pushing with her front paws against Jess' chest, digging in claws that had the power to scratch but not to make Jess bleed ... at least, not for long.

But Jess found the magical place behind the cat's ear which so few felines can resist; soon Eclipse purred and cuddled against her, unconcerned about anything as fickle as dignity with such adoration readily available. Jess persisted in her caresses until the cat relaxed, and then brought her face next to Eclipse's.

Between her purrs, Eclipse's soft breaths breezed across Jess, miraculous after their long absence. Not for the first time though certainly for a singularly unique reason, Jess found herself jealous of a cat.

"You're alive," Jess repeated, awe suffusing her words; Eclipse butted her head against Jess' stilled hand in response. "You're really alive."

Jess dared to touch her nose to the Eclipse's and delighted in its warmth. She quickly resumed petting cat, interpreting her now-twitching tail as a precursor to renewed escape attempts.

Throughout Jess' interchange with Eclipse, Love's door remained firmly shut. This unusual fact concerned Jess, but with Eclipse alive—*alive!*—in her arms, she hesitated to knock. She supposed she could talk to Love later and find out then if the other woman knew how long Eclipse had been back.

She suspected her own time in isolation dwarfed that since Eclipse's rejuvenation.

"We have to do something; you need a litter box and food. Water, too."

Establishing Eclipse's water supply seemed easiest remedied so Jess hurried to her room to do just that. At the threshold, though, she paused, concerned.

How long had she been in Zane's room? Jess found she had no concept of the duration of time she'd spent in gloomy communion there. She could have been there mere hours, or ... could she have been there weeks?

She opened the door to her room and peered inside. Aside from a straightened quilt, the room looked just as when she'd been in it last. There didn't seem to be anyone else about, and so Jess gently deposited Eclipse on the bed and proceeded to the bathroom.

There, she evicted the desiccated soap from its dish and separated the slotted surface of the lid from its lower half. The inner surface was as dry as the cracked soap had been above, reassuring Jess that no one claimed her room in her absence. She used a washcloth to scrub out soap dish's shallow bowl as best she could and then filled it with fresh water.

On the bed, Eclipse bathed, her tongue working her fur with furious energy unlike anything Jess observed from the cat previously. Jess set the bowl on the floor next to the desk and wondered if this fervor resulted from being alive—if, by plain virtue of breathing, Eclipse resumed the vibrancy of which she'd been dispossessed within Between's static environment.

Jess watched Eclipse wash her belly, her legs, and her paws. She looked on, a superfluous sentry, until the cat yawned and settled herself; then Jess mindfully reiterated her determination to find the cat some food, and something to serve as a litter box.

But because Jess dreaded what Joe would say when he saw her downstairs again and feared Warren might give her a good estimate of how long she'd stored herself upstairs, she continued to wait until Eclipse slept deeply before she slunk from the room.

Joe and Warren remained at the bar, still or always in their favored positions. Jess almost waved but since neither one looked up, she aborted the half-hearted effort and instead turned away, back toward the storage closet.

Inside, Jess stared at the available options, comparing the memory of her mother's improvisation for Ruthie with the currently available tools for Eclipse. She found a half-full box and emptied it, arranging the pristinely new glasses it had contained back on the shelf where she found the box. She also appropriated several heavy-duty garbage bags, a stack of paper towels, and a box-cutter. After extruding the blade and finding it suitably sharp, Jess moved to close the door and came face to face with someone she did not know.

Breathing or not breathing, she could not suppress a little shriek.

"Delivery day," the strange man said; the music of his voice registered with Jess more readily than his words.

"Out of the way, Jessamy!" Joe called from the bar. "You're finally out of Zane's room and now you got to block the hall on delivery day?"

"I-I-I'm sorry." Jess hurried to shut the closet door and clear her improvised supplies from the hall. She noticed the handcart standing inert next to the wall, stacked with four boxes.

The man didn't smile, but he did give a short nod as he went back to his task, readying the cart for the instant Jess moved.

And move, Jess did. She scuttled clear of the hall, bumping into the first table she encountered; skittering around that obstacle, she paused, still clutching the items she'd procured from the storage closet.

Warren roused from an apparently intense study of the bottom of his glass.

"What's going on? Oh, delivery day."

Joe ambled toward Jess.

"Dumbass central, that's what you stuck me with when you set up with Zane. What's all this?" He gestured broadly with the glass he held even as his eyes locked on the supplies Jess carried.

Jess tore her gaze from the delivery man, who maneuvered the handcart toward the bar now that a clear path presented itself. Jess didn't have time to speak to Joe before the bartender swung open the bar's gate and came forward to greet the delivery man.

The two shared identical coloring, though the delivery man stood a head taller than the bartender. As she approached, he stopped the handcart and extended his left hand to the bartender's face, just as she mirrored his gesture.

When they touched, each one's hand to the other one's cheek, Jess sensed the contact as if directly against her own skin. The sensation surging through the invisible contact felt like the sound the wall of names made when carved.

"Ah!" Warren tipped his head back, and Jess understood she wasn't the only non-participant absorbing the soundless song between the pair near the bar's end.

"I love delivery day." Joe raised his glass in an encompassing toast. "To delivery day!"

"To delivery day," Warren responded, sounding more like himself. His eyes, which he turned to Jessamy as the delivery man and bartender broke contact, brightened. "You're back."

"Eclipse!" Jess roused then, shaking off the diminishing sensation of touchless contact against her face. "She's alive. I need to get her something to eat, and ... I need to make her a litter box."

Joe aborted the mouthful of whiskey he'd been about to guzzle as laughter overtook him.

"Hoooo-ie!" he drawled.

"I can do it," Jess said, glancing at the bartender who now engaged in silent review of the clipboard the delivery man proffered. "I can, too; when Ruthie was sick and couldn't jump, Mama made her a shallow box she could walk into and used newspaper for litter."

"Never said you couldn't do it." Joe backed away with his hands slightly raised, all available fingers extended. Jess briefly feared for the glass he held with only his thumb and stubby index finger.

"Good to see you back, Jessamy." A small smile crossed Warren's face as Joe rejoined him. "You didn't miss much."

Jess set her collected supplies on the table and pulled out a chair.

"No new regulars?" She realized the inanity of the question—the Between equivalent of a weather inquiry.

"Nope," Joe said. "Not a one, and nobody much stopping in, neither."

"There was that woman ..." Warren began.

"Sure, that woman. Her's that memorable. So's the guy what come in after her. Or maybe I'm thinking of some other ..."

"Idiot." Warren broke Joe's belittling litany, but didn't put much effort into it.

"Dumbass." Joe's jibe, too, imbued more resignation than camaraderie.

Jess looked over at the delivery man, removing boxes from his cart. He stacked two, set one beside the pile on its own, and handed the last directly to the bartender. She took it behind the bar, carrying it without apparent effort, even though the box was large and bulky. She went into the kitchen without a backward glance. The delivery man didn't wait, either ... following the intense and silent song of their reunion, he simply wheeled his empty handcart away, vanishing into the hallway's shadows.

Jess didn't hear a door open or close, but she knew he'd left. Her hand stilled against the side of the box she cut.

"That's it?"

"What's it?" Joe asked, not shifting from slouched perusal of his whiskey.

"One cart?"

Warren didn't move, either, but shrugged with his words.

"He comes when she needs him to come, brings what she needs him to bring. One cart at a time."

"Don't know what she needs here. Bottles don't run dry. Eli don't run outta food."

Jess renewed her efforts with the box she held, breaking her pause as a rush of depression penetrated her mind—despair's lethargy came easier now, she realized, after her time practicing it with Zane.

"Convenient," she forced herself to say. The hollow word, degraded by worry, stood alone, incapable of limping the feeble conversation even one step farther.

Jess worked in the following silence, carving the box and lining it with the garbage bag, doubling the plastic over the box's bottom and shortened sides.

"Is there any duct tape in the closet?" She didn't expect a response but after a moment, Warren stood. He moved like he'd aged decades since Jess last saw him, though his physical appearance endured, unchanged. Jess recognized his slow and deliberate motion as a manifestation of the same desperation she felt.

"I think so." The words came faintly—an afterthought—as Warren neared the closet door. "I'll check."

Jess waited, listening to Warren's movements.

"Yes, here's some. It even has cats on it."

"Cats?" Joe interjected a small shot of interest in his tone.

"Cartoon cats," Warren said, waving a pink roll in the air as he returned.

"That ain't duck tape; duck tape's gray!"

"Duct tape," Warren responded, and hearing the emphasis he put on the "t," Jess felt her lips move upward.

Her face felt stiff, the motion and emotion behind it odd but familiar, like a long-lost relative returning home.

"Let me see." Joe rose and tried to snatch the tape away from Warren.

"Hang on ... Jessamy asked for it, so let her get what she needs and then you can play with it."

Joe snorted at this rebuttal but went back to his bar stool.

Warren not only presented Jess with the tape then, but helped extend and hold the proper lengths as she used the box cutter to slice it. When she taped the final piece into place, holding the garbage bag lining to the box, she nodded.

"That's enough. And it's 'Hello Kitty,'" she explained, starting to shred paper towels. "It's a cartoon—from Japan, I think. I used to have a 'Hello Kitty' watch. And duct tape comes in all kinds of colors now."

"Hollow Kitty? What kind of name's that?" Joe took the tape when Warren held it out to him, grimacing as he examined the cat faces on its surface.

"She said 'Hello Kitty,' idiot, not 'Hollow Kitty.'"

"Still dumb!"

Their banter came so close to lively, Jess felt a smile cracking her facial barriers again. Then Zane's voice entered into the mix.

"Hey."

Connections

Zane stood at the bottom of the stairs, his voice reflecting the burden of the small but significant urgency he'd managed to find upstairs when Eclipse's actions broke them both out of their self-imposed prisons.

Now, without any inflection, Zane's words had little to commend them.

"What?" Jess looked back down at the paper towels she tore, and began to crumple them into pellets.

"Who's gonna clean that up?" Zane said. "That pee?"

When neither Joe nor Warren spoke, Jess sighed. She started to stand, but her motion caught as the streams of thought in her head flooded, forming a single-minded river.

Her decision made, Jess sat back down.

"It's your room. You should clean it."

"Ooh. Getting goooood." Joe spoke under his breath, but Warren shushed him anyway.

"I didn't leave the door open." Zane raised his voice then, but not much.

"No, but I'm making sure Eclipse won't pee in there again, and you did tear all the paper off the walls," Jess said. "It's not my fault or Eclipse's that you made your room look like a big litter box. We're all stuck here. You should clean it up.

I think I saw bleach in the storage closet. Or you could try to find baking soda. That might be better to start with."

"Baking soda," Warren said. "Eli should have that in the kitchen."

"Baking soda," Zane repeated.

Jess kept working in the silence following the refrain—the ripping and crunching sounds soft, but somehow appropriate.

"Baking soda absorbs the pee and smell," she offered, hoping this additional information might spur Zane to action.

"Baking soda," Zane said, yet again. "Okay, I guess. Okay. In the kitchen?"

"In the kitchen," Warren confirmed.

Joe opted for less subtle direction.

"Eli! Eli, you got some baking soda?"

The bartender emerged from the kitchen first—Jess had forgotten she was in there—and Eli followed her out, wiping both his whole and partial hand on a towel. The bartender glanced around the room and then returned to her work with the boxes, next selecting the one segregated from the others; she carried it down the hall to the closet.

Eli took a little longer to survey the situation, nodding only after he had thoroughly dried his hands and stared at Joe, Warren, Jess, and Zane.

"How much soda is it that you need?"

Jess barely gave Zane a chance to not speak before answering for him.

"Zane doesn't need much. I could use some, too; I'm making a litter box for Eclipse."

"Ah." Eli's bright eyes flashed as a smile spread over his face. "This is the cat that came into Between with you. She is restored."

He didn't say it like a question, but Jess nodded.

"I will make her a meal each morning and night." Eli turned toward the kitchen. "We will help grow her strength so she is ready when the kittens come."

That got everyone's attention and became a new chorus of repetition, with inflection ranging from Jess' stunned excitement to Zane's flat dismay.

"Kittens?"

"Kittens?"

"Kittens!"

"For the love of Pete." Joe broke the trend. "Something in the water, Warren. Lucky we drink whiskey."

Eli paused before re-entering the kitchen.

"Jessamy and Eclipse are aligned in more ways than one." Eli's eyes bored into Jess'. Her hands, which stilled when Eli mentioned kittens, dropped into the makeshift litter box she crafted.

"I guess we are," Jess responded, when Eli appeared to be waiting for her agreement.

"It is not only the kittens I mean," he said sternly, moving his stumpy hand up to his temple, tapping it twice and then pointing at Jess.

When Jess gasped, grasping his meaning, Eli nodded and continued on his way.

Provoked once more, the last spot Lucas struck resumed its throbbing. Jess felt like crying but the wave of emotion rushed past, requiring neither acknowledgement nor release ... it just rolled. In this way, it reflected the aching pain beside Jess' eye— there whether she noticed it or not, a shock of sudden intensity, and then reduction back into jaded omnipresence.

Jess lifted her hands to return to laboring over the nubbed confetti in the litter tray. "Well." The word stood alone, waiting, but Jess could find nothing more profound to join to it and so she went back to work.

Joe stalked over to the table, yanked out the chair across from Jess, and sat, pounding his whiskey back as he did so.

"Give me some," he said, waggling the fingers of his outstretched hand at Jess until she separated a portion of sheets from the stack and followed his directive. "Don't seem too hard, and I'd rather help you than Zane."

Jess smiled slightly, though she wiped her expression clean as she glanced at Zane. He didn't appear to be listening, standing motionless by the stairs. Joe's enthusiastic shredding soon outpaced Jess' efforts and they continued to work even as Eli reappeared, handing two boxes of baking soda to Warren.

Warren brought one box to the table and set it next to Jess, raising an eyebrow at Joe.

"What're you looking at, dumbass?"

"Maybe not as big of an idiot as I thought," Warren replied, swatting Joe across the shoulders before carrying the other box to Zane.

"Come on, Zane. I'll make sure you don't use too much."

"See what I done?" Joe jerked one thumb in the direction of the stairs. "I stuck Warren with Zane, that's what I done."

"There's not much he can do wrong," Jess said. "All he has to do is ..."

"Yeah, well, you seen Zane. If there's a way to screw something up, he'll find it." Joe shook his head. "What he done to his room! Why not count whiskeys? Or beers?"

"He must be like that outside." Jess spoke slowly to give the words time to organize, clothing the bare idea forming in her head. "Paying attention to time, I mean. He's probably really careful to be on time outside Between. People like that can't stand to lose it ... the way they keep track of time, I mean."

"Warren tracks time in his head."

"Yes, but I bet he can do that outside, too. Some people know when it's noon because that's when they get hungry."

"Go on!"

"No, it's true. Bess—she's a customer in the first restaurant I worked at—she'd come by every day in the summer and knit, she didn't have a watch and didn't look around, just sat and knitted in the corner where she couldn't see the clock. Every day, almost to the minute, she'd call me over and tell me she was getting hungry and every day it happened right around noon."

"That's just dumb," Joe scoffed. "Who gets hungry on the clock?"

"I don't even remember being hungry." The thought seemed like it should have been frightening, but it wasn't. Jess set down the paper towel she was holding. "I think this is enough for now."

"Until the cat pisses again. You're gonna need extra ready."

"True ..." Jess frowned, wondering how many paper towels she would need to keep Eclipse supplied.

She looked down the hall where the closet door still hung open, the bartender working to put away whatever supplies she lugged there.

"Wait. Why ..." Jess looked back at Joe, a question agitating in her mind like a child hopping from one foot to the other. "Why doesn't Eclipse have to leave now that she's alive again?"

Joe shrugged.

"Don't got to leave when you're alive. Just can."

"But ..."

"Jessamy." The quiet power of her name instantly halted the rise of skittering anxiety. "You're still looking for this to make sense. It don't make sense. It don't got to make sense. It's just the way it is in Between. That's all."

That's all?

"You gonna get more stuff? Or do I got to?" And Joe winked.

Jess smiled back.

"Fine." She rose, and walked to the closet.

The bartender was closing the door, an empty box in her hand.

"Excuse me," Jess began, arresting the bartender's motion and focusing her ancient stare. "I ... " Jess fumbled for the remains of the $50 bill Lucas thrust at her, so long ago it might as well have been something that happened to someone else, or been something Jess read in a book. "I can pay ... well, I can give you everything I have left."

The bartender waited, looking into Jess' eyes rather than at the crushed mess Jess extended.

"Eclipse—the cat—she's alive and she needs a litter box ... well, I've got a box, but ... wait!"

The bartender moved back toward the bar in her uncanny, gliding gait. Jess scurried after her, peripherally aware of her comparative lack of grace.

"I'm using paper towels for litter and I don't want to use more than she needs but ..."

Jess struggled to continue her explanation as the bartender moved, setting the empty box on top of the remaining stack. Then she picked up both the empty box and one full box beneath. She turned back to Jess, who still struggled to articulate Eclipse's situation.

And then the bartender foisted the boxes from her own arms into Jess'.

"You want me to help you? To earn the supplies? I can do that, I can ..."

The bartender grasped Jess' forearm, cutting off her frenzied speech and movements. A jolt of connection surged through the bartender's brief touch; when Jess peered around the empty box's flaps, the bartender's face remained unreadable, but Jess would have sworn she glimpsed a hint of amusement underneath that smooth facade.

170

The bartender tapped the boxes Jess now held—the solid bottom box first, followed by the hollow top box. She pointed at Jess and then to the table where Joe sat, one arm draped over the back of his chair, watching the scene.

Finally, the bartender bent, picking up the last box from the floor, and carried it behind the bar.

Joe broke Jess' trance.

"Box you're holding's full of paper towels."

"How do you know?"

"Says so on the side of the box," Joe chuckled. "She's giving it to you."

"But I can pay ..." Jess still held her fistful of bills and nearly dropped both boxes as she tried to show Joe.

"Stop trying to make sense of this crap!" Joe bellowed. "You think getting free paper you got to rip up for a cat that's back to alive's any weirder than anything else? Like drinking for free in a bar because death's outside, and your heart's not beating and you're not breathing, or ..."

"Okay, okay." Jess brought the boxes to the table and set them down with a thud in front of Joe, halting his ambivalent tirade and causing a few loose pieces from the makeshift litter box to jolt out onto the floor.

Joe stared as she stood there, embroiled in the insanity.

"Put the money away, Jessamy." Joe's voice was absurd in its gentleness. He stabbed a finger at Jess' hand. "Put it away and take care of the cat. Make your list of names. Maybe play a game of the dice. Stare at the walls in Zane's crappy room if you want to—just don't try making sense where there ain't none. That's what'll drive you nuts."

Jess looked down at her hand.

"Only that?" She didn't expect a reply since she didn't mean to ask the question but she waited for an answer anyway. When none came, Jess relaxed her grip and released the money onto the table, smoothing the bills before folding them and returning them to her pocket.

"Gimme the cutter," Joe said, assumed gruffness back in his tone and secure as an armored truck. He extended his hand.

Jess did he bid and when Joe tossed a packet of paper towels to her, she only fumbled a little as she caught it.

"I'll do one more bunch and then I got to wet my whistle," Joe proclaimed, shoving the empty box between them.

"Fair enough." Jess feared the risk of falling back into her own world again, descending into despair's certain, waiting trap. Despite Joe's confidence, Jess suspected the key to sanity in Between lay more in connection with others than in avoidance of personal rumination.

That notion drove her to try to explain.

"I think," she said, raising her voice slightly so as not to be overpowered by the shredding, crumpling torrents she and Joe created, "Between is like God's trying to make us go to therapy."

"God? Therapy?" Joe barked. "Oh, you're already gone ... all the way around the bend."

Jess looked up from the paper towels and frowned.

"It seems like therapy to me. At least, like what I've seen on TV or heard people talk about. I don't know if it's God or Between or something else, but this place ... it came to us and it put us together and there's nothing to do but talk or go crazy, so how is that not like therapy?"

"Jessamy's got a point," Warren called from the stairwell. When Joe and Jess looked, he raised the broom and a handful of empty trash bags he carried like trophies. "Zane's cleaning up!"

"Riiiiight," Joe drawled, temporarily diverted. "See you next year then." And he brandished his middle finger in Warren's general direction.

172

"Idiot," Warren replied, sounding positively cheerful. He waved, trash bags fluttering through the air with the motion, and headed back upstairs.

"Dumbass!" Joe yelled. "He's trying to get the last word again."

"Him? Both of you."

"You might be right about that," Joe chuckled. "But if Between's therapy, it's lousy."

Jess scooped up a handful of shredded paper pellets and deposited them in the designated box. She bent to pick up the bits that scattered earlier, too.

"Maybe ... " she said, when she settled back into the rhythm of her work, " ... maybe you only get out of it what you put into it."

Joe paused, staring at her so hard Jess felt it and looked up, meeting the steel of the older man's eyes. She supposed her own eyes must be flickering, even though she wished they could be as steady as Joe's, and the imagined flinching made her remember her bruise.

In this moment, the memory of receiving the blow hurt far worse than its current, monotonous pulsation. In the past, the shock of remembered shame might have made Jess drop her gaze but this time, she tapped her experience's dark energy and used it. She held onto Joe's eyes with a resolve she couldn't remember feeling before.

Determination, Jess thought, felt good ... and it felt good by itself, regardless of outcome.

"Maybe," Joe agreed at last, breaking off his stare with an abruptness that deserved an audible *snap*.

"Just maybe?" Jess asked.

Joe laughed. "Yeah. But still, maybe."

They finished tearing the paper without words, but not without communion.

Benighted

After installing Eclipse's litter box in the unused shower of her room, Jess hurried to Zane's to rescue some "used" wallpaper. She found Warren sweeping detritus while Zane manned the dustpan.

"Let me have one of the big pieces," Jess said, and extracted one such from the open trash bag near the site of Eclipse's original, makeshift bathroom. "Oh, good! You haven't gotten this yet."

She tore the envelope-sized piece of wallpaper she'd selected in two and crouched, using the smaller portion to slide some of the urine- and baking soda-soaked bits onto the larger piece.

When she stood again, she found Warren and Zane watching her: the former with bemusement, the latter with disgust.

"I told Zane to do that last so he didn't make everything else stink, and then to wash the broom."

"Exactly … the smell is important. I'll put this in her new litter box and it will help her know where to go next time."

"Ah." Warren waggled his raised brows before bending back to his task.

"Gross." Zane shook his head.

Jess hid her smile and went back to her bathroom to sow the textural and olfactory seeds she'd obtained for Eclipse. As she finished, the cat rose from her nap and arrived to supervise Jess' activities. Jess coaxed the cat nearer with gentle petting and then pulled one paw into the box, dragging it through the papers in a scratching motion.

Eclipse arrested her demonstration, pulling away and stepping backward. But then she sniffed and re-approached the litter box.

"There, now! You know what this is for."

A soft knocking drew Jess' attention from the cat and she left Eclipse to peruse her new, human-approved cat bathroom.

Love waited as Jess cracked the door open, her hand still raised from her tentative taps.

"Come in." Jess waved. "Come in and see; we made Eclipse a litter box. She's alive!"

Love glanced down the hallway to Zane's room, where audible evidence of continued cleaning efforts emerged. Then she ducked into Jess' room and closed the door behind her. At Jess' beckoning, Love slowly crossed the room, peeking into the bathroom when Jess pointed.

Standing near Love as the woman watched the cat inspecting her facilities, Jess' own attention fell on Love rather than Eclipse. She wondered again how long she'd sat in Zane's room; like her impossible impression of Warren's senescence, Love, too, seemed to have aged.

"She's staying?" Love asked, pulling back from the corner of the bathroom.

"I guess so. Eli said she's going to have kittens."

Love pressed her hand over her mouth, but Jess saw the smile forming there.

"Isn't it exciting?"

Love nodded, fingers curving from their original flat position, as if the expression beneath drew them up.

"I'm keeping her in my room ... well, I have to because she peed in Zane's room." Jess hurried to explain when Love's eyes widened at her initial statement. The other woman's fingers slipped away as her lips formed an "O"—then she giggled and her hand returned, hiding her mouth again.

"She didn't!"

"She did. Don't worry; you can come in anytime—you don't even need to knock. You will help me take care of Eclipse, won't you?"

The pause before Love answered lasted long enough to thoroughly confuse Jess. From Love's early protection of Eclipse to the moment when she'd bowed to Eclipse's preference to stay with Jess, the woman always put the cat's best interests ahead of anything else. Yet now, she did not answer immediately and Jess wondered why.

She realized what the reason must be and dismay pushed past bewilderment like an elbow to the gut.

"Maybe we should move the litter box to your room? She must have been with you while I was ... while I was in Zane's room. She'd probably be happier with you."

Love gasped then, grasping one of Jess' hands with both of hers.

"Oh, no. No! Eclipse likes you best. She should stay with you." The sincerity of Love's words carried not only in the way they rushed out, but through the warmth of her hands pressing against Jess'.

Just as quickly as Love reached out toward Jess, she pulled away.

"I understand. Sometimes everyone needs to be alone. Being with Zane is the most alone anyone can be here, I think. I can sit with Eclipse sometimes. If you need me to."

Relief wrapped Jess in its embrace as if it were a physical being and briefly, Jess wanted to hug Love, too. But Love moved before Jess could act on her impulse, hurrying away in a strange gait that evinced the urgency of a hunted animal.

Near the door, Love turned, her tone apologetic.

"I have to go. I don't want to talk to the boys. They won't be nice, because they don't like cleaning."

Giving Jess no time to respond, Love hastened from the room, closing the door behind her.

"Mrrrt?" Eclipse wound her body around Jess' ankles as Jess stood there, not sure what to make of Love's brief visit. Jess dropped to her knees and dedicated her full attention to the cat, inspiring a rapturous purr from Eclipse.

"I don't know, Eclipse. I don't know." Jess gave voice to the lingering confusion Love's visit inspired, and then listened to the sounds of Warren and Zane passing.

"... alive, it should leave!" Zane raised his voice, a soaring irritant compounded by the distinct whine injected into its heart.

Before Jess could bristle, Warren replied, his voice firm and smooth.

"Zane, we all choose when we come into Between and we all choose when we leave, even cats. It's not your decision."

Jess stood to move closer so she could hear every word, but it wasn't necessary. Warren's voice was perfectly clear; he must have stopped outside her door.

"But ..."

"Let it go."

"But it's alive."

"The cat is alive, yes. And the cat is pregnant, just like Jessamy is pregnant. Think about it, Zane. You see why no one wants to force the issue?"

This time, Zane's voice carried a grudging understanding.

"Yeah. Girls are weird even when they're not pregnant."

"I wouldn't put it quite like that but I do think we can deal with a little inconvenience if it helps a pregnant lady feel better about her time here."

"I guess."

There was a crinkling then, followed by a splatting noise that sent Eclipse into high alert, fur lifting along her spine as muscles tensed, ready for flight.

"Really? You can't carry a bag of trash? Give me that." Disgust dripping from Warren's words. "You take the broom and dustpan."

"It's slippery." Zane's defensive tones carried even though they modulated as he moved away down the hall. "And it smells!"

"Excuses, excuses ..."

Jess looked down at Eclipse, who resettled herself and casually groomed one flawless paw.

"You're staying as long as you like, Eclipse. I'll make sure you're safe."

Eclipse didn't pause in her work, didn't look up with her fiercely fragile eyes, but Jess remembered her first encounter with the cat and felt a rush of will. Nobody was going to mess with this cat ... not while she had something to say about it.

"I should go talk to Eli again, before you get hungry or Zane comes back," Jess told an oblivious Eclipse. And then she suited action to words, exiting the room with renewed purpose.

Purpose she hadn't possessed since before Lucas.

Jess brought her thoughts up short even as she continued down the stairs, arresting her mind with the same earnestness that backed her defense of Eclipse.

Not since Mama died.

No. While accurate, too, that assessment felt just as wrong as the reference to Lucas. Such correlations carried blame and Jess didn't want the weight of culpability—right or wrong—bearing down on her when she cared for a cat who needed someone dedicated to *her* and not to self-reproach.

Not since ...

178

Jess paused on the final step, feeling for a marker that could summarize her life's struggles without constraining her. She'd framed so much around the cornerstones of her mother's passing and her own, self-destructive involvement with Lucas. Even as powerful as those delimiters were, they needn't be a straightjacket on her.

At least, not in Between.

The idea surged, a revelation. Though edged with fear as sharp as broken glass, entertaining it also served as a release. Jess gripped the handrail hard as her emotions manifested physically, trembling out of her in a rush so close to joy that it was nearly a dance.

I haven't felt like I could do something myself since ... no ... It's been a long time since I felt like I could do something like this. A long time, that's how long it's been.

Too long.

At the bottom of the stairs, Zane's presence infringed on Jess' small triumph, unseating it immediately. He stood near the middle of the bar's floor space like an unwelcome centerpiece, empty hands dangling listlessly, focus dour. It seemed to Jess as if he trained his unpleasantness on her as soon as she appeared.

Jess straightened her shoulders and walked toward the bartender, determined to bypass Zane. Joe called out before she could reach her goal.

"Jessamy! Zane thinks he's got a match for you."

And Zane, all awkward and grim, actually smiled. It wasn't an expression that would sell a free blanket to a penniless soul during winter, but it bespoke an attempt at positivity. Jess tried to meet it with a smile of her own even as she found her brows knitting together, trying to understand what "match" Joe meant.

Fortunately, he waved the notebook in the air, resolving the question.

"Oh!"

"Zane says 'Andy Interesting' is the same as the scabby name."

"What?"

Zane cleared his throat.

"Same lines. Same writing."

"Really?" Jess hadn't forgotten her mission for Eclipse, but this resurrection of the name-matching project intrigued her. "Can you ... will you show me?"

"Yeah. Yeah, okay."

Zane moved to the wall, turning around twice as he traversed the short distance, making sure Jess followed him.

"Here." He waved his hand in front of "Andy Interesting" without actually touching the letters. "Here's 'Andy Interesting' and then here ..." Zane stretched out one long, spindly arm to the undecipherable, three-dimensional etching; the expanse of space between the two not even far enough that he had to shuffle his feet.

Jess cocked her head and frowned.

"But we can't read that."

"We can. We can!" Zane put his hand down on the unreadable name this time, pressing three fingers flush against the pattern. "Feel it. It feels the same." He pulled back from the wall and pointed at Jess, moving like an accuser, stabbing as if with a knife. "You try. Go on."

Jess stepped forward, looking from the jagged wound in the wall to Zane. He nodded, another jerky motion, and Jess returned her gaze to the wall. Then she lifted her hand and pressed it against the leftmost edge of the textured wood.

Though the wood looked the same and she did not move her fingers, she would have sworn she felt the letter "A."

"Goofy, huh?" Joe called from the bar.

"Very goofy," Jess heard her own voice speaking, even as she shifted her fingers slowly to the right.

"A-N-D-R-E-W ..."

"'Andrew Adams.' That's what we get," Warren said.

"That's what it says." Zane's correction sounded almost smug.

"Shut it, parrot," Joe cackled, laughing.

"You shut it," Zane said, and gasped, seemingly surprised by his own rejoinder. Jess broke contact with the wall, more jarred by the obscure pleasantry of Zane joining in Joe's jibes than by the fact that she'd just read a name with her fingertips.

"It feels the same. I mean, I haven't felt the other one, but ..."

"We know what you mean." Joe nodded his agreement with Warren's statement when Jess turned to look at them.

"All this time, we never touched them, one and the other, on the wall." Joe shook his head. "Never."

"Why would we?"

"Don't know, dumbass, but seems like we could of done something other than the same old."

"Why?" Warren persisted.

"It is the same in Between as it is outside," Eli said, exiting the kitchen. He carried a plate that might as well have been a doll's, delicately small by comparison to his hand. "We do what is familiar and easy more readily; what is new and difficult challenges us too much."

"Ain't hard to touch a wall," Joe argued as Eli approached Jess with the plate she realized was intended for Eclipse. "Easy as lifting a glass."

"But it is not familiar to read a word by touch that you cannot read with your eyes."

"Unless maybe you're blind," Warren said.

"I'm not blind." Zane roused himself to outrage, his voice squeaking a bit on the final word.

181

Eli set the plate of ground beef into Jess' hand, where it instantly assumed normal proportions.

"We are all blind in ways beyond our eyes. You," Eli said, extending his stubbed hand at Jess first, "are blind to your strength. You," and he turned to Zane, "are blind to your value."

Eli trained his sights on Warren next.

"You are blind to your independence, and you ..."

Joe leaned back against the bar, awaiting Eli's pronouncement like a dare.

"You are blind to your kindness."

"Kindness!" Joe rejected the label with his entire body, turning away and pounding his glass on the bar. "Dumbass crap. Gimme another whiskey."

No one else had anything to add. Jess started toward the stairs before she thought of something and turned back.

"What about you, Eli? What's your blindness?"

Eli blinked, and a slow smile spread across his broad face.

"I cannot see what it is that blinds me. That is my blindness."

Joe snorted. "Mumbo-jumbo."

Warren looked as if he were considering Eli's words carefully and when he spoke, his tone affirmed it.

"Sounds like the definition of a blind spot, Eli. And a general definition at that. I'd guess, just based on what you said there, your blindness is more specific ... I'd guess you're blind to your fear."

Eli's smile faded, wiped clean as if by the force of Warren's words. He dipped his head to Warren and walked back into the kitchen without another word.

"Weird," Zane said, moving to the bar.

Even with the lump sum of Between's timeless at her disposal, Jess knew she could found no reason or notion to argue with that. She went on her way to feed Eclipse.

Heat

As Eclipse grew rounder, a new series of customers entered—and left—Between. The influx, and subsequent exodus, became so steady that Joe and Warren stopped guessing which of the newcomers would become "regulars." None did, and those who entered in a group rarely stayed at all after finding Between empty of both electronics and table games.

"What a shithole." The lead member of the latest collective of entrants was significantly shorter than any of his companions but carried himself as if he were a King. "Come on, boys ... there must be something better around, even in a podunk town like this."

Joe and Warren exchanged glances as the group left, one cranky member knocking the nearest chair out from under a table as he went.

"Wonder where we are today?" Warren said, after the door slammed shut behind the chair-kicker. He didn't sound as if he cared.

Jess rose from the bar where she'd been waiting for another plate for Eclipse and went to right the chair.

"Do you think I have value?" Zane asked. Since Eli delivered his insights on blindness, Zane had taken to asking the question every time a customer left the bar.

Joe sighed.

"Yeah, Zane, we all got value in the wonderful world. Even little old Zane gots value."

The sarcasm-laced reply was, with little variation, Joe's response to Zane's question. Jess was glad Joe took it upon himself to answer, however, since Zane would ask again and again until someone did.

Jess pulled the chair up and settled it back into position, her hands weighing down on its back. The chair held firm, its stability unaffected, even though it had been hit so hard that it clattered into one of its fellows. Jess looked up from the dimpled wood—the chair had seen other trials in its time—and rested her eyes on Sandman, perpetually slouched at his table.

Then she sighed, the expulsion of breath she still did not need striking her as wasteful, somehow.

Why, if it weren't for Eclipse and the stray customers who entered, we all might as well be stuck in a vacuum!

Although, if she remembered right, the void of space would rip their bodies apart ... in the real world, anyway. Jess wondered where Between existed when not settled onto some random stretch of Earth.

"Has anyone ever come in who didn't speak English? I mean, does Between go to other countries?"

Warren looked up from his glass and frowned, even as Eli emerged from the kitchen with Eclipse's food.

"Who cares?" Joe's shrug needlessly emphasized his answer.

"I have only known people to enter Between from the western states," Eli told Jess.

"So, only from the U.S.?"

"Yes, and then only west of the Mississippi River."

"Thanks, Eli. And thanks for Eclipse's food, too."

"Has she grown larger again today?" Eli's smile shone like a beacon.

"Today and every day," Jess replied. "She's like a furry watermelon on stilts."

Eli threw his head back and laughed, a sound so infectious even Warren's frown cracked a little along its edges.

"Jessamy," Warren said when Eli's mirth had been expunged, "why do you keep asking questions about Between? What good does it do?"

Jess felt her brows knitting as she thought about it. The motion pulled at her temple, flexing her perpetual bruise and reminding her she remained wounded here.

She remained always wounded here.

"Because I wonder about it, that's all. What harm does it do?"

"No good, no harm, yippee-ki-yay, how about another round," Joe said.

"Not for me." The needlessness of Zane's assertion rang as hollow as his words.

"Don't you wonder?" Jess asked. As the words left her mouth, she thought it was a very *Jessamy* thing to do, to ask a question like that.

She didn't have time to ponder what on earth the notion of a "Jessamy thing to do" meant before Warren replied.

"Wonder what?"

"Anything. Anything at all."

Now Warren took time to consider, and Jessamy—Jess— could tell from his expression that he didn't like the direction his thoughts traveled.

"I guess I don't. Not anymore." Warren looked beyond Jess to Sandman's table and then turned back to the bar, rapping his glass against it with unnecessary force.

Jess picked up Eclipse's plate and nodded her thanks to Eli. Eli nodded back, his face as serious as Between's discharged atmosphere.

Joy never overstayed its welcome in Between—not by a millisecond, it seemed. Smiles might linger outside the bar, happiness passing through time as lazily as a summer sunset, but inside Between, pleasure ended as abruptly as a switch cut electricity.

Climbing the stairs, Jess tried to remember if it had been this way from the start of her time in Between and couldn't recall. Time worked differently without anything so natural as sleep or daylight to bookend its segments; fact interchanged with experience more readily, too. Confusion constantly fogged what Jess might otherwise name intuition, and trust? Trust was something that only existed when life and death properly paired.

Trust served no purpose in Between where walls bled tears, you couldn't see past your personal death outside, and only passers-through possessed life.

Jess stopped at the top of the stairs, trying to grasp the idea's flipside. Outside, life surrounded people regularly with death hanging on the periphery; in Between, death waited just on the other side of the door and life absented itself. Life, tangible but uncertain outside, assumed an exceptional ambiguity within Between ... maybe it existed for other people but it shunned Between's regulars, flitting just out of reach like a specter.

Entering her room, Jess felt like shivering but did not. Her skin, smooth to the eye, nevertheless curdled, wanting to crawl ... a sensation both disconcerting and entrancing.

Eclipse rose from the puddle of towels Jess made for her on the far side of the bed and scurried into view, meowing imperiously as she smelled and saw the plate Jess carried.

"Yes, yes. Here it is, Eclipse."

Jess squatted next to the cat, placing the plate carefully as Eclipse rose on her haunches to meet it. The cat remained graceful, even though she looked ungainly in the extreme, her midsection swollen and taut. Eclipse settled back to dine, mumbling little cat praises between bites of dinner—or was it breakfast?—and Jess lowered herself to sit, too.

Eclipse did not look up from her meal.

"You know I won't steal your food, don't you, Eclipse?"

As Eclipse feasted, Jess petted the cat's glossy fur, keeping her strokes short and near Eclipse's shoulders, lest the cat feel compelled to raise her squat body to meet the caresses. Jess didn't want Eclipse to overdo anything at this stage of her pregnancy, but she also found it soothing to care for the cat.

"I wonder if I ..." Jess caught the rest of her thought and bit it back so it wouldn't pass her lips. But the notion's entirety remained, insistent, even as Jess continued to pet Eclipse's warm, furry body.

I wonder if I would have had my baby by now.

It wasn't the first time she'd considered holding a living, breathing version of the dormant life trapped within her. But lurking reality always tempered her imagination's sweetness, leaving Jess with the cold shock of knowing Lucas could have killed them both in a rage by this time as well.

Somehow, some way, if she ever got out of Between, Jess had to find the means and opportunity to escape. The idea seemed impossible before Between and it still did. Jess frowned. Except ... Between itself was impossible, so maybe ... maybe nothing was impossible.

Eclipse finished her food and rose, stretching. She positioned herself to meet Jess' hand with her head, bumping up against the downward pressure of Jess' stroke.

"Maybe it's not so impossible after all, huh, Eclipse?"

The cat purred and nuzzled Jess, tipping her waitress with the particular currency unique to cats. Jess returned the gratuity, savoring the latest temporary joy she found with a depth of appreciation that eternized the experience, however briefly.

When Eclipse curled forward to groom her chest fur, Jess shook her head. Between was strange enough without it seeping into her thoughts. Though Jess could remember Mama saying something—what was it?

"Jessamy, are you putting puzzles together behind your eyes?"

Yes. That's what Mama said when Jessamy daydreamed, or when she asked a question her mother couldn't answer without taking them both on a trip to the library. The happy memory stung because of loss, but Jess smiled through the pain.

"I'm putting puzzles together, Eclipse." Jess worked her fingers deep along the cat's tail fur.

"Maybe you'll make sense of it and maybe you won't, but you keep trying. My Jessamy, you never stop trying."

Jess pressed the fingers of one hand against her lips and then pinched her eyes shut against the sudden shock throbbing at her temple.

"... you never stop trying ..."

But she had. Jess became aware of her stomach, which troubled her not the least in Between; it was a strange sensation indeed, to be surprised by nausea's lack. Jess wished she could be sick, longed for a proper response to this unsettling realization instead of the renewed reverberation of unrelated agony around her eye.

Although ...

"It's all the same, isn't it? If I hadn't stopped trying, then I'd never have stayed with ... or Lucas wouldn't even want to be with ..."

Jess hunched forward, the gravity of her thoughts a burden past bearing.

She stayed that way for a long time until Eclipse, once more, strolled into the jumbled mess inside Jess' head, scattering puzzle pieces as she went.

The cat curved around Jess, rubbing against Jess' stagnant self with her own beautifully living body. The press of kittens within and Jess' immobility without conspired as if by intent and when Eclipse stood still, purring, Jess thought she felt the subtle squirming ... life within life.

"Eclipse! You're so close."

Jess raised her head, regarding the furry face so near her own. And then she smiled softly as she lifted her hands to meet the cat's touch with hers, wondering if her own skin felt as cool to Eclipse as Eclipse's felt warm to her.

Hot and cold, life and Between. Another odd dichotomy and Jess didn't want to entertain more enigmas—she found herself spectacularly tired of thinking.

But it nagged her, long after Eclipse settled down for a rest.

Hot and cold.

It poked Jess, prodding a memory that wouldn't quite surface.

Hot and cold.

And then ...

"Oh, no. No! Eclipse likes you best. She should stay with you." The sincerity of Love's words carried not only in the way they rushed out, but through the warmth of her hands pressing against Jess' skin.

... the warmth of her hands pressing against Jess' skin.

Hot and cold.

Hot and cold!

Jess stood as if pulled up by a string, flew to her door like she'd sprouted wings. She burst across the hall, entering Love's room without knocking and startled the woman from sleep—*Love could sleep!*—sparking terror into her bleary eyes.

"You're alive!" Jess exclaimed, too shocked by Love's secret to do more than whisper it.

Love's face drained of color except for her cheeks which glowed, blistering red.

"You're alive!" Jess repeated it, her voice rising without intent.

"Shh!" Love scurried from her bed, violently casting off covers in her haste. She shut the door tight and then pressed her back against it, facing Jess. "You can't tell—you can't!"

"Why ... when ..."

"It doesn't matter." Love's voice quavered and its tremors got Jess' attention; she realized Love was shaking, too.

"Are you all right?"

"Fine. I'm fine, I'm just ... I'm tired. It's hard. Sometimes it's harder, sometimes it's not so bad, but always, I can't ... I can't leave. I can't leave without Bear."

"But you ... he ..."

Love launched from the door toward Jess, who reached out to catch her. Jess gripped Love, though not as tightly as Love reciprocated the embrace, clinging to Jess with her warm, living hands—beyond warm, in fact.

Hot!

"You've got a fever. You're sick!"

"No." Love shook her head and lurched away, stumbling back to her bed. She sat on the edge, fingers clawing at the disarrayed quilt. "You can't tell."

"Love!" Alarmed, Jess started to close the gap between herself and Love.

"NO!" Love panicked, her jerky movements escalating past mere trembling to outright quaking. "I can't leave Bear! Don't you understand?"

Alarmed by Love's intensity, Jess sat next to the woman and wrapped one arm around her spasming shoulders.

"Okay, okay. But we have to get you better. I can't promise not to tell if you don't get better. I can't do that to you or to Joe."

"Thank you," Love sobbed the words. As she did, Jess felt—or imagined she felt—the slightest release in the heated, tensed muscles underneath her arm. "I'll get better. I promise I will."

190

That it wasn't something Love could know with certainty didn't lessen the strength of her determination. Jess let her go with one final squeeze around those too-warm shoulders and stood.

"I'll get you a cold cloth now and later, I'll bring the ice bag from the bar. I'll get a glass of water, too. You'll need to drink a lot more water to get well."

"Okay. Okay, I will."

Jess left Love with a cold, damp hand towel wrapped around her fevered head. Her own head filled with what she should do next ... and then she turned from closing Love's door and saw her own door standing open.

"Oh, no."

Though she looked everywhere in her room, twice, Jess did not find Eclipse there.

The cat had escaped.

Nesting

"How could she get out?" Warren asked as Jess pressed the ice bag lightly against her temple. She worried about Eclipse and didn't want to waste the ice on herself with Love ill upstairs ... another concern! She was torn.

"I shut *my* door." Saturating sanctimony dripped from Zane's four small words.

"That's good, Zane." Jess managed to say it without bitterness. "Eclipse is close to having her kittens so she'll want the best spot to do it. I should have been more careful."

"Well, there's not too many places she can go." Warren rose from his stool. "Come on, idiot, let's find this cat before anything else happens."

Jess pressed the ice bag against her head more firmly, thinking about Love.

"What's in it for me?" Joe griped, but he stood as he spoke.

"What else? Saving the whiskey. The cat could knock over a bottle otherwise."

"She wouldn't ..." Jess lifted the bag to look directly at the men.

Joe met her eye and winked.

"Save the whiskey." He slapped Warren on the shoulder. "I'm in."

Warren and Joe walked to the back of the bar, evidently planning to begin their search with the storage room and bathrooms. Jess couldn't imagine Eclipse could enter the storage room without being seen, and even a nice bathroom—which Jess didn't suppose any bar featured—would be lacking suitable coziness.

Jess set the ice bag on the bar and looked to the bartender where the woman stood, endlessly polishing glassware.

"I'm sorry, but can I look for Eclipse behind the bar? And in the kitchen? I promise I'll be more careful with my door."

Before Jess finished her words, the bartender answered with a silent nod and tip of her head.

"Thank you."

Jess rushed past Zane, slowing as she stepped behind the bar. Gleaming glasses and bottles lined the space there, except near the sparkling sink which stood empty, bereft of a single dirty item. Jess took her time searching but there were no hiding places she could find and no cat to be seen, either.

Jess thanked the bartender again regardless and moved toward the kitchen. She pushed open the swinging door just enough to let her voice travel unimpeded inside.

"Eli? It's Jessamy—Jess. I'm looking for Eclipse, she ..."

"She is here." Eli's deep voice might as well have been a purr, carrying the words Jess longed to hear with gentle depth.

"She is?" Jess fought the urge to fly inside, slowing her progress only with great effort. Eli stood before the griddle, cleaning its surface with vigor; the scratching and scraping echoed in the small space even though Jess hadn't heard it from the bar.

"She chose well, you see." Eli pointed at a shelf next to the door. Following his direction, Jess found Eclipse halfway up the shelving and contrasting sharply with the bright white towels on which she lounged.

The cat looked at Jess and yawned.

"I'm so glad she's here!" Jess bent next to Eclipse and stroked the cat's bouncing head as she applied her tongue to the curl of her toes.

"I'm sorry, I didn't mean to let her get out ..."

Eli chuckled, going back to his cleaning. Unlike the bartender's perpetual efforts, Jess noticed Eli performed a task that actually needed doing.

"Cats like softness," Eli said, speaking loudly to be heard over his work. "Cats with kittens to come ..." He left the thought unfinished but for the quirk in his voice.

Jess put her own spin on it.

"She wanted what she wanted. And she took the opportunity when she saw it."

"Opportunities do not come when we choose," Eli agreed. "Only when they come."

Jess smiled, thinking what Joe would say about this conversation. On the surface, it held little more than repetitious nonsense but the words encompassed inner layers thick with meaning.

Jess felt her smile fade.

"I'll tell Joe and Warren we found her." She straightened. "Do you think ... I want her to be comfortable, but ... maybe I could just take a few towels?"

Jess looked at Eli then, finding him regarding her with a serious expression, one unwarranted by her question.

"Do not let opportunities pass you, Jessamy."

"I ..." Jess bit her lip, aborting the sentence she couldn't form.

"You must care for yourself, just as Eclipse cares for herself."

Intensity filled the moment, pressing on Jess harder than her teeth bit into her lip. She eased her jaw but held Eli's shrewd gaze with her own.

Since neither of them needed to blink, the stare-down went on, enduring for a long time even by Between's standards.

"I'll tell Joe and Warren we found Eclipse," Jess said at last, resorting to repetition.

"Yes." Eli renewed his scrubbing, though without the vehemence that saturated his advice. "When I am finished here, I will bring Eclipse and the towels she has marked to your room."

As Eclipse rubbed her cheek against the top towel, Jess didn't question Eli's choice of words. With almost each word he said, he reinforced her belief that he purposefully phrased everything passing his lips. She supposed he might have done this prior to entering Between, but she had the impression he perfected the habit after he became a regular.

She wondered if he would ever leave.

She wondered if he ever wanted to leave.

The questions fluttered drunkenly, butterflies glutted with the distilled ambivalence of "what if."

Jess pushed through the door and stepped out from behind the bar, calling to Joe and Warren.

"I found her; she's in the kitchen with Eli."

Joe popped his head out of the men's room almost at the same time Warren emerged from the women's.

"The whiskey's safe?"

"Yes, the whiskey's fine. I guess Eclipse wanted some softer towels, that's all."

"Well, she could of said so," Joe groused, exiting the men's room and glaring at Warren.

"No, she couldn't, idiot. She's a cat."

"No excuse." Joe straightened, gesturing so expansively that Warren pulled back. "The wall sings, we ain't breathing but we're still walking around, and oh yeah, colors of death sit outside. Why don't the cat talk, too?"

195

"She's alive," Warren pointed out, stepping into the hallway and moving quickly past Joe.

"Dumbass details." Joe trailed Warren back to the bar. "Messes up my possibilities."

"Warren's got a point." Zane withered in an instant when both Joe and Warren favored him with daunting scowls.

"Shut it, Zane, or you're buying the next round."

"But I ..."

Jess ducked back into the kitchen, the sound of grating metal purely melodic compared to mockery's din at the bar.

Since Eli showed no signs of lessening his efforts, Jess settled onto the floor in front of Eclipse's cushioned lair.

"Do you think they mean it? Joe and Warren, when they make fun of each other?" Jess voiced the question aloud, not knowing if Eli would hear or answer but hoping he would do both.

Eli released his deep, rolling laugh. The virulent contagion caused Jess to giggle in harmony. She answered her own question after they both finished.

"They don't."

"They do not. It is their way to speak without showing they care. It is their protection."

"Protection from what?"

"From hurt. Pain is all we seek to protect ourselves from. It comes in many guises, so we give it many names. In the end, it is only pain."

In the end, it is only pain.

Jess petted Eclipse and thought about it.

Only pain. Only pain drove people past speech, sent some careening off life's ledge. Only pain broke Jess when her mother died.

But pain also numbed. Jess stayed with Lucas in spite of the hurt, or maybe because of it. She became so inured to emotional

196

agony—punctuated by occasional physical abuse—that she'd cocooned herself in her pain, wrapping the layers around her until she couldn't feel … or, at least, couldn't believe she felt anything beyond her imprisoning chrysalis.

She'd been in pain's dark so long that when she saw light, pure light, through Between's door, she found it beautiful.

The thought singed her, affecting a pretentious intensity like Zane's focus on time. Jess hated the idea she'd trapped herself long before stepping into Between's inexplicable snare.

Not that Lucas was blameless. No, Lucas bore blame like a cartoon pack mule, barely visible underneath its burden but walking on as if oblivious to the heap on its back.

"I am finished." Jess looked up at Eli. He stood next to her and might have been there for some time.

"Me, too," Jess said. Like the words they'd spoken earlier, this small exchange upheld more than one meaning.

Eli didn't say so but Jess felt as if he was pleased by what she said—and more so by what she meant.

After their brief and silent unity, Eli slid one hand underneath Eclipse and her towels and wrapped the other around behind her. The cat reached out with her front paws, claws digging into the shifting surface upon which she reclined, but she did not take flight.

Eli paused and then lifted slowly. Eclipse peered over the edge of the arm now sheltering her. She seemed curious, not concerned.

"Let us go, quietly and carefully."

Jess nodded.

She opened the door and waved, pressing one finger to her lips when she'd gotten the attention of the three men at the bar. Then she stepped aside, holding the door for Eli and his round feline passenger, cushioned by towels.

"Kodak moment," Joe said, elbowing Warren.

"Quiet, idiot. You want the cat to run off again?"

"She's huge!" Zane exclaimed, and promptly suffered renewed, stabbing stares from Warren and Joe. "Well, she is." That, he whispered, and Joe snickered.

"Warren, you'd best have *the talk* with little Zane here."

Jess bit back a smile as she and Eli approached the stairs, glancing back at the unlikely trio.

"Go ahead," she told Eli. "I forgot the ice, but I'll catch up."

She waited until Eli began negotiating the steps and then flew as swiftly as light footsteps would take her back to the bar. The ice bag weighed heavy in her hand when she picked it up, and she took the time to thank the bartender for refilling it.

The bartender half-nodded her usual, wordless reply, but the sharpness of her eyes made Jess feel like an insect taking a specimen pin straight through her core.

Eli would need her help to open the door upstairs, too—which she now realized she ought to have left open for Eclipse, should the cat have returned on her own. Jess forced a blink and broke free from the bartender's intense gaze.

As Jess rounded the corner out of the stairwell, she saw Eli waiting by her door. Both he and his odd burden of cat cushioned on her towel bed appeared calm, and it tickled Jess so much that she grinned.

"Sorry." She spoke softly, the words carrying her good humor like chimes. Eli smiled back, and Eclipse looked up at Eli and over at Jess as if perplexed by her servants' delay.

"She's been over on the far side of the bed," Jess told Eli as she opened the door.

Eli navigated the sparse room so readily that Jess wondered why she'd thought she had to provide directions in the first place. As he lowered Eclipse and her towels, the cat shifted and leapt onto the nearby bed, meowing.

"She will watch," Eli chuckled, "to be sure we do as she wishes."

Jess joined Eli's laughter again, and it felt good. Together, they settled the towels, crafting a new nest atop the old one until Eclipse meowed again and dropped down into the middle.

"Our part must be done now." Jess watched as the cat began to knead the towels herself.

"It must," Eli agreed. He reached out and stroked Eclipse, who purred appreciation but did not moderate her own efforts to perfect her kittens' birthing place.

"I must return to the kitchen." Eli stood in a fluid motion. He extended his hand to Jess—the same hand he'd petted Eclipse with, the same one he'd touched his death with—and she took it, rising easily with his aid.

Then Eli brought his other hand down over Jess', enveloping her hand and making her feel small. That living heat remained absent from the clasp did not make it any less life-affirming; Jess savored the gentle pressure, returning it through her fingertips.

"Thank you," she said when Eli released her hand and turned to leave.

"You are welcome," Eli replied without looking back. His voice, deeper by far than the bartender's, nevertheless paced and inflected the words just as she would have done.

Eli left, the door clicking shut behind him and Jess stood still, caught in an elastic moment that stretched without breaking.

Eventually, she remembered.

The ice. Love!

Jess assured herself that Eclipse remained content—she did seem so—and scooped up the ice bag from where she'd set it near the foot of the bed. She checked and double-checked that she closed her door before ducking into Love's room.

Love popped up in bed as if a button had been pressed, releasing a spring and Jess hastened to reassure her.

"It's okay." Jess rushed forward, pressing the older woman back against her pillow. Love's forehead, when Jess touched the back of her hand against it, still burned with fever.

"I g-g-got the washcloth c-c-cold again. Twice," Love's tone blended a peevish whine with miserable vibrato.

"That's good." Jess tried to keep her voice light. "The ice bag will be better." And she brought it down lightly against Love's skin as she spoke.

"Ohhhh. That is better!"

"I'm sorry it took me so long," Jess began, settling back a bit. "Eclipse ..."

"What about Eclipse? Is it the kittens?" Love's eyes popped open under the ridge of the ice bag.

"No, no kittens yet. And Eclipse is fine." Jess grabbed Love's free hand and rested its heat between her own hands' cool neutrality. How different Love's touch was from Eli's! Jess patted the woman's skin, choosing her words carefully. "She's getting everything just right for when the kittens come, that's all. Eli gave her some very soft towels."

"Soft is good," Love said, her eyes flickering open and shut. "Ice is good. You are good."

"I ..."

"You are. *You*. Are good."

Love seemed certain and because Jess wanted her to rest, she didn't try to speak again but simply waited until Love's breathing softened into sleep.

Reclamation

No shadows lengthened in the room but the ice bag slowly lost its lumpiness, helping Jess track the passage of time. She released Love's hand the first time the bag shifted and held it in position thereafter until its interior sloshed with the least movement.

"I'll be right back," Jess whispered. "I'll be as fast as I can."

Love murmured something unintelligible as Jess lifted the ice bag away. She exchanged it for a hastily-dampened washcloth and left the room.

Jess ducked into her own room to check on Eclipse. The cat, returning from a trip to the litter box, stopped when she saw Jess and meowed pleasantly.

"I'll get you some more food, too, Eclipse."

Eclipse did not agree or disagree with Jess' proposal, but eased her swollen body back down into her cushioned towel nest and began to wash behind an ear.

Back in the hallway, Jess paused, intensely aware of her position between two living, breathing beings who relied on her. On her! Someone who wasn't even alive herself. The situation's strangeness clung like burrs, encased like a gall.

She wasn't alive, but she hadn't died. Straddling these two worlds, she still mattered, exerting an influence that surprised her. Jess actually felt more alive now—now that she wasn't alive—than when she'd been with Lucas.

But there was more to her unique importance than juxtapositioning ... more to her significance than randomness or fate, whichever ruled in drawing people to Between or it to them. Jess found herself representing a willingness, a driving need to be involved, and a deep longing to integrate into the lives of others.

The ice bag gurgled as Jess lowered her hands to her belly, and the literal "bag of water" she held without pressed against her own arrested life, and that of the developing life figuratively frozen within her.

She didn't dream of becoming a mother while with Lucas because such a notion could only manifest as a nightmare. How benedictory that her dream dared to defy her, materializing regardless of her will ... how tantalizing that Between excluded Lucas, stopping his interference without neutralizing his threat.

In one sense, Jess still felt like she inhabited a nightmare. But she couldn't deny that her Lucas-free abeyance in Between's unnatural realm gilded the experience, enriching it in spite of its vapidity.

Nothing could harm her here in Between, not while she occupied the narrow space bordering life and death. Nothing could harm the baby she wanted—beyond anything—to bear. Outside, something always lurked, ready to steal certainty and diminish determination. Here, even if a dream petrified, it remained viable. Just out of reach but unmistakably possible.

Between singularly excluded the enemy named time, forcing it to pass without most of its usual influences. Its ban extended to even lesser outside barriers like Lucas, denying such simple entry and, to some degree, affectation of divisive form.

Physically, at least.

Jessamy stood straighter, shaking off her ruminations and moving more purposefully toward the stairs. Love and Eclipse needed her and she would not let them down.

She began to believe she wouldn't let herself down, either.

Jessamy marched to the bar and nodded to the bartender.

"Can I get the ice bag refilled, please? And can I have a cheeseburger?"

"Maybe not in that order," Warren drawled.

"Maybe not."

Joe narrowed his eyes and frowned.

"And what's got you all ..." he fluttered the fingers of one hand upwards, grimacing, "whatever you are?"

Jess thought about it, finally deciding on a partial truth.

"Kittens. It won't be long now."

"I don't wanna rip more paper."

"Nobody cares what you want, Zane," Joe said, dismissive. "You ain't good at it anyways, so don't worry about getting asked again."

Thinking about further depleting Between's paper towel supplies sparked a matched set of ideas. Jessamy extracted the contents of her pocket, dumping them on the bar, and separated the remaining cash from her barrette, Tracy and Todd's address, and stray lint.

"Excuse me." She waited anxiously until the bartender favored her with the searing attention of those dark eyes. Then Jessamy slid her remaining money to the bartender. "Could I ... could you use this to order some cat litter? And ... some ibuprofen?"

"Ibuprofen!"

"What the?"

Warren and Joe spoke within split-seconds of each other, their voices fighting for top billing.

"Well, it might take the edge off this headache I have every single minute of every single day."

Warren looked thoughtful; Joe, suspicious.

"Don't get drunk here but you think you can get rid of pain?"

"She can't get rid of you, idiot; she's talking about her other headache."

"Ha-ha. Dumbass."

"It was just an idea," Jess said, hoping it sounded as if she didn't care.

"Too late to go back now." Joe nodded at the bar, where the bartender had selected several bills, leaving the remainder next to the gleaming barrette and rumpled paper.

She also left a single-dose ibuprofen packet.

Jessamy whisked the money and ibuprofen into her hands, bundling it back into her pocket.

Joe watched with his sharp, hooded eyes.

"Not gonna take your meds here?"

"You're supposed to take it with food," Jessamy said, lifting her chin. Joe opened his mouth, ready to object again, and so Jess rambled on. "Besides, I've always been awful with pills. I'll probably have to smash it into pieces and put it on my cheeseburger."

She grabbed her barrette and tapped it against the bar's polished wood. The sacrilegious thought of crossing her fingers behind her back while holding her mother's barrette outweighed the logistics of the act; she hoped her lie was forgivable under the circumstances.

"I don't know what's gotten into you, Jessamy, but I like it." Warren stamped his approval into each word.

Joe snorted.

"Beats her sitting in Zane's room like a dumbass, but then what don't?"

"Hey!"

"Hay's for horses, Zane. If you don't got something interesting to say, shut your hole."

"I got interesting things to say." Zane's outrage audibly dwindled as he spoke. "I do, too."

They sat in silence for a few moments, so quietly that Jess heard Eli working in the kitchen. She could even hear squeaking from an irate glass suffering the indignity of the bartender's ubiquitous polishing efforts.

"Been a while since we had a round of 'I Miss,'" Warren said.

"I miss what?" Zane asked, and Joe groaned.

"Warren, are you trying to drive me out the door?"

"Shut up, idiot. Zane's got interesting things to say and I bet Jessamy does, too. I'll start."

Warren's voice dropped, firmness usurped by a deep and painful longing.

"I miss hot nights when the sun sets and the breeze starts up. When it feels like the wind's carrying the ocean right to you, no matter how far away you are."

Joe sighed again.

"Right, then. I miss vodka."

"I miss!" Zane exclaimed. "I miss catching stars on the ground."

"Stars on the ground," Joe guffawed, but Jessamy interrupted him when he would have started back on Zane.

"Fireflies."

Zane met Jessamy's eyes, nodding.

"Your turn, Jessamy."

The flood in her mind threatened to drown her with the rush of things—so many things—she missed. One notion forced its way through the hoards wanting to win out to be first.

"I miss the rain. I miss the way it sounds when it falls, hard on the roof and soft on the ground. I miss the way puddles ripple and the way droplets try to fly back home to the clouds when you jump in with them. I miss how cool and sweet the rain tastes. I even miss how it smells afterwards ... like ... like ... caterpillars."

"Caterpillars? How the hell do rain smell like caterpillars?"

"I don't know." Jess ducked her head, though Joe sounded more perplexed than deriding. "It just does."

Between's supernatural silence descended again, a stultifying, smothering heaviness. And it stayed, doing its worst, until Joe spoke once more.

"Fine. I miss sunlight on my face. I feel like an old owl sitting in this bar all the time, and I don't want to remember that because of some dumbass game."

"Why, Joe. I didn't know you had it in you." Warren clasped Joe's shoulders and Joe shoved him away with a grumble. "Zane, Jessamy, this is a great day, and you've both witnessed it ... this is the first time in the history of Between Joe said he missed something besides vodka."

"He said that, too," Zane pointed out.

"Shh." Jessamy didn't try to hide the grin and giggle bubbling behind the finger she raised to her lips.

"Oh, yeah." Zane mimicked her pose.

"Dumbasses, all of you." Joe shoved at Warren with renewed vigor. But his words, disarmed of their barbs, were scarcely more than sounds.

This time, everyone could tell.

"Order up," Eli called, ringing the bell. He peered through the window, smiling at Jessamy.

"I have added a portion for Eclipse and a tray to carry it all."

"Thank you." Jessamy waved to Eli. "Thank you," she said again, this time to the bartender as the woman transferred the tray to the bar.

The bartender inclined her head as she so often did, and then picked up the ice bag and moved to refill it. Jessamy wondered if perhaps a tip of the head carried more weight than words with the bartender and mimicked the gesture when the bartender placed the refreshed bag on the tray.

The small part of Jess hoping for an approving smile from the bartender was disappointed but she knew her gesture had been noted.

That would have to be enough.

"Back in a jiffy." Jessamy sang to the men at the bar. "Maybe we can play another round of 'I Miss' then?"

Joe groaned, dramatic and loud, and Warren guffawed.

"I miss!" Zane piped up. "I miss cake. Cake is good."

"Zane, you ain't going all Poet Laurel on us with 'stars on the ground' for fireflies and then talk about cake, just... 'cake,'" Joe complained.

"Sure he can," Warren said.

"I miss birthdays," Zane went on, apparently undeterred. "Cake on fire."

"Warren, do you see what you done? You got him going ..."

Jessamy left the conversation behind, focusing her attention on the stairs. In all her waitressing experience, she'd never had the occasion to carry a tray up or down stairs, so she felt as if she ought not take such a skill for granted.

It turned out to be easy enough, at least for someone with Jess' background, and soon she arrived at Love's door.

She knocked gently and opened the door a crack.

"Love? It's Jessamy. I have some food and medicine ... and more ice!"

"Medicine?" Love's voice wavered. "I don't like medicine."

"It's only ibuprofen," Jessamy explained, setting the tray on the desk and carrying the ice bag to the bed. "It might help your fever."

"Oh. Okay."

Jessamy extended the ice bag to Love and in exchange, Love offered the washcloth that had slipped from her brow to dampen her pillow. Love's hands still shook, and it worried Jess.

"I forgot to bring a glass of water." Jess rose to return the cloth to the bathroom. "But you have one here, so it's okay."

After Love swallowed the ibuprofen, Jessamy brought the burger.

"I can't eat that," Love protested. "It's too much."

"Just eat a little. You're sick; you need to eat something."

"Can we share?"

"Sure, we can share." Jessamy smiled, and watched Love smile back underneath eyes glistening with fever. "Here, I'll break it in half; I'll take a bite of my half for every bite you take of yours."

They got Love propped up against her pillows and put the plan into action.

"You don't need it like me but it's still good," Love noted.

"It's delicious; Eli is a great cook."

"I never had the cheeseburger before." Love took another small bite. "I only got the eggs from behind the bar."

"The pickled eggs? Oh, Love, is that all you've been eating?" Aghast, Jessamy raised her voice without thinking.

"Shh! No, Eli gives me other things sometimes, if there's leftovers. We have to be careful so Bear doesn't notice. He would make me leave."

"He can't make you leave, Love."

"He can, too." Love's fingers plucked at the bun, sending a sesame seed shower onto the plate. "He can give guilt just as much as Mother ever could. I wouldn't care if he pushed me, I really wouldn't. But he'd make me go with words. And words hurt worse."

She looked up from the plate, catching Jessamy's eyes with the bright glare of her own.

"You can't tell, Jessamy."

"It's okay, Love. Don't worry, please ... have a little more. You need to be strong for Bear. He doesn't know it but he needs you, too."

Love didn't blink.

"Bear might need me but Joe doesn't. Joe doesn't need anybody."

"Everybody needs somebody."

"Not Joe."

"Well, you need food." Jessamy winked. "You can't let this amazing cheeseburger get cold. What would Eli think?"

"I don't know what Eli would think. I don't know what I think now." Despair soaked Love's words as badly as perspiration soaked her brow.

"That's just the fever. Come on, just one more little bite?"

With "just one more," Jessamy persuaded Love to eat almost all of her half. When the sick woman's eyelids began drooping between bites, Jess backed down.

"Rest," she said, patting Love's hand. "I'll take Eclipse her dinner and check on you later."

Love half-nodded, sliding down her pillow's incline. This set the ice bag into motion as well, but Jessamy caught it before it got too close to the edge of the bed.

After Love drifted into restless slumber, Jess picked up the tray and crossed the hall to her own room, where Eclipse greeted her with a meow interrupted by a yawn.

"It must be late; I do have dinner, though."

Eclipse accepted Jess' offering and after she finished her portion, settled back and began to purr.

Knowing that Love slept, Jessamy stayed with Eclipse, petting her until the cat dozed off, too.

Restoration

Aided by ibuprofen and cheeseburger halves, Love recovered. Jessamy felt Joe watching her closely each time she placed an order for the curative combination but if he had suspicions, he determined not to voice them.

Besides, a new regular arrived.

Her name was Bella and she took the bar by storm. She came into Between covered in snow, stomping her feet to dislodge chunks of the stuff, and called for a round of beers. When she turned to close the door, she saw "fire like lightning, leaping down from the heavens and lighting up the whole world" and slammed the door shut.

The fact that she still existed hours after seeing what she'd seen, along with a brief self-demonstration at Joe's behest, sufficiently convinced her of Between's strange character.

"'No point in this game!' That's what she told Joe after he talked her into holding her breath while he drank his beer ... and then tried to take hers," Warren explained to Jessamy when she arrived to order another cheeseburger.

"Nobody takes my beer." Bella cuffed Joe on his shoulder as she slid down from her barstool perch. She walked over to Jessamy and gave her a once-down/once-up appraisal. "I'm Bella, which means 'beautiful' and goes to show the Almighty has a great sense of humor. If He knew Mom planned such a misnaming and then went on and let it happen anyway ... well. The angels must have got a kick out of it, that's all."

"I'm Jessamy." Jessamy shook the hand Bella extended. Her beauty might be debatable but Bella had a presence and comportment anyone would envy.

Anyone ... and in particular, Zane, whose eyes followed Bella's every move with admiration approaching worship.

"What do you see?" Bella asked, and it took Jessamy a minute to realize that she spoke about what lay outside Between's door rather than the petite powerhouse standing within it.

"White light. Nothing but white so bright it hurts to look at it."

Bella stared, then shrugged and turned away.

"Beats fire, I expect." Bella snapped the words, punctuating their pace with her boot heels as she returned to her spot at the bar. "Another round, with one for Jessamy, too."

"Oh, no. Thank you, but I couldn't."

Bella waved Jessamy's protest into the ether, dismissing it as easily as an insect.

"Bring it." Bella aligned the direction of her words with the bartender. "Somebody'll drink it before it gets warm. Same as somebody'll drink Zane's."

The bartender nodded her acknowledgement and then inclined her head to Jessamy.

"A cheeseburger, please."

"What? No ice, no ibuprofen?" Joe coated his tone with innocence, a sickly sweet syrup.

"It helps," Jessamy lied. "But not enough to keep doing it; not all the time, anyway. Bella's here, and Eclipse ..."

"Eclipse? Oh, the cat." Bella answered her own question. "Between's not your average bar even without what's happening outside, I'll give it that."

"We're waiting for the kittens," Jessamy went on, propelled by Joe's continued scrutiny. "So there's a lot to do."

"You was waiting for kittens before, so I don't see ..."

"Joe, you've got an ice-cold beer in front of you—why are you fussing?" Warren's interjection seemed a little too quick to Jessamy but she was grateful, regardless.

"To Between." Bella raised her glass. "May it always keep its secrets and may you always keep yours."

Joe's rising glass paused, hovering awkwardly just above the bar, when he heard the remainder of Bella's words.

"What kind of toast's that?"

Bella sipped her beer, eyeing him over the top of the glass.

"My kind." Her tone added that there would be no disputing her toasting style.

"Oh, your kind. Well, that's all we got to know. Bottom's up." So saying, Joe drank.

Warren cleared his throat half-heartedly, a clear prelude to speech rather than the result of tickling air.

"Bella found Between on her way to a friend's place during a blizzard," he told Jessamy. "She thought she got off route somehow and came in to ask directions."

"Didn't make a bit of sense." Bella shook her head. "I know my way around, storm or not. It doesn't take more than 15 minutes—normal weather, I mean—to get me to Ceci's place so when I saw this freaking bar, I nearly plowed my truck into a snow bank. Figured I had to be lost."

She shook her head again. "Should've known something was crazy."

"Maybe it ain't the bar. Ain't the bar what's crazy, I mean."

Bella's gaze narrowed, zeroing in on Joe and obviously requiring no clarification. If the fire Bella saw outside was anything like what she could muster with her dark brown eyes, Jessamy knew it must be a furious blaze.

Then, Bella laughed. And Jessamy imagined she understood why divine intervention failed to materialize upon Bella's naming: her laugh transformed her, revealing all that her physique and demeanor hid.

While Eli cooked Jess' cheeseburger, Jessamy watched as Bella casually pushed aside Warren's teasing and Joe's intimidation. Warren described how Bella took Zane under her slight wing, saying, "You come here, boy, and I'll go all mother hen on these sons-a-bitches the next time they bother you!"—and how Zane refused to stray from her side after that.

"I like her," Warren finished.

"You like anything with tits," Joe proclaimed, and Bella punched Joe in the shoulder, putting some real force behind it. "It's the truth!"

"Truth isn't reason to talk. And if it was, there'd be nothing but silence in the world."

"Nothing but silence in the world." Zane affirmed Bella's words and it rang like bells.

Joe met Jessamy's gaze and mouthed the word "parrot" without breathing sound into it. The beginnings of a giggle escaped Jessamy; she hastily converted the sound into a deranged cough.

"Gonna make it, girl?" Joe gave her a gentle pat on her back.

"Sure, I'm fine, I just ..." Humor stampeded over Jessamy's attempted suppression of it as she realized her faux excuse had no merit. "I was going to say I must have swallowed wrong but I couldn't have. I don't even know what happened."

The absurdity captured Joe right along with Jessamy, and soon their shared laughter morphed into its own storm, sweeping Warren, Bella, and even Zane up into its ridiculous delight.

Immersed in her fit of hilarity, Jessamy didn't notice when the others' mirth faded. She tried to get herself together, gasping for air and wiping tears from her eyes, but that took a while, too.

"Sorry," she finally managed, barely able to spare the breath to do so. "It's been ... a long time since ... since I had a laugh that good!"

"Sit down, Jessamy," Warren said, rising and directing her to the nearest chair.

"What ..." Jessamy eased into the seat and applied herself more completely to the task of stopping her raging giggles. The job became significantly easier when she focused on the eight eyes drilling into her, sad and stern, above four unsmiling mouths.

Jessamy felt her pulse picking up pace.

"What? What is it?"

... felt her pulse picking up pace ...

... pulse ...

"I'm alive again. Oh God, *oh God*, I'm alive again!"

Jessamy wrapped her hands over her belly as black terror, insistent and surging, bored through her body and into her soul.

"Put your head down, Jessamy," Warren urged.

"Barkeep—bag of ice and quick!" Joe shouted.

Bella materialized in the seat next to Jessamy's and wrapped a protective arm around her.

"There, now. It's all right."

"It's not all right. It's not! Lucas ..."

"Keep your head down and breathe." Helpless, Jessamy grasped for the steadiness carried through Warren's words. "It's been too long. You've forgotten you need it."

Jessamy followed Warren's instruction—or tried to—and listened. Her heart pounded in her ears, ringing like crazed church bells, abandoning tune for ratcheting vigor. She heard Joe's heavy, rushed plodding as he circled back to the table behind her and felt the cold weight of the ice bag land as lightly as a butterfly on her nape.

She listened as Zane forced a huge sigh and then another as he confirmed to himself that he still didn't need air the way Jessamy now did.

Panic reared, bucked.

"He'll be out there when I open the door!"

"Whoever he is, he can't hurt you," Bella replied. "We won't let him."

"We won't let him!" Zane repeated, but with a strength that lifted Jessamy's head from the table. She looked at Zane and found his skinny face earnest; she turned to Bella and found her countenance fierce. Joe, when Jessamy searched his face, nodded, as did Warren.

The circle around her, lifeless though it was, encompassed fear's drowning agony and buttressed it with determination. Jessamy felt a surge inside her like a living being ... like *another* living being ... and she knew she would face Lucas this time.

She must face him. She must not back down.

Bella clearly read it in Jessamy's expression for her smile came back, edged with steel. She took her hand from Jessamy's shoulder and slammed it onto the table.

"Beers all around!" she shouted. "So we're ready for whatever comes next." She pushed back her chair and made her way to the bar.

"Like Klingons going into battle."

"I like you more when you're a parrot, Zane. What the hell're chingens?"

"Klingons!"

"Don't be ridiculous, Zane." Bella made her way back to the table, laden with beer. "Klingons wouldn't go into battle when they'd been drinking. Warren, take one of these; you, too, Joe."

"Here, Jessamy." Joe pressed the ice bag into her hand so he could free his own. "Take it. Wishing you had a beer while you could, ain't you?"

"But what about ..." Zane began to protest. "Hey, how do you know about Klingons?"

"I read." Bella set the last beer on the table and returned to the bar for the other two glasses the bartender prepared.

"But Klingons are on television. And in movies."

"They're in books, too, Zane. There's even a Klingon dictionary."

"A Klingon dictionary!"

"Hallelujah—parrot's back."

Jessamy managed a smile then, though not much of one.

"Come on over here, Jessamy." Bella settled into the chair opposite the one Jessamy currently occupied. "We'll all sit where we can see the door."

Warren started, sloshing his beer.

"I suppose we should," he said, brushing at the spillage.

They rearranged positions and shuffled chairs. The five of them ranged out from the circle of the table in an uneasy rainbow, and Zane fidgeted in his position on the end farthest from the bar. Flanked by Bella on her right and Joe and Warren on her left, Jessamy let the cheeseburger the bartender delivered grow cold, tension holding her erect in a visible sign of her will to protect herself and her baby.

Eventually, her stomach growled.

"What was that?"

"Don't be dumb, Zane. Girl's hungry's all." Joe delivered his pronouncement with a glare and then pointed at Zane's untouched beer. "Pass it over. Beer must be as warm as the burger's cold, but I don't give a crap."

"You'd better eat, Jessamy." Warren spoke across Joe. "You're going to need the energy."

Realizing he was right, Jessamy picked at the burger, eating it slowly and trying to savor its slightly clammy texture.

"Could he have left?" Bella asked, her voice as gentle as Jessamy had heard it yet.

Jessamy shook her head, swallowing the tiny bite she'd been chewing into nothingness and struggling to speak in spite of the paucity of interference.

"He wouldn't. But ..." she considered, remembering her interrupted day with effort, "... it was late, when we got here. Maybe ... he fell asleep waiting?"

If he did, her absence would only serve to enrage Lucas when he awoke. It was a hard realization but Jessamy knew it made no difference in what she had to do.

"You ... " Jessamy glanced at each of her unlikely, unwavering allies. "You don't have to ..."

"Shut it, Jessamy." Joe banged the glass he'd just drained onto the table. "We don't got to, but we're gonna and you ain't gonna make us not, you hear?"

"What the idiot is trying to say is that we're with you, Jessamy."

"Dumbass," Joe said, and belched loudly.

"Just once, Joe ..." Warren stopped, whatever he was about to say lost as he stared. Jessamy followed his eyes and saw the color drain from Joe's face.

"You're ... Joe! You're alive, too," Jessamy whispered the words, but she didn't think Joe would have heard her if she'd shouted. "Joe, breathe."

Pushing away from the table, Jessamy reached around behind Joe and pressed the sloshing mess of an ice bag against his neck as he'd done for her so recently.

"Bartender! Please, I need more ice ..."

Even as Jessamy found herself growing more frantic—now worried for Joe—he panted, sucking in air.

Color rushed back into his face.

"I'm fine. I said I'm fine!" He pushed Jessamy's hand away so hard that she dropped the ice bag onto the floor. And then Joe caught her hand and held it, his clenching grasp replete with desperation. "I'm fine. I'm fine."

Joe gasped again, reasserted autonomous action at war with the oddity of its long absence. Jessamy knew how he felt. She squeezed his hand as much as she was able with her own held so tightly already. Mercifully, Joe lessened his grip, though he didn't release her.

"Idiot." The wretchedness in Warren's tone tore into Jessamy's heart. "You made it. You really did."

"I ain't leaving yet, dumbass," Joe replied, the bare bones of his former cockiness rematerializing. "Got to see Iris safe. Jessamy, too."

Warren's expression warred between loss and relief, but before the battle could be won, Love barreled down the stairs.

"Jessamy, Jessamy, the kittens are coming!" She stopped, a meteor wrecked in a crater, as the arch of five swiveled to look at her ... as the recognition of what each understood—if they hadn't already known—upon seeing her flushed face, hearing the breathlessness she so carefully camouflaged before.

Love's excitement plummeted as she realized her mistake. Then the door burst open with galvanizing sharpness and Lucas invaded Between.

"What the hell is going on?"

Daybreak

Jessamy stood and leaned forward against the table, letting it support her.

"What's taking so long, baby?" Lucas' eyes sparked as he made his way toward her, the open door behind him revealing hints of light beginning to cut through the fading night's fog. The thick haze that shrouded the world when Lucas stopped at Between was fast dissipating.

"Shut the door." The strain of saying it wore the edge of Warren's tone ragged. "Get out and shut the door behind you."

Lucas stopped, regarding him.

"Who are you people?"

"Dumbass probably don't know how to shut a door, Warren." Joe rose. "I'll get it."

"No, I got it." Zane skittered up and around the perimeter of the room to avoid Lucas. As the door slammed shut, Warren stood, too, as did Bella.

"Jessamy's staying," Bella said. "You're leaving."

Lucas looked at them all, eyes wide.

"Crazies, that's who you are." His eyes fell on the table, on the remains of the cheeseburger there. "Is that my burger? You'll have to pay me for that."

"No." Jessamy paused on the lonely word, her voice hardly the firmament of denial she wanted it to be. "No," she repeated, and it came out better that time. "You took all my money. You owe me, really, but it doesn't matter anymore. I want you to leave."

As she spoke, Lucas' lips thinned, a compressing line synchronous to the bloating rage impelling it.

"All your stuff is in the truck. You're coming with me."

"No, I'm not."

"The hell you're not," Lucas snarled, stepping toward her again.

"The hell she is!" Joe barked out, stopping Lucas in his tracks. "You ain't gonna try to make her, neither, and if you do, I'll stop you." He raised his fists as he said it.

"All of us will stop you." Bella delivered the correction, her voice as icy as the winter she'd left.

"Just me." Joe stepped around the table. Warren stayed next to him as he approached Lucas.

Lucas refused to give any ground.

"This is none of your business."

"Yeah, it is," Joe replied, and Warren nodded. "Jessamy's a friend."

"A friend. After a couple of hours in this hole-in-the-wall?" Lucas snapped his head into direct alignment with Jessamy. "What did you do? Or who did you do?"

"That's enough!" Warren clasped Joe's shoulder in an attempt to hold him back.

"More than enough," Joe agreed. He didn't bother shrugging off Warren's hand before punching Lucas in the face.

Lucas saw the blow coming and dodged the brunt of it; he came back with his own swing. But Bella moved, grabbing Lucas by his shirt, yanking with all her might.

"What's wrong with you people?" Lucas raged, shoving Bella into a nearby table. Zane rushed to Bella's side as she stumbled, but she righted herself without aid. "Jess, come on!"

"My name is Jessamy." Jessamy's slightly quaking voice resounded almost in stereo with Warren's firm one, "The lady's name is Jessamy."

Lucas stared. His hair, rumpled in the way it always did when he slept, struck Jessamy as sloppy now—not remotely vulnerable, as it appeared the first time she'd seen it. The memory came with a pang but conviction tempered her sense of loss and it only took a blink for the twinge to fade.

"Come on, Jess. Time to go. Be out in the truck in five minutes ... or else."

Jessamy knew what "or else" meant, and it both terrified her with its promise and reassured her with its consistency.

"I'm not coming with you. Not ever again."

A burst of applause startled Jessamy but even with all eyes turning, Love kept clapping. Her face, paler than it had been, now beamed with what Jessamy recognized as pride.

Lucas tore his distracted gaze from Love back to Jessamy. "Bunch of crazies and a retard."

Without a word, Joe lunged at Lucas again. Warren struggled to hold him while Bella positioned her body in Joe's path. Zane danced between Bella and Lucas, protective of Bella and wary of Lucas.

"You'll be sorry." The way Lucas said chilled Jessamy. He started to move away from Joe, who continued to fight to reach him. Lucas' chin jutted out and his jaw clenched as he turned, staring at each member of his opposition individually. He reached the door and opened it.

"All of you will be sorry." And Lucas isolated Jessamy with his dark glare before exiting, slamming the door behind him.

Jessamy sank into her chair.

"Bring it on, little boy!" Joe shouted. "Get off me, dumbass."

"What is happening?" Eli asked, emerging from the kitchen and wiping his hands on a towel.

Before Jessamy could answer Eli's question, Love leaned over the back of the chair and wrapped her in a hug.

"You were so brave."

"It's easy to be brave with friends." Jessamy patted Love's arm as long-denied tears started to flow.

"It's never easy to be brave," Bella asid. "It's easier with friends, but it's never plain easy." She waved to the bartender. "Another round. And I'll buy one for this lady here and the big guy over there, too—where were you when the horse-apples hit the fan? You could've scared that rotten one away and saved me from getting slammed into a table!"

Eli looked bemused and Jessamy smiled at his expression. Then Lucas' threat replayed in her head.

"Joe," Jessamy called, pressing Love gently away.

Joe whirled, still fuming.

"Joe, thank you, but you shouldn't have ... " Jessamy struggled out of her chair, flinging herself straight at the older man and hugging him as tightly as Love just hugged her. "You can get hurt now, too, you know. You can, because you're alive."

Joe—perhaps because he was stunned—hugged Jessamy back, and then they were both nearly flattened as Love intercepted and expanded their embrace.

"Bear? You're alive? Bear!"

Someone wept noisily, but not until Love and Joe exited their group hug did Jessamy realize she was the one crying.

"I'm okay. It's just ... I don't understand ... everything is ... and it's all happening—happening so fast ..."

Bella took charge, steering Jessamy over to the bar.

"Sit down, Jessamy, and tell me why you're worried about Joe here and not my delicate self." She called back to the others, "Belly up to the bar and let's have a toast!"

Warren took it upon himself to explain the vaster implications of being trapped in Between. Because Bella accepted the situation from the start, no one had demonstrated a regular's inability to get permanently injured—she'd only learned about the vagaries of breathing and ordering.

Jessamy got a water and refreshed ice bag from the bartender and offered the bag to Joe for his hand. He waved her away, staring alternately at her and at Love, who still beamed at the abundance of renewed life in Between, far beyond herself and Eclipse.

"Eclipse ..." Jessamy murmured.

"The kittens!" Love exclaimed, clearly anxious as she remembered. "I'll go check. I'll go now!" She turned away, then back. "Bear? Bear, you'll wait for me?"

Joe's eyes focused, slow and disquieted, and he frowned, prompting Love to flutter. Fear poured from her and she wrung her hands, vibrating with anticipated rejection.

"Sure," Joe rasped, and then steadied his voice. "Sure, I'll wait."

The sun none of them had seen in aggregated days long uncounted could not have outshone Love's face on hearing those words. She nodded, full eyes glistening, and whirled, flying back up the stairs like a personified version of the surname she'd chosen for herself.

Joe focused his attention on his beer but lowered the glass back to the bar before so much as sipping.

"Suppose I'd best take her slow now."

"Yes, idiot, leave drinking to real men."

"Dumbass." Joe's tone was flat, a gravelly mirror of Warren's.

"Are none of you going to introduce me to this fine hunk of a man?" Bella sighed, walking over to where Eli stood, still as a statue, watching them all. "Hi." She extended one short arm over the bar. "I'm Bella."

Eli enveloped her hand in his own.

"I am Eli."

"Eli's a really good cook," Zane offered, hovering next to Bella.

"Are you, now?" Bella looked up at Eli and clasped her other hand around his, not shy about extending their contact. "I must try your specialty—all your specialties—and soon."

Joe, watching the scene with Jessamy and Warren, burst out in a guffaw.

"Zane, your face!"

Zane turned fully toward them then, glowering.

Bella, after slowly disengaging her hands from Eli's—and unlocking her eyes even more slowly—wrapped one arm around Zane's shoulders.

"Zane, my first friend in Between, I know you don't drink beer ... what can I get you?"

The apoplexy that had frozen Zane relaxed its hold and he offered Bella a hesitant smile.

"Root beer?"

"A root beer for my friend Zane." Bella extracted a wad of money from her coat pocket, laying a $100 bill on the counter. "Eli, what will you have? Jessamy, anything for you? We still haven't had our toast."

Eli agreed to a root beer as well, but Jessamy demurred, anxiety directing her mind back to the door.

Would Lucas come back? Could he?

"He's not going to find Between again, Jessamy." Warren intercepted her glance as the bartender filled three glasses with root beer. "I promise you that."

"Here, Jessamy." Bella slid the third glass past Joe to her. "I know you said you didn't need anything, but you do." She picked up a glass of beer from the bar—there were many to choose from—and raised it, waiting.

"Come on, come on! You want the beer to get warm?"

When they all raised glasses to join hers, Bella beamed. And Jessamy wondered whether Warren made promises he couldn't keep, what Bella would say, whether Zane was jealous or ... could Warren possibly right? Did Between stand still for its regulars while moving for others?

"To friendship," Bella crowed, putting a full stop to the seething mess of questions in Jessamy's mind. "Wherever it finds us, however it binds us ... to friendship. To us."

"To us," Warren echoed, his voice both jubilant and dull.

"To friends." Joe clinked glasses with Warren first, then with Jessamy.

"Hear, hear!" Zane exclaimed, and did so repeatedly, moving about the bar to touch his glass against every other—including those yet unclaimed on the bar.

"For the love of Pete, Zane, watch it. You're gonna spill the beer," Joe complained, but he dutifully clinked glasses with Zane when his time came.

"Who's Pete? And I won't ... I won't even spill the root beer." So saying, Zane lifted his glass up to Jessamy's. When he finished with Warren, he turned back to the sight of Bella cozying up to Eli, deep in conversation across the barricade of the bar. "She likes him, doesn't she?"

Joe snorted.

"Zane, a lump of coal could see she likes him."

"She likes you, too, Zane." Jessamy tried to sound reassuring, but she had to fight through the worry gripping her. "Just ... "

Warren grinned.

"Just differently than she likes Eli. Seems like she likes you and Eli best, though."

"You think?" Zane seemed excited by the possibility.

"Yes, I think so." Jessamy dared to elbow Joe in the ribs as he opened his mouth. Joe shut his lips tightly together, but he winked at Jessamy. "I think she likes us all or she wouldn't buy us drinks, but she likes you best. And Eli, well, we all like Eli, right?"

"We all like Eli." Zane nodded. "Eli's a really good cook."

Joe rolled his eyes and Jessamy elbowed him again, more softly this time.

"Warren ... can Lucas really not come back?"

Warren nodded, but didn't meet her eyes.

"You don't know," she accused. "Not for sure."

"I've never seen anyone come back, other than Tracy, and I've been here—what did you say?—50 years?"

"She said about 50 years, dumbass."

"Fifty years, almost 50 years ..." Warren shrugged. "Might as well be forever, but anyway, I'm as sure as 50—or almost 50—years can make me."

"That's good." Joe looked at Jessamy, and she had to agree.

"That's good," she repeated, and wished it would be good enough.

But it wasn't.

"Don't you go parrot, too," Joe scowled, poking Jessamy when she didn't continue. "Got enough on my plate without that."

Jessamy's crushing concern made it impossible for her to acknowledge the joke and move on.

"I could check. I could open the door and see if the truck is gone. The sun was just about to rise, I think, and the fog is lifting, so I could see ..." she glanced at Warren. "I'd look really quick? Just to make sure?"

Warren glanced at Joe.

"Are you asking us? Or telling us." He smiled—a slight smile, but not a forced one, as far as Jessamy could tell. She smiled back.

"Asking and telling."

"Go ahead, Jessamy," Warren said, tiredness radiating from his time-frozen face. "I'll survive."

"Survive? You ain't even alive." Joe stepped around Jessamy and slapped Warren on the back.

"I'm not likely to forget that, either, Joe. Though with a little luck, I might forget you."

Joe froze, the hand he'd clapped on Warren's shoulder visibly clenching there. What little mirth he'd managed to convey with his dour features vanished as if it never existed at all. He swallowed hard, Adam's apple bobbing up and then dropping back down.

"Suppose you will, too," he said. "Wish I'd be so lucky ..."

"I'm the best friend you ever had, dumbass." Warren shoved Joe's hand away. And then he wrapped his surprised friend in a full-on hug.

"Hey. Hey! That's my line, you idiot." Joe sounded hoarse, his voice nearly inaudible, and he pounded Warren's shoulder with one hand and while gripping his friend tightly with the other.

"I thought they didn't even like each other," Zane squeaked in Jessamy's ear.

Jessamy smiled, peeking sideways at Zane before returning her eyes to Joe and Warren. They separated in that short interval and began working to obliterate evidence of any lingering strong emotions by arguing about which glasses at the bar remained unclaimed.

"Like it matters, idiot," Warren said, pointing. "Take that one. It's all the same."

"Maybe to dumbass regulars, but I got to worry about germs and crap."

"On a glass of alcohol? Are you nuts?"

"I guess they don't like each other again," Zane said, shaking his head. He angled away, weaving toward Sandman's table.

Jessamy watched him go, wondering how Sandman escaped Lucas' notice. Realization came quickly: someone Lucas didn't want something from—or who didn't stand in his way—would never capture his attention. It was that simple and that ugly.

But Lucas is gone now ... isn't he? Jessamy's eyes flicked back toward the door.

"Go on, Jessamy." Warren nodded to her when she looked back at him. "You'll feel better when you know. It's way past five minutes."

"I'll go with you," Joe said. "I ain't scared of the door."

"No, I'll do it." Jessamy inhaled courage, exhaled half of it, and then walked straight to the door. Behind her, Bella continued to murmur sweetly to Eli and Warren resumed his half-hearted attacks on Joe's capacity for alcohol.

Jessamy opened the door and heard the first tentative bird call of morning. She felt the cool tendrils of the dwindling night against her skin, smelled daybreak's crisp scent. She saw oblique sunlight glinting off the dull surface of the truck, still parked across the street ...

And Lucas leaped from the entryway's sheltering shadows and grabbed Jessamy, twisting her around and pressing a knife hard against the agitated pulse in her throat.

Nepenthe

"Jessamy!" Zane squawked from Sandman's otherwise silent table. His alarm alerted the others.

"Back off!" Lucas shouted through Between's open door. "We're leaving, so just back off. Tell them!"

He jabbed the knife harder against Jessamy's neck and she raised terrified eyes from the length of the blade—so great she could see it peripherally—to the aghast group inside Between.

"Lucas … Lucas, you're hurting me …" Jessamy fell back into old habits, pleading with him, although her voice sounded closer to calm than she could remember from past experiences.

"Can't be helped, babe. Not unless your *friends*," and he spat the word, as if it tasted foul, "back off."

Bella ceased her stealthy forward advance—even turned away. Joe stopped his overt progression as well but he stayed in position, eyes sparking like molten metal in the cauldron of his resolute face.

"Let's make a deal." Bella said it if she didn't care one way or the other. She extracted her wad of cash again, this time, raising it. "You leave Jessamy, but you take this. It's all big bills—lots of 50s and 100s. Look."

She unfolded the money, fanning the bills seductively and then waving them at Jessamy and Lucas.

"You people are crazy." Beneath Lucas' feigned outrage, Jessamy picked up on the pungent tang of greed.

"Look, kid, it isn't a big thing. This isn't even mine." Bella grinned but Jessamy saw the strain, noticed Bella's eyes shifting ever so slightly from Lucas to the open, gaping maw of death behind him. "I supply medical marijuana to people who need it ... I've gotten robbed before and I can give a perfect description of the thief. See that big guy behind me?" Though the thumb of Bella's free hand jabbed in Eli's direction, her eyes remained locked on Lucas. "He did it and I'll swear to it on a stack of Bibles, as God is my witness."

Once again, Bella lived up to her name in Jessamy's mind, advancing as she spoke, weaving her words in a pattern more convincing than the most truthful tale ever told.

"Stop. Stop!" Lucas dropped the knife from Jessamy's throat to her ribs and wrapped his arm like a snake where the knife had been.

The serpent constricted, too, making Jessamy's vision darken in an instant.

"Hey, it's no skin off my butt." Bella flipped the switch, indifferent again, and raised both hands in the air. Lucas relaxed slightly and Jessamy gasped. "But the offer's only good if you put that knife down and come get this money." She flung the cash onto the table beside her. "Jessamy reminds me of my sister, see. I'm just trying to help her."

Lucas shuffled Jessamy sideways; she realized he must be trying to see the money more clearly, to estimate its value.

*To estimate **her** value and compare it with the cash.*

She knew without a sliver of doubt that she would not come out ahead in Lucas' eyes.

"Let's say I take the money." Lucas' voice oozed blatant avarice. "How do I know you'll do what you say?"

"You don't," Bella responded. "Except I always do what I say. I'm guessing that doesn't carry much weight with someone like you ... but there it is."

Lucas didn't bother to refute the insult Bella didn't try to hide.

"You're really not coming with me?" Lucas asked Jessamy then.

The question failed to carry any interrogative quality. Perhaps the fact Lucas knew her answer enabled Jessamy to provide it honestly, or maybe experience and her friendships emboldened her.

"No." Her answer, flatly certain, needed no embellishment. She saw Joe tense and willed him to remain still.

"I always knew you'd leave." Lucas pressed the words into Jessamy's ear with the edge of his tongue while his knife poked into her side. She swallowed hard, recognizing his need to prove he still held power over her even in the face of her resolve.

"Even a broken clock's right twice a day." Joe took a step forward as he spoke.

"Here's what's going to happen, old man," Lucas raised his voice and thankfully pulling his Marlboro-scented head away from Jessamy's. "You're going to go sit at the bar and that skinny little shit over there is going to bring me my money. Then I'll let Jess go."

"No, that's not the deal." Bella amplified her voice with disdain. "*You* put the knife down. *You* come get this money."

"I can do it."

Bella cast Zane a stern glance. "Of course you can. But like I said, that's not the deal."

Zane started to speak again but Lucas overrode his effort.

"Well, your deal won't work, either. You'll just pick up the money and here I'll be without my girl or my cash."

Jessamy looked at the faces in front of her, pale except for Joe's which was still suffused with anger's favored shade. Eli's countenance might as well have been a mask, stern and foreboding.

And the bartender—the bartender picked up an empty glass from the bar and bent to wash it as if nothing untoward was happening.

Jessamy swallowed, tasting bitter bile as her muscles contracted and released. She felt the knife pushing, ready to pass through cloth, skin, and vital organs. It, and the man wielding it, were capable, willing, and able to bleed her body dry.

"What if ..." she began, surprised at the firmness of her voice. "What if Zane picks up the money and takes my hand ... then Lucas holds the money with Zane ... then Zane lets go of the money and Lucas lets go of me at the same time?"

Bella sighed.

"That might work."

"Ain't good enough. What if he don't let Jessamy go? He'll pull her right out with him, and your money, too!"

"You got a better idea?" Lucas challenged. "I'll leave Jess, don't you worry. The question now is if I leave her with a hole in her or not."

"You'll be dead before you get to your car," Joe snarled.

"Truck." Smug condescension all but dripped off the word. "I'd say you're blind, old as you are, but it's not light out so there's that. Let's do this. Get the money, Skinny."

"Zane, take Jessamy's hand and let him grab the money, but don't let go of the money until Jessamy counts three."

"I won't! I can do it."

Zane shuffled up to the table, collecting the cash Bella had flung across it with care, straightening the bills and clasping them tight in one scrawny hand.

Was it the hand he'd kept time with, now holding the balance of her life within its narrow confines? Jessamy wasn't sure, but she thought so.

232

Sensations she'd long been without intensified as Zane approached. She realized she had to pee and felt the pressure in her bladder with an appreciation she knew she'd never experienced before. Her body worked again! She lived, processing accounts long dormant, her heart racing with the terror of her situation, her mouth dry in a way it had never been while she'd been a regular.

Jessamy wanted her life, wanted the messiness and the pain, because whether designed or accidental, the only option life provided was a mix of good and bad ... wishing for only the good was like running in a hamster wheel, going nowhere.

She marveled at her sudden clarity of mind: her friends, Lucas, and Between all contributed to it, a conglomerate composition of good, bad, and even indifferent. What happened next could only occur because of what came earlier, in all its awkward—and sometimes hideous—glory.

Zane drew close and he extended his free hand to bridge the gap between himself and Jessamy; she lifted her hand, moving gingerly on account of the knife still pressing into her flesh. When they touched, Jessamy felt Zane's dry, room-temperature skin against her own with singular fascination. It seemed so odd, the contrast of their conditions, and it made her wonder how her flesh's clammy warmth felt to Zane.

"Hurry up," Lucas demanded, releasing his hold on Jessamy's neck and thrusting out his own hand.

"When you both have hands on the money and Jessamy counts three, you let go and pull Jessamy away from that knife, Zane, you hear?"

"I hear you." Zane looked at Jessamy, but his eyes—like Bella's before—flickered. Death, Jessamy knew, had a peculiar ability to hypnotize, at least when one stood directly before it.

She couldn't see her death as she once had, but she now felt its mesmerizing physical presence through her core.

"Hurry up!" Lucas' urgency transferred not only in his voice, but through his digits, more reminiscent of claws extending and contracting than fingers straightening and curling.

Zane raised the money in his deliberate, slow way, watching Jessamy, Lucas, and death lurking behind them. He swayed and Jessamy felt a moment's panic at the idea that he might shove her and Lucas and rush past them, but then he steadied.

And in the next instant, Lucas clasped his hand around the top half of the cash.

"Count, Jess."

Jessamy didn't hesitate.

"One."

Joe tensed, extending his body to its full height.

"Two."

Lucas wiggled the knife, and Jessamy felt an unsurprised hatred that he would do such a thing. She waited just a heartbeat longer, gathering courage.

"Three."

Zane released the money and pulled on Jessamy with all his might, spinning her away as the knife scraped a farewell against her side. Jessamy clutched the wound until relief at the slow seep of blood—not a gush—penetrated her mind.

"Jessamy!" Joe and Warren joined her in an instant, supporting her and pulling her further back into Between. Lucas stood in the doorway, grinning obscenely, staring at the money he held but brandishing the knife with his other hand ... a knife now edged crimson with Jessamy's blood.

"Is she okay?" Jessamy heard Bella ask as she turned her head away from Lucas.

"I'm okay." But she lifted her shirt to assure herself that it was true.

"It's a scratch. Skinny pulled the wrong way."

234

Zane whirled to Bella.

"I did it right ... I did! He ... he ..."

"We know, Zane." Bella sounded disgusted, hastily procuring a towel for Jessamy to press against her injury.

"You did it right, Zane." Jessamy trained her own distaste fully on its rightful target. "Lucas did it wrong."

"Damn you." Lucas' eyes blazed. He pointed at Jessamy with the bloodied knife. "I did it wrong? You do everything wrong. You know it's true."

"You have the money." Ice spiked from each word Bella chipped out. "Get out."

"It's too dark," Lucas said, an edge to his voice. "I'll wait until morning."

Jessamy looked up then and saw full daylight behind Lucas, bold and bright. And she realized what she should have already known.

"Lucas! You have to come inside!"

"What the ...?" Joe stared.

Warren started to laugh. "Him, too? Well, if that doesn't beat all ..."

"It won't be long. I'll stay right here at the door," Lucas said, frowning. His knife-holding hand stabbed in the direction of the bar. "And you stay over there."

Warren continued to laugh and since he needed no breath to sustain it, the sound slithered continuously, eerie and unnatural

"Stop laughing."

The admonition drove Warren's cackle to more demented heights. He clasped Joe's shoulder and turned away.

"Stop it, or I'll make you stop!"

"We can't let him go out there." Jessamy searched the others' faces for support. "He doesn't understand."

"Sit down, Jessamy, and keep pressure on that. You need to keep it clean so it will heal." Bella directed Jessamy to the nearest chair.

"Come on over," Warren called to Lucas as his fit finally abated. "Bring your knife and try—just try—to make me do anything. Come on."

"Shut it, dumbass. He made his bed, let him lie in it. When he realizes morning ain't coming, then we deal with him."

Now Lucas laughed. "Morning always comes."

"Jessamy, you have to come ..." Love burst back onto the scene, stopping still at the sight greeting her. "What's he doing here again? He has a knife! He has to go ... he has to go away."

"He has a knife, all right, but what he doesn't have is a clue." Bella shook her head, turning from Love to Warren and Zane. "He can't hurt us. Let's take him."

"What is wrong with you?" Lucas protested. "I have the knife, and I'll use it."

"I'm not going over there." Warren slapped the bar. "I'm staying right here and having more whiskey. Let the devil take his due."

"I'll help. I can do it!" Zane said.

"I will not send another along a path I dare not travel." Eli held up his hand with its death-nipped stub.

"No." Jessamy stood. "You can't just kill him!"

Bella's neck cracked as she twisted her face into opposition with Jessamy's.

"After what he did? What he'd do again? Besides, we can't let him in here. He could hurt you. He could hurt her." Bella pointed at Love. "Or Joe."

"Let me explain," Jessamy protested, her eyes darting to Lucas'. "It's not right that you don't know, no matter what ..." Lucas, scorn written on his face so clearly it might as well have

236

been in permanent marker, turned away. "Lucas, it's death out there! You'll die—it's ... "

"The hell with this." Lucas cast the words over his shoulder, even as Jessamy started toward him and Joe and Bella blocked her. "It's just a dark night in the middle of no- ..."

As Lucas moved past the supernatural portal masquerading as Between's entryway, his words ceased.

So did he.

Bonds

From Jessamy's perspective, Lucas simply vanished between the bar's entrance and the truck beyond. But this was more than the simple visual disappearance she'd seen before ... Lucas' exit from Between—his *death*—carried with it a sense of obliteration, while Todd and Tracy's passing through the doorway felt distinctly transitional.

Although it looked like a magic trick, Jessamy knew it wasn't. Shock held her captive more surely than any of the others ... she froze, unable to look away.

"Wow," Zane said, breaking the utter silence.

"Get the door, Zane." Joe's gravelly voice approximated gentleness. "Come on, Jessamy."

Jessamy let him guide her back to a chair, her gaze locked on the doorway even after Zane shut out the various realities it revealed. She felt someone pressing the towel against her side again and forced her eyes down.

"You didn't tell him."

Bella looked up, steady and unfaltering.

"You can't tell some people anything. They take what they want without caring who they hurt—without even thinking about who they hurt—and you can't tell them what's right in front of them. They see it, and you still can't tell them."

"But you didn't try." Jessamy looked around the bar. "None of you tried!"

"You tried," Love said.

"That's right. You did," Zane agreed, nodding.

238

"You tried, Jessamy." The depth underneath Joe's small words drew tears from Jessamy's eyes. "Didn't do no good but that don't take away that you tried."

"He only came to take," Eli said. "He did not come to listen."

"But he should have!" Jessamy cried. "He didn't have a chance."

"His chances have already been taken."

"Have my chances been taken?" Zane asked.

"You are still here," Eli said, as if that was an answer.

"Eli, can we get another cloth?" Bella asked. "A wet one this time. I think she's fine, but I want to clean this up."

"Jessamy's hurt?" Aghast, Love resorted to fluttering, moving in to hover over Jessamy. "You haven't even seen the kittens yet."

"She'll be all right." Bella sounded certain.

"The kittens are here?" Jessamy willed herself to be diverted, and Love beamed.

"Three. There's a black one with a white patch, like Eclipse, an orange one, and one that's all black."

"If I had a kitten, I'd name it Mister Bananas," Zane said, and Warren snorted.

"You'd better pick a boy then, Zane."

"I can pick?"

"Not yet," Love exclaimed.

"The kittens need to spend time with their mother, Zane." Jessamy's focus flickered between Lucas' death and new lives' arrival.

"Oh." Zane sounded as if he hadn't considered that possibility. "I guess. Can I have more root beer?"

"You sure can," Bella said, and Warren passed the order to the bartender, adding, "She's buying."

"Your money," Jessamy gasped as Bella pressed the hot cloth Eli brought against the rent in her flesh.

"Easy." Bella dabbed at Jessamy's skin. "It's long, but it's not deep. Bet it hurts, though."

Jessamy felt the welling of additional tears unassociated with her own pain. "It does."

"He hurt you." Outrage twisted Love's soft tone and Jessamy knew she understood, even without her following question. "What makes you cry for him after he hurt you?"

"I ... he ..." Jessamy swallowed her confliction, weighed the pain from the last injury Lucas would ever inflict, remembered him vanishing. "He was kind in the beginning. He could have been kind again ... someday."

"He took all his chances."

"What do you mean?" Jessamy craned her neck to see Eli's face.

"He took his chances at the expense of others. He took without giving at every opportunity. It is not the way of things to take forever—there must come a reckoning. Now, there is balance."

"Not exactly 'balance.' I'm out quite a bit of cash." Bella's hands remained light, but her tone dripped blistering acid.

"You gave what was not yours to give," Eli observed. "You lied."

"Lied?" Jessamy frowned, accosted by yet another piece of unpalatable knowledge.

"I don't deal in medical marijuana," Bella said flatly. "Not that it matters, but I don't have a sister, either."

"What do you do?" Love asked.

Bella smiled.

"I deal in drugs that aren't medicinal."

Jessamy realized her mouth gaped open and closed it, gritting her teeth as Bella pressed the cloth against what must be the deepest part of her wound.

"That's not good," Love said.

"It ain't," Joe agreed.

"Your chances are nearly gone."

"I don't doubt that, Eli. But I need the money."

"Then what were you doing, giving it to Lucas?" Jessamy whispered, wanting to know.

"Saving your life." Bella delivered her answer with the loving charm of a weather report.

"That's good."

That Love's disapproval morphed so readily into approval resonated deep in Jessamy's heart. Her lips responded to that call even as her mind struggled with the incongruities: Bella, truth, and lies.

"You people ... you're all crazy." Then Jessamy's tears returned as if they'd never faded—she recognized the echo of Lucas' words in her own. She wasn't alone in hearing the reverberation of words from beyond.

"You're crazy, too, girl. Crying for that son-of-a-bitch." Joe sounded as if he still couldn't believe it.

"Let her be, idiot."

"Shut it, dumbass."

"Can you hold this in place?" Bella asked Jessamy, adding the slightest pressure to the towel on Jessamy's side. "I need to talk to Eli."

"Yes." Jessamy steadied herself, blinking furiously.

"Right here. No, a little more forward ... there."

"I've got it. Thanks."

Bella moved away and when Jessamy looked back, she'd locked arms with Eli.

"You drink beer, big guy?"

"I do not."

"What do you drink? Other than root beer, I mean. I have more money in my pocket."

"For the love of Pete! She held some back," Joe breathed, easing into the seat next to Jessamy.

"Do you want to see the kittens?"

Joe halted Love with a glance.

"She needs to ..." he began brusquely but stopped himself, starting over with care. "She got hurt, remember? So she's gotta rest. Go and watch the kittens. Jessamy'll be up soon."

"She's okay?"

"She's okay." Joe smiled, and that was all it took.

Love left, and Zane watched her go.

"Can I see kittens?"

"Later, Zane." All gentleness left Joe's tone. "You know kittens pee, right?"

"I have to, too," Jessamy said, feeling the resurgence of need.

"And kittens play!" Zane was undeterred as Joe supported Jessamy to standing.

"I'm fine. I don't even think it's bleeding anymore but I'll put pressure on again as soon as I get back." Jessamy divested herself of the towel, tucking folds over the red marks marring the fabric, forming a sloppy sort of origami.

"I like it when kittens play."

"Zane!"

"It's okay, really. Zane, the kittens don't even have their eyes open yet. But they'll play soon and you can play with them then as long as you help feed them and clean up. All right?"

As she spoke, Zane nodded, shook his head, and then resumed nodding.

"I'll be right back." Jessamy noted Joe's disgusted glares at Zane with the briefest touch of amusement.

The bathrooms seemed as distant as the lunar surface as Jessamy made her way back to them. Joe hovered near her at first but he stopped near Warren, settling next to his friend.

"What swill you drinking now, dumbass?"

"Same as always, idiot."

Jessamy smiled, even though the weight of what just transpired remained crushing.

Death was never easy to witness, she supposed. She wondered what afterlife Lucas could expect and if anyone other than she would miss him. Not that she missed him as much as she missed the *idea* of him ... and ... and what would she tell her baby about its father?

Jessamy made it into the bathroom before despair wrenched gasps from her. Inside, she breathed as deeply as she could through overwhelming worries, escalating fears, and a desperate need to process the unfathomable, yet again, here in Between.

While she might not be able to understand what happened, to justify the singular tragedy of a life lost too soon and wasted too thoroughly, she could attend to her own physical needs in this moment. As banal as urinating had ever been, Jessamy found it practically novel after so long a time without the necessity.

Relief at the relaxation of pressure, delight in her body's full functionality ... the inexplicable triumph of returning to the full experience of living carried an intensity Jessamy could have never imagined prior to Between. She breathed! She cried. She even peed.

She supposed she'd get tired of that soon, as the baby grew.

The baby! Alive again, inside her. It was too wonderful to believe.

Jessamy washed her hands and carefully lifted her shirt, examining the gash in her flesh. Blood seeped, a slow and diminishing ooze; she supposed she might end up with a scar, especially at the spot where the injury appeared most ragged. Scar or not, it would heal with time and care.

Her face, when she looked at it, clearly commemorated recent events. Her eyes were bright and wide with shock and the sheen of tears; her skin was blotched, red here and pale there. After drying her hands, Jessamy took the damp paper towel she'd used and dabbed the dark circles under her eyes. Then her hands stilled as she took in the bruise at her temple—the brand she'd worn since her arrival in Between—and she realized the colors already started to shift, moving incrementally from the bold shades of impact to the tarnished palette of healing.

"Jessamy!" Joe knocked raucously.

"Yes?" Jessamy tossed the paper towel in the trash and stepped out into the hallway.

"Making sure you're okay," Joe said, his face flushing.

"Joe," Warren called from the bar. "That's the women's room."

"Dumbass!" Joe yelled back, then lowered his voice. "Sorry, Jessamy."

"Don't be. You two picking on each other is the most normal part of everything right now."

Joe snorted.

"Well, go back and sit down, take care of that cut." He shook a finger in the general direction of her injury. "Don't want to make the resident dealer mad."

"I heard that," Bella sang from the bar.

"You're suppose to," Joe replied. "Excuse me, Jessamy, but I got to take a leak myself ..."

244

"It's kind of great." Jessamy's confidence took Joe aback, shifting his neck in a visible jerk away from her.

He shook his head. "If you say so."

"I do." Jessamy tossed the words over her shoulder and walked back to the bar.

How can I do this? When ...

But she could do what she had to do, just as she had when Mama died. She could and she would, and ... and she was free. She would do better—she had to do better.

To take care of my baby.

Jessamy picked up the cloth she'd left behind and moved to Sandman's table, pressing the wadded material against her wound. The pain—while not insignificant—paled in comparison to what might have been and so Jessamy bore it, listening to Bella flirt with Eli, watching Zane observe the dance. And Warren ...

Warren slouched as Jessamy never saw him do before, slumping like a man worn out by living rather than one held in stasis. Even when Joe rejoined him, Warren's posture appeared senescent, his demeanor dejected.

He looked like a man who'd lost his best friend.

Or was about to.

Jessamy waved to the bartender, who glided to the table.

"Can I have ..." Jessamy began, then stopped. "How long can we stay here?"

The bartender tilted her head, primordial eyes inscrutable—unshuttered, but guarding the secrets behind them as securely as the best vault ever conceived. Joe glanced over his shoulder, then back to the bar.

A battle can only be won when the other party engages in the fight. Though she'd known the bartender would not—maybe could not—answer the question, Jessamy asked anyway. She wondered what foolishness drove her to inquire and if it could be related to whatever stopped the bartender from answering.

"Can I have a cheeseburger?" She formed the question only after the bartender straightened her posture and began lowering her hands from their prepared stance.

The bartender nodded, writing and moving away quickly. As she passed Eli, he straightened, disengaging from Bella and following the bartender.

Bella called after them both. "I'll have what she's having."

"Just a cheeseburger."

"And we'll both take an order of fries," Bella added, watching as Eli disappeared into the kitchen.

"Mmhmm … that is a fine figure of a man," she proclaimed, clasping Zane's shoulders.

"He's a really good cook, too."

"So you said, Zane, so you said."

"Barkeep, give us the dice." Joe pointed from himself to Warren.

Warren finished his whiskey and signaled for a refill. "Why are you still here, idiot?"

"You kidding? Her ain't leaving without one of them kittens, and them kittens is weeks from leaving their ma."

"Weeks? Are you telling me I have to put up with your idiot presence for weeks?" Calculated disgust cascaded from each word … but not enough to conceal Warren's delight.

Joe nodded sagely.

"Maybe months."

Warren groaned and Bella caught Jessamy's eye, winking at the feigned agony in the sound.

"Make it two," Warren told the bartender when she placed his whiskey in front of him.

Joe rattled the dice.

"Call, dumbass."

"And keep them coming." Warren didn't turn around, but Jessamy heard his smile in his words.

Time

The former and present regulars formed new routines so quickly that remembering they'd ever done anything else became increasingly difficult. Except for the kittens, who grew from blind slugs to mewling caterpillars to wobbly scamps, Between's inhabitants resumed their mostly mundane existence.

Jessamy's and Joe's returned lives, and Love's freshly acknowledged restoration, tempered their combined experience less than might have been expected.

The kittens—and her own again-growing child—kept Jessamy from veering too close to an abyss; however, she continued to think of Lucas, wondering if she'd done all she could to stop him.

"Don't," Joe said, during one of her musings.

"What?"

"Don't think about it." He joined her. "You sit by Sandman and you think about it."

"You can tell?"

Joe rolled his eyes.

"Everybody can tell."

Jessamy placed her elbows on the table and rested her chin in the cup formed by her upturned palms.

"But ..."

"But nothing. You got to take care of yourself and your babe. You don't got to beat yourself up about not being able to take care of somebody who don't look out for nobody but himself."

"People have to look out for each other." Jessamy didn't meet Joe's eyes, but she drove determination into her voice. "Even Bella looked out for me."

"Jessamy," Warren called from the bar. "You have to take care of yourself first. That's what you're missing here."

"That's right," Bella agreed. "You ever fly?"

"Fly?"

"In an airplane."

"No."

"Well, when you fly—when the plane's getting ready to take off—they tell you what to do if the plane has trouble. One of the things they tell you is that if the oxygen masks come out, you should put your own mask on first before helping anybody else."

"But ..."

"Think about it, Jessamy. If you don't help yourself first, you might not be able to help anybody else."

Jessamy did think about it, even as Joe slung an elbow over the back of his chair and started to argue with Bella.

"Ain't got nothing to do with this, unless you're gonna say sometimes you got to knock a dumbass out before he steals your mask."

"That's not part of the pre-flight safety presentation, no."

"It should be, at least when there's not enough masks to go around."

"What plane wouldn't have enough oxygen masks for all the passengers?"

"I don't know." Joe's hands raised, waving dissidence away. "A bad one, I guess—the Titanic of the sky!"

"Titanic of the sky!" Bella repeated, and promptly dissolved, laughing loudly.

"I'm going to go see the kittens," Jessamy said, even though Bella's laughter contained contagion, and Joe caught it as surely as she.

Warren even joined in the conversation.

"Joe's familiar with the Titanic. He remembers hearing the news on the radio when it sank."

Jessamy rolled her eyes at Warren as she passed him and he winked back. Bella continued to meld into Between's clique of regulars and anyone could see it had a positive effect on Warren.

Still, Jessamy worried about how he would feel when Joe finally left Between.

She mounted the stairs with deliberation and when she reached the top, could already hear Love and Zane. Before the kittens became too mobile, the three of them worked to even more thoroughly clean Zane's old room. The last delivery to Between included an enormous supply of cat litter that Jessamy paid for and so they'd moved Eclipse and her kittens into their own space. They put one makeshift litter box in the shower stall as Jessamy had done in her own room and one in the spot where Eclipse had delivered her version of "tough love" to Jessamy.

Jessamy paused outside the door, listening to the laughter inside. She guessed Love and Zane were tossing paper balls, which the kittens loved to chase. Joe and Warren's old notebook sacrificed page after Tic-Tac-Toe-marked page for the kittens' entertainment, but Jessamy kept the sheet on which she'd scribbled names to ensure its safety.

"Good throw, Zane." The sound of galloping kitten feet pounded after Love's words.

"Aw, you threw yours under the bed. You throw like a girl."

"Well, I am a girl, so I can't throw any other way. Don't worry, see? Mister Bananas is going to get it back."

"Good kitty, Mister Bananas. You're the best kitty ever."

Jessamy tapped on the door and entered just in time to see Mister Bananas, the orange tiger kitten, emerging from under the bed. In his mouth, he carried a wad of paper; if the toy hadn't seen better days already, it never would—it looked more like a squashed egg than a ball. Mister Bananas' ears, appearing oversized on his head at this stage, carried trace evidence of spider webs.

As Mister Bananas spat out the paper near Zane and promptly launched into an impromptu game of kitten soccer, Jessamy wondered about the webs. She supposed life surrounded them all along, even here in Between ... even if they hadn't known quite where to look.

"Mew!" The solid-black kitten—another male—shot out from behind Love and Jessamy felt for the door even though she'd already closed it behind her. But neither Hum, so named by Love for his vibrating, melodic purr, or Mister Bananas showed much interest in the door. Shadow, on the other hand ...

Jessamy looked down and there she was, gazing up with a beseeching expression, rubbing against Jessamy's ankles and then stretching her front paws up next to the door frame.

"She tries to get out all the time," Love said, enticing Hum back to her by tapping her fingers against the floor. "Except when you're here. Then she wants to be with you."

Jessamy picked up Shadow and the kitten promptly began kneading her chest, splaying her tiny claws out and curling them in. Shadow rarely made a sound, but her purr was a tangible thing and Jessamy felt it now.

On the bed, Eclipse reclined, observing her small litter with an apparently satisfied air.

Jessamy took Shadow over to the bed. Compared to Eclipse, the kitten looked like a perfect little miniature, albeit one with slightly longer fur than her mother. Eclipse's tail twitched, catching Shadow's eye, so Jessamy turned herself and the kitten slightly away. They watched Love playing with Hum, Zane playing with

Mister Bananas, and Hum and Mister Bananas occasionally tackling each other.

Jessamy petted Shadow and scratched the perfect spot along her jaw, listening to Love and Zane and delighting in the kittens' antics. Eventually, she had to ask.

"Love, are you hungry?"

Love gasped.

"I forgot again, didn't I?"

"Yes," Jessamy affirmed, but Love already knew the answer and scurried about, giving Hum one final paper ball, tossed lightly toward—but this time not underneath—the bed.

"Good throw, Love," Zane cheered, looking up from Mister Bananas' activity. "Ow!" he exclaimed as the kitten sunk his claws into the exposed flesh of his ankle. "Naughty kitty."

Love blew a kiss to Hum and slipped from the room; Zane continued to gently scold Mister Bananas.

"You have to play nice, Mister Bananas," he explained as the kitten caught sight of his own tail and gave chase.

It was good advice, Jessamy mused, since Mister Bananas had a sorry habit of biting his tail on the occasions when he captured it. This time was no exception.

The sound the kitten made when he bit himself defied description, but it was always the same—as was Zane's reaction.

"Oh, no. No, that's your butt. Stop biting that ... here's a ball."

It gave Jessamy hope. Zane still grumbled about the odor of cat urine but he doted on Mister Bananas, with all his rambunctious quirks, and the other kittens as well. Jessamy showed Zane how to remove the clumps of litter as soon as one of the cats used the box, thereby minimizing the smell. Though he continued to complain, Zane was often the first to attend to the litter box.

"You're doing a good job taking care of Mister Bananas," Jessamy said, while Shadow continued her soundless purr and fervent kneading.

Zane smiled at Jessamy and it struck her as if with physical force how it transformed his thin face.

"Maybe someday … someday, I can work in a pet store."

"I bet you can. Or an animal shelter." He could, too, Jessamy thought, though she supposed neither one of them would have considered those possibilities before Mister Bananas and his siblings arrived.

It made Jessamy think that just as Between harbored life even when they hadn't known it, transformation, too, happened … with or without regard for its processes. A curious sensation—like a somersault in her gut—distracted her from deeper consideration.

Then it happened again.

"Oh!"

"Did Shadow get you?" Zane quickly tossed a ball for an ever-playful Mister Bananas. "You have to play nice, Shadow …"

"No. It's … I think it's the baby, Zane … my baby. I think my baby just rolled over."

Zane frowned. "Rolled over?"

"Yes." Jessamy stilled one hand on Shadow and brought the other to her belly. "I'm not sure, but I think it was my baby moving."

"Gross." Zane returned his attention to Mister Bananas.

Jessamy pressed both hands against her growing midriff and Shadow butted her head against them, pausing long enough for her inaudible contentment to distinctly vibrate through her kitten's skin onto Jessamy's.

I can't stay much longer.

That thought terrified Jessamy. Lucas' truck was gone; she'd peeked out the door one morning after his death and saw a bright orange tag on the window. The next time she looked, the truck was gone.

"Towed," Joe said when she told him about it. "Life is messy and we forgot while we wasn't alive—it's all lots less messy when you ain't alive. But out there, time goes on and stuff happens; that's how it works and we got to remember now."

"Stuff" happened, indeed. Jessamy's baby kicked!

She moved her hands away from herself, setting them around Eclipse's furry baby. Shadow ducked her head and nestled into the caresses, her little body so attuned with Jessamy's that she might have been another appendage if not for her distinctly feline attributes.

We can't stay much longer.

This time, Jessamy wrapped herself, her baby, and Shadow into her determination. She needed to find a doctor's care, a place to live, and a job. Her baby and Shadow needed her ... needed the life she could build for them all.

Shadow squirmed and Jessamy wondered if the contortions of the kitten's body in any way resembled the ones her own baby made. Certainly, Jessamy felt her own mental struggles—trying to adjust to the idea of leaving Between seemed nearly as difficult as the process she'd gone through adapting to being stuck there in the first place—surpassed any writhing wriggle either her baby or Shadow could manage.

Shadow scooted away across the bedspread before circling back, crouching, and shaking her butt. This prelude to a pounce was followed by a direct attack and Shadow struck Jessamy's right hand. Jessamy rewarded the kitten's efforts with a playful response using her left hand, and giggled at Shadow's studied seriousness.

But the depth of Jessamy's inner turmoil remained, churning underneath laughter's shiny veneer. In its own way, the duality mirrored Between's slurry of lifelessness merging intermittently with life. Jessamy rested underneath Shadow's continued strikes, thinking about how she'd been so afraid to leave Lucas in spite of knowing that doing so was essential to saving her own life ... Shadow sank her teeth into Jessamy's skin but the realization that what she truly feared was bigger than Lucas had ever been—the great, shadowy *unknown* underlying every new experience—pierced Jessamy to a depth impossible for mere kitten fangs.

She would always be afraid of the future. Why shouldn't she be? Not knowing what hazards lay ahead could frighten the bravest soul. But she couldn't let unknown obscurity—which could hold wonders right along with its danger—force her into accepting known, clear perils.

She couldn't allow herself to exchange potential for fact, presumption for familiarity.

Jessamy swallowed hard and extracted her digits from Shadow's teeth. The dimpled but unbroken skin glowed pink, evidencing the continuing flow of life throughout her body. Jessamy inhaled, felt Between's stale air come into her lungs, and savored it.

How good will a crisp morning smell when I step outside again? How warm will the sun's rays feel against my skin? How green will grass look and how glorious will birdsong sound? How fresh will rain taste and how loving will wind feel?

"I'm back!" Love crowed, stepping into the room.

Jessamy caught Love's eyes and the other woman searched the room for Hum, and disrupted her focus.

"I'm leaving. I ... we're leaving."

Conviction settled over Jessamy like a cozy blanket, covering her with superficial warmth. She smiled her bravest smile and after she formed the words with her lips, they tasted right—as right as they could get, anyway. She made her decision, choosing to embrace possibility with or without the approbation of probability.

"Tomorrow," Jessamy continued. "Shadow, the baby, and me—we're leaving tomorrow."

Love bobbed her head, a swift movement of singular accord.

"It's time. Time for me and Hum and Joe, too."

Zane gathered Mister Bananas to his chest and rubbed his face against the kitten's head. Jessamy thought he might be crying—or would, if he could.

"Time." That's all Zane said, raising his head only when Mister Bananas mewed, squirming.

Zane, as he released Mister Bananas, nodded too.

Sincerity

"You sure?" Joe asked, when Jessamy told him later. Warren raised his hand to the bartender. "Whiskey." His voice sounded flat— decidedly firm. "Bring the bottle."

Joe's eyes shifted from Jessamy to Warren.

"It's time," Jessamy responded, the two small words sufficiently vague to summarize the vastness of their situation.

When Joe didn't answer, Warren did.

"It's past time." He struck the bar with a flattened hand and Bella jumped even though she'd been listening, as she always did.

"Past time," Zane echoed, and Joe heaved a sigh.

"Shut your hole, Zane."

"It's not him that's the problem here," Bella interjected, moving around Warren to insert her body between him and Joe. "It's you and Jessamy, and you both know it."

Bella's unblinking eyes burned bright and her glare seared.

"Us? How's us the problem?"

"Seriously?" Bella turned to Jessamy, incredulous, and raised both hands, palms upward, as if the air would drop Joe's answer into them.

"Yeah!" Joe rejoined as Bella's hands remained empty.

One of Bella's cuplike palms folded and then her index finger extended from the brief fist to point at Jessamy.

Jessamy knew the answer—knew Bella wanted her to give it.

"Because you don't want to leave Warren, and ..." Jessamy drew a shaky breath and then rushed to finish her thought, "... and I don't want to leave you—any of you. You're ... you're my f-f-friends."

The words out, Jessamy sank onto the stool next to Joe's.

"I don't have anyone out there," she said, her head drooping. "Me and my baby ... we're alone."

"You'll have Shadow." Zane sounded outraged that Jessamy hadn't mentioned the kitten.

"And you got me," Joe added. "Me and ... me and her, we'll find you again, somehow. That's a promise."

Jessamy smiled through the tears clouding her vision, though she didn't raise her head.

"You can't promise that."

"If you believe it, you promise it," Bella said, "and then you do everything you can to make it happen. What else is a promise? It's not a guarantee. It's a promise."

"And I promise. What? You think I got all kinds of friends myself? You're better than them. And prettier."

"Joe likes pretty girls," Love affirmed, joining them.

Jessamy looked up then. She hadn't heard Love come downstairs.

"Me and her," Joe jerked his thumb at Love even as he smiled to soften the fact that he still struggled to use Love's preferred name, "we need all the friends we can get."

"Who doesn't?" Bella arrested the bottle the bartender placed in front of Warren and took a long draught.

Warren raised a brow and Bella winked, holding the bottle out to him. Her fingers caressed his before she relinquished her grip.

"Believe I been replaced," Joe said sourly.

"What are you talking about?" Bella huffed. "I only have eyes for Eli."

258

Warren laughed, a short and startled burst, like a single bark from a sleep-addled watchdog.

"Not like anything can happen in here," he commented, pouring whiskey into his glass. "But I'd give Eli a run for his money if it could."

"It could happen." Bella frowned as Warren shook his head. "Sure, it could."

"Think about it." Joe leaned forward. "Blood don't move through your veins, so how you figure ..."

"Joe!" Warren hastened to cut him off, even as Jessamy realized where Joe was headed with his reasoning.

"It's true."

"Well, I'm a lady and I don't see why you need to be a prick about it," Bella exclaimed.

"Pricks don't work here, see—that's what I'm trying to tell you."

"Yours does," Bella said archly. "And you're going to be here until tomorrow, aren't you?"

Joe's face reddened and his mouth fell open, but no words escaped.

Warren laughed again, this time uninhibitedly.

"She's got you there, Joe," he said when his mirth was exhausted, slapping Joe hard on the back. Joe snapped his mouth shut.

"Give me another hit of that whiskey, would you, Warren?" Bella fairly preened at her success in silencing Joe.

"Take it all," Warren responded. "Worth it to see the great Joe Drabyak at a loss for words."

"I ain't out of words. I ..." Joe began, but Love halted him with one hand on his arm.

"Joe, can you help me find something to carry Hum?" Accumulated concern eked out from beneath her words, carried in the light trembling of her fingertips.

"I can help," Jessamy offered. "I'll need something for Shadow, too."

"Thanks." Love's eyes didn't leave Joe's face. "But I want Joe."

The dismissal felt more cutting than it should have, but Jessamy knew more pain would come when morning approached.

This was only the beginning.

"Crazy to think about it," Bella remarked as Joe headed to the storage closet with Love. She directed her full attention to Jessamy. "You're all going to walk out the same door there, but you're going to step into one place and time, and they'll be going somewhere else, to some other time."

"Maybe that's what Love's worried about," Warren said. "She followed him into Between so they didn't come in at the same time. Maybe she's afraid she won't find him outside."

"I don't think that's it," Jessamy disagreed. "All the problems that were there for her before ... they'll still be there."

"Not yours, though. Your problem's dead and gone." Bella met Jessamy's shocked stare without blinking.

"I ... well ... I still have to deal with Lucas even though he can't hurt me ... can't hurt me or my baby anymore."

"He's dead." This time, Bella said it with aching slowness. "What's to deal with?"

"What kept me staying," Jessamy replied. She blinked, but only because she had to. She kept her eyes on Bella's, giving up nothing even though she felt like she was losing everything. "That's what I have to deal with. What kept me staying with him, what makes me miss him sometimes, what I'll say to my baby about her—or his—father. And my baby! There's a lot of Lucas left behind, whether he's dead or not."

"He's dead." Bella belabored the point with the intensity of her repetition, ratcheting it exponentially with each cycle. "You're not. That's a good thing."

"But ..."

"But nothing. Forget it."

"Jessamy's right." So saying, Warren drew Bella's frown. "She is. The problem with Between is that everything you leave behind … it waits. If you go back to your life, no matter how long you're away from it, all of it is still there. You need to deal with it; you can't 'forget it' or it'll find a way to kill you, too ... slowly and painfully."

"He's not there," Bella insisted. "There's nothing to deal with."

"He's not alive there," Warren responded. "But he's there."

"Bull."

Warren shrugged.

"Well, I see what Jessamy means, but maybe that's because I have a reminder." Warren didn't look at Sandman then, but Bella and Jessamy did.

It felt like another loose thread in the flimsy fabric holding her together, Jessamy thought. She refocused on Bella, watched the other woman frown.

Bella must be made of canvas, or concrete. Or perhaps she was deaf to the things she left behind when she entered Between, unable to hear the whispers and shrieks of her past—of her mistakes.

"I don't get it," Bella said finally. "But I guess it's not mine to understand." Her static eyes bright, she turned to Jessamy. "I hope you figure it out. Whatever you need to deal with, do it right away." She leaned in, her words growing heavier, passing from her lips to

Jessamy's ears, deepened notes underlying an otherwise inaudible song. "Get on with your life while you have it."

Jessamy nodded, staring at the motionless kaleidoscope of Bella's irises.

"I will. I promise."

They both smiled crookedly after Jessamy uttered the disputed phrase.

"Yes, I understand." Jessamy forced a laugh as she spoke and rubbed her eyes with the back of her hand as a single tear escaped. "It's a promise, not a guarantee, but it's still serious."

"Right." Bella nodded. She glanced down, noticing the bottle in her hand with visible surprise. "I forgot I had this. Shouldn't waste good whiskey."

She lifted the bottle, gulping with forced enthusiasm, until she'd drained her desire to drink.

The bottle, Jessamy noted, did not appear depleted at all.

"Easier to drink without having to breathe," Bella declared with a grin. "No burn."

"If you don't like whiskey—if you're just wanting to do a shot and it 'burns'—you're drinking it wrong," Warren opined. He raised his own glass. "Just wait to inhale until the stuff goes down your throat. When it's down, there's no burn."

"Get out of here!" Bella declared. "Well, not literally. I like you—don't want you dead. But you've got to be kidding me. And how would I test that?"

Warren shrugged. "Practice while you're here. Should be easy, since you don't need to breathe anyway."

"Practice not breathing?"

"You're still doing it sometimes." Warren swiveled in his seat and pointed at Bella. "You get riled up about something and you breathe. You miss the habit so you force it."

Bella frowned, her face the perfect picture of concentration.

262

"You're not doing it now. Now you're thinking about it. That's the opposite of what you want to do with whiskey. When you're drinking whiskey, you think about the drink and concentrate on breathing."

"You said concentrate on *not* breathing."

"Yes, but when you're alive, you have to think about breathing to not do it; here, it's the opposite."

"Bartender!" Bella called. "Get me a shot glass over here. Maybe if I drink more of this stuff, Warren'll make sense. You want another?"

"I wouldn't count on me making sense whether you drink or not, but if you're buying, I'm drinking."

Jessamy left them to their bickering—different from the exchanges Warren had with Joe but similar, too. These conversations masked anything deeper, tinting the serious underbelly of lifeless existence with light nonsense.

But ... but ...

As she made her way upstairs, it struck Jessamy how much of life was similar. Few invocations of a casual, "How are you?" ever met with a considered response. Common discussions about the caprices of weather and sport vastly outnumbered talk of life and death matters. Solemnities most often occurred in doctors' and lawyers' offices, or under the shielding umbrella of baptismal, marriage, and funeral ceremonies.

Jessamy stopped on the landing, a place where the happenings of downstairs and upstairs resounded but where neither could be clearly discerned. Perhaps she only thought this way because of a leeriness to engage at a more profound level herself. Maybe people would respond more directly to even an ambiguous question if the person asking it seemed sincere, not merely perfunctory.

"How are you?"

Jessamy tried to remember when she'd last asked that question and waited to hear an answer. Surely she'd posed the question a thousand times, pouring coffee in the diners where she'd worked. Had she ever waited to hear more than a generic, abbreviated affirmation?

Had she ever wanted to hear more?

The questions roiled, embers of unfulfilled power possessed of a base ability to consume.

What if ... what if someone had asked me how I was and waited to hear the truth ... the truth about Lucas?

Jessamy drew a shuddering breath, felt her baby spinning inside, and half-sobbed, half-laughed.

"What's the matter?" Love hurried down the stairs, Joe fast behind her.

"I'm fine ... I'm ... I'm ..." Jessamy started to wave the question away, and then she stopped. "I'm thinking. I'm wondering what you would ask people, if you were a waitress and you came to give them coffee. You wouldn't ask, 'How are you?' would you?"

Love shook her head.

"I don't like 'how' or 'why,' you know that."

"I do know," Jessamy affirmed, smiling a little in hopes of softening Joe's frown. "So what would you say? What would you ask someone you didn't know, just when you were meeting them at their table in a restaurant?"

"I'd ask them, 'Would you like some coffee?'" Love replied, her brow knit tight in confusion. "If I knew them, I might ask them about what they were doing today, or something like that."

"And if you didn't know them?"

"If I didn't know them, I'd ask them where they came from, or where they're going. Most people like to talk about those things."

"Most people like to talk about themselves," Joe observed.

"Yes, especially if someone is listening," Love agreed.

"That's just what I was thinking, except I was thinking how most of the time, people don't listen. Outside," Jessamy added, when Joe opened his mouth, apparently ready to argue. "In Between, I listened. I didn't do that much out there."

"You listened good in here." Love paused. "Except when you didn't. When you went in Zane's room, you didn't."

"No, that's true, but when I went in Zane's room I wasn't pretending to listen. I think … I think maybe I'll be more careful about listening. It's good to do and okay to not do, but I don't want to pretend to listen anymore."

"Fair enough," Joe nodded, though Jessamy thought his listening in this moment was mostly feigned.

Joe sidled around Jessamy and Love then, absconding in a silence that did nothing to disabuse Jessamy's suspicion of his pretense.

"He's scared of leaving," Love said. "I'm scared, too, but I guess I believe in him more than I don't, and more than he does."

Jessamy listened, considered, and thought she understood.

"I bet you're right." She dared to hug Love briefly. "I know you're right."

Symbols

Alone man entered Between later that evening and glanced around the room at its regulars. He retreated back out the door well before it closed behind him.

Jessamy turned to Joe and swallowed the mouthful she'd been struggling to process. Joe spoke before she could.

"We look that bad?"

"You smell that bad, maybe," Warren called from the bar.

The joke dissolved, not capable of falling flat.

Jessamy picked up the remains of her cheeseburger, then set it down with a sigh.

"Get some sleep, Jessamy," Joe advised, swirling the glass in his hand.

"Do you want the rest of my burger?"

"Nuh-uh. Not hungry."

"I guess I'm not hungry, either."

"Why the long faces?" Bella asked, looking away from the bar.

She jumped off her stool and swaggered over to the table where Jessamy and Joe sat.

"Land of the living out there might be a mess, but it's better than the land of the lost in here." Bella's tone indicated her certainty.

"Hey!"

Bella shushed Warren's indignation with a wave and grabbed the chair next to Jessamy. Reversing the chair, she straddled it and sat.

"Have a seat, why don't you." Joe's voice was dry, and not from lack of drinking.

"What's wrong with you two now?"

"I ..." Jessamy began, but stopped. Joe just shook his head.

"Don't bother, Jessamy. Let her say what she come to say and then maybe she'll go away."

"And where would I be going?" Bella said, her smile restored. "Look. Yeah, you're leaving this homey establishment and all us fine regulars, but you're going back to a whole world of choices. That guy who came in here a few minutes ago? He didn't like what he saw, so he left.

Choices! That's what makes the problems—whatever problems you think you've got—worth putting up with. You go where you want, do what you want, be who you want, and if you don't like where you are, what you're doing, or who you've become, you get a do-over. That's what it means to be breathing, understand?"

Joe looked at Bella as if she'd sprouted a second head; Jessamy wondered if Bella liked who she'd become.

"Not bad." Again, Joe spoke before Jessamy could. "You should make cards. For the card people."

"Hallmark?" Jessamy suggested.

Joe snapped his fingers and then pointed at Jessamy. "That's them."

He turned his attention back to Bella, accusatory finger redirecting as well.

"Ain't none of your business but it's kind of a big deal, going back after so long."

Warren swiveled in his seat. "Joe, you're making too much out of this."

"Warren," and Joe did not turn, but raised his voice instead, "you're a dumbass. You know what it's like, looking after someone

267

besides yourself? I got to look out for Iris—Love," he corrected, though with effort, "and I got her to look out for my whole life, since our ma died. It gets hard. And ... that's when I do dumb crap like what got us both stuck here; when it gets hard, I get stupid."

Warren stared, and Joe must have felt its weight, because he finally faced his friend.

"How can you think I don't understand?" Warren's voice, burdened under the weight of what it conveyed, dipped lower, his words slowing their pace. "I got Sandman the minute I came in here. Had him all this time, looks like I might have him until the end of time. You really think you have the raw deal?"

Joe leaned over the back of his chair and the taut rigidity in his body raised the fine hairs on Jessamy's neck. She exchanged glances with Bella and found the other woman tense, too.

"I told you before and I'm telling you again, if you get the chance to walk out the door, you take it. It don't matter if you ain't taking Sandman with you. You didn't do nothing to get him stuck here and you can't do nothing to get him unstuck."

Warren's eyes sparked like a waning fire poked hard with a stick.

"I'm never going to get out of here. Never. Sandman's asleep, so he'll never see life again and we crossed together so I'll never see it either. My only choice is if I stay here with him or drag him and let the devils outside take us both. What kind of choice is that?"

Silence descended on the room, hanging like a fog. Even the bartender's rote actions seemed muted, quieter.

"Warren," Bella said, and the sound following such an intense dearth of speech made Jessamy jump, "now you're the one making too much out of this."

Warren frowned, lines of his face drawing down more than the slight change in expression warranted.

"Bear with me." Bella straightened, warming to her task. "Here's how I see it: when you think you know your options and you got it all figured out, that's when you're in this place even if you're not."

"Whaaat?" Joe gaped.

"Wait." Warren's frown remained in place but it looked less like a mask and more like a flexible expression. "I want to hear this."

Joe shook his head but extended one hand to Bella, bidding her to continue.

"You get trapped out there the same way you do in here; the only difference is that out there, you're trapped in your own head. You think you know what you can do, what you can't do, what you can change, and what you can't change. But it isn't the world telling you how it is, it's you thinking you see everything there is to see. You might as well be here in Between when that happens. You get trapped by what you think you know.

What do any of us know, really?" Bella's eyes moved from Warren to Joe, and then to Jessamy. "We don't know what this place is—all we know it takes some and not others. We know what Between does, but that's not the same as knowing what we can do."

"You saying we just choose to see the world again?" Joe interrupted. "You saying we make this place get us and we make it let us go?"

"Maybe. Mostly I'm saying it doesn't matter who makes it do what it does or how it all happens, or even why it happens. The only thing that matters is that we don't lose ourselves over what's going on so much that we close ourselves off from what could happen next."

"What could happen next," Warren repeated, prompting Joe to glare at him.

Jessamy reached over and put a hand across Joe's mouth, muffling—but not silencing—the word, "Parrot."

"What could happen next," Jessamy said it, too, and winked at Joe when he pushed her hand away. "It could be anything. It could be walking into a bar and getting trapped by your death. It could be making friends out of people you'd never have met otherwise. It could be ..."

"It could be anything. But what you believe might make you miss it all." Bella looked directly at Jessamy. "Take that piece of ..."

"Work," Warren supplied.

"That piece of 'work,'" Bella went on. "The one who cut you. He didn't believe what was happening. And it killed him. Rightfully so, I'd say, but ..."

"Stop," Warren said. "I see what you're saying."

"I don't!" Joe glowered. "And even if I did, how's that any different than Jessamy having to deal with that piece of crap— that's right, piece of crap, not piece of 'work;' what's that supposed to mean?—even with him gone?"

"Look, I'm just trying to help." Bella stood, abandoning her backwards-facing chair, and shrugged dramatically. "Some things make sense, some don't. You take what works, you make your choices, you do your thing. But when you walk out that door, you know everything is possible. Even in here, you can't know what all is possible. Why's it so hard to believe life is crazy when you've seen crazier stuff right in front of you here?"

"Crazy don't mean crazy-good," Joe said, dryness persisting. He stared down into his glass of whiskey, swirling the untouched amber liquid. Jessamy watched, too, as the liquor attempted to cling to the sides of its prison only to slide down under the inexorable forces dictating its possibilities.

Jessamy didn't know exactly what all conspired to draw the edges of the whiskey back down to the base of the glass, but her observations made her think.

"What about the things we can't control?" Her question arrested Bella as the woman moved to return to her barstool.

"What about them? You don't really know until you try your whole life, do you?"

"Try to fly off a building," Joe snarled. "See what that gets you."

Bella raised one brow and answered without hesitation.

"Hey, you have to be smarter than pavement."

Warren laughed, breaking the grim lines remaining on his face.

"If I ever get out of here, I'm getting that tattooed on my backside."

Joe snorted. "Get it on your forehead, so you see it in the mirror."

"Then he'd have to get it tattooed backwards." Bella boosted herself back onto her stool and waved to the bartender.

"Don't got to be able to read it to remember what it says," Joe replied, unrepentant.

"I'm going to try to get some sleep." Jessamy rose. "You can have the rest of this if you want," she added, sliding her plate toward Joe.

"Maybe I will." Joe scooped the generous remnant half of cheeseburger off the plate in a swooping motion. "Wouldn't want to say it ain't possible this' the best burger I'll ever eat."

"See? Now you're getting it." Bella sounded proud. "You might be smarter than pavement."

"Dumbass," Joe replied.

"Idiot," Warren said, with Bella seconding the epithet just a moment out of synch.

Remembering the exchange tugged a smile from Jessamy as she trudged up the stairs to face her last night in Between. Her thoughts swooped and spun, whipping around like fruit in a blender. Sometimes, ideas banged up against each other and got stuck; sometimes, they merely passed in the vortex. It was hard to imagine being outside this time tomorrow.

It was practically impossible to imagine.

Jessamy spent a few minutes in Zane's room, giving Eclipse a good cuddling as Zane played with Mister Bananas and Love entertained Hum—through it all, Shadow nuzzled up against Eclipse and Jessamy both. Then Jessamy entered her own room for the last time; as she laid down in her bed, she still could not decide if Bella imparted wisdom or nonsense in her diatribes downstairs.

The chance of getting trapped in her own mind was a given, she determined. She could remember many a night when she'd thought she'd never be free from Lucas, yet here she was! At least, free of physical harm from him. She couldn't see how but Jessamy thought about Bella's speech, remembered Tracy's urging, and it did seem possible now that there must be some way she could find to escape the mental ties she still felt.

She'd be a mother. A mother with a baby and a kitten, and that meant she'd have someone to love just as her mother had loved her and Ruthie. Jessamy swallowed a lump in her throat as she turned out the light and crawled into her bed. She could do no less for her own child and cat than her mother had done.

Her challenge would be to do even more ... so if death managed to devour her too soon, her child would be able to face life without her. But if platitudes thrived on simplicity, life laughed at plans.

No guarantees, only promises.

And you have to be smarter than pavement.

It made Jessamy laugh and cry, both—which was an improvement over crying alone.

A soft knock on her door startled her, yanking her away from her musings.

"Yes?" she called, batting feebly at her eyes.

Love cracked open the door, admitting a band of dull light from the hall.

"Don't cry." Uncertainty fringed Love's voice.

"I didn't mean to scare you." Jessamy heard echoes of the past in their present. "I'm a little scared tonight myself, that's all."

"Me, too." Love's nodding head made ripples through the shadow she cast.

"Do you ..." Jessamy began, and then started over. "If you'd like, you can get your quilt and come in. If we can't sleep, we can talk."

"Okay." Love whirled, letting darkness settle into the room once more.

Jessamy blinked away the last of her tears and scooted over to bed's far side, making room for Love. The woman returned quickly, shut the door behind her, and faltered only a little as she made her way to the bed.

Jessamy thought Love moved more surely these days.

"It's hard," Love said, while the springs complained about the addition of her weight.

Jessamy knew what she meant.

"I know. I guess I didn't think how hard it would be. And I haven't been here as long as you. It must be even harder for you."

"I don't know about that. I don't know how you feel, except I heard you cry so I know it must hurt some. I know it hurts me, too. I don't know why ..."

"But you're not a how or why person." Jessamy smiled. The springs grew silent, and even the whispery movements of the fabric Love tugged into position around her body ceased.

"I'm not. It doesn't make me stop wondering, though. It just helps me stop asking questions with too much space for answers."

"I understand." And Jessamy almost thought she did.

"What should we talk about next?" Love asked.

It didn't take Jessamy long to find the right answer.

"Cats?" she suggested.

"Yes, let's talk about cats."

So they did, starting with enthusiastic particulars of their own growing friends, their voices strong and certain in the beginning and losing volume and speed as they moved on to generalities. Eventually, they both slept.

Jessamy's last conscious thought centered on Love's tiny snore ... it was almost like purring.

Portent

J essamy snapped into wakefulness, startled out of a dream in which she lay alongside a burbling stream, watching a smaller version of herself splashing near the water's edge.

She struggled, transitioning from vivid sweetness into unrelenting darkness. Finally, she sat up and pushed the blanket back.

And she remembered.

She pressed her palm against the place where Love had lain; the surface there felt warm, and Love had taken her own quilt with her when she left.

Jessamy ran both hands through her hair, spreading tendrils of the lingering dream's touch as she separated strands. She could take a shower but didn't have any interest in the process. She could make a messy bun, secure it with Mama's barrette, and figure out something else when she got where she was going.

Where **am** *I going?* she wondered, padding toward the door with arms outstretched to locate the light switch.

"Ouch." In spite of the care she'd taken, Jessamy jammed one finger against the wall before she found her target.

Under sudden illumination and by comparison with the recent memory of sublime outdoors, the room she'd claimed as her own for so long appeared stark and dismal. The two sentry lamps, one with shade and one without, remained as she'd found them, casting what light they could. The desk at which Jessamy had never sat reminded her of a doll house fixture, designed more for ambiance than functionality. Even the bed, with rumpled coverings testifying to some semblance of sleep, seemed ambiguous in nature.

Jessamy shoved her hands through her hair again, then dropped her arms mid-ruffle. Surely she only added to the gritty mess by doing this. But without a comb, her grooming options were limited.

After unnecessarily detailed consideration, Jessamy took a quick shower and wrapped her hair in the towel. She'd washed her underwear the preceding day, so it was as close to clean as it could get in Between. She'd even showered in all her clothing not too long ago, removed the wet fabric with some difficulty, wrung it dry, and spent a veritable eon waiting for the dripping sounds to subside—longer still for the clothes themselves to dry.

She'd done what she could and in the process, she developed a devout appreciation for the spin cycle of a washing machine.

Redressed but no less pensive, Jessamy made the bed with deliberate care. Whatever else Between was, it had been her home … longer, she supposed, than some apartments she'd lived in. That she didn't know exactly how much time passed during her stay in Between no longer discomforted her.

After all, she knew what day it would be when she stepped outside. She'd tracked the passage of time since it restarted for her.

Jessamy patted the pocket of her pants, feeling the distinct shape of Mama's barrette and hearing the reassuring crinkle of paper, too. She had Tracy's address and the list of names she'd made with Joe and Warren. She had her baby, and she'd have Shadow.

Having virtually no money didn't faze her as much as it would have once done … her renewed strength, measured in nameless units of supernatural experience, enriched her more than any bank account sum could ever do. Even though Jessamy trembled as she hung her towel, she truly believed she would be all right now.

Turning, she faced her reflection straight on. The discoloration which marred her entry into Between and the throbbing pain that carried through her transition back to a living being had both faded into oblivion. Jessamy Buccholz would re-enter the only world most people could imagine without bearing any visible trace of what befell her before she'd stepped outside it.

Knowing her trials were no longer obvious felt like wearing secret armor. Jessamy managed a small smile for the girl—no, the woman—she saw in the mirror.

It seemed unexpectedly wondrous and not at all ordinary when the mirror-woman smiled back.

Jessamy worked her hair into a loose bun and clipped it there with Mama's beautiful barrette. Her barrette now, and if the vision she'd dreamt came true, her daughter's one day in the future.

In spite of her nerves, Jessamy met her eyes in the mirror more easily this time. She tucked a clump of hair behind her ear to prevent it from shadowing the spot that no longer bore Lucas' brand. Her body, her temple, her whole being—all *hers* forevermore. She would care for herself, her child, her cat, and if there came a time when she could not, she'd find someone to help ... somehow.

"I promise," she whispered. And then said it again, louder.

Jessamy turned away from her reflection then, walking out of her room in Between without another hesitation. She found Love in the hallway.

"Are you ready? Are you scared?"

"Yes, and yes," Jessamy replied. "Are you?"

"Am I what?"

"Ready? And scared?"

"I'm ready. I'm only a little scared." Love spoke with her usual openness and Jessamy found joy in it.

Love's face mirrored Jessamy's blossoming grin.

"Let's go get Hum and Shadow." Love moved fast, but Jessamy caught her arm.

"I think we should have breakfast first, and ... say our goodbyes. Hum and Shadow might not like being in their boxes for long."

"Oh, that's a good idea. You're right. And I almost forgot to eat again."

"You know, I bet if you ate when you feed Hum, you'd never forget a meal again. All you'd need to do is feed Hum three times in a day instead of two and then eat your own food at the same times."

"That's a good idea, too. I'll go tell Joe." Love converted words to action in an instant, hurrying ahead of Jessamy.

If only all problems were so easily fixed.

Still, Jessamy supposed, sometimes you could spy a solution just by thinking about a problem in a new way. She took the stairs slowly, feeling each step's impact as she descended, letting each footfall drive the notion home. The rhythm converted into an abbreviated version of an old adage: *Try, try, try again!*

So simple, yet so complicated.

Jessamy joined Love at the bar where the other woman beamed at Joe, Warren, and Bella.

"All this time stuff is messing with my head but I'm pretty sure that ain't gonna work, us going back together." When Love's face fell, Joe added, "Nice idea and all; I just been thinking and I don't think we can. But I don't want you worrying."

"I know." Love put a hand on Joe's arm. "I just ... we didn't come in together. Time and space and more separated us. That's over, so I want us to leave together. It feels right that we should. And it feels like we could."

"But you was alive way before me. Don't make sense that ..."

"You could look out," Jessamy suggested. The idea jarred the others, to judge by their expressions. "Well, you could. You could look out and see what's there. All you'd need is an animal or a person or a car ... then you'd know if you were both on the same time."

"How could that be?" Bella said.

"I don't like how." Love frowned right back as Bella's disapproval deepened. "I do like Jessamy's idea. Joe, let's go look."

Love got up, conviction driving her determined strides.

"Warren, man, sorry about this."

"Do what you need to do," Warren replied, picking up his drink and moving in the opposite direction. "So will I."

Love flung open Between's door.

"Don't got to open it that much!" Joe yelped, rushing over to join her. "Think about Warren and Bella, will you?" He grabbed the edge of the swinging door, holding it tightly.

"I am. The more we see, the faster we'll know. Yellow bug car."

"Ain't moving ... don't help. Look over there—black bird."

"The big one? In the tree? It's just sitting!"

"The big one sitting in the tree, yeah. Hey. Hey!" Joe raised his voice to a roar and flapped his arms wildly. "Fly, you bastard!"

"There it goes," Love said, nodding.

"That's it." Joe shut the door. "We're back in time together, so we go together. Aw, crap. My car ... I bet it got towed, too."

"It was probably a junker," Warren offered, rejoining Joe. "Where do you live?"

"Where? What's that got to do with ... oh. It's Ma's old house and paid off, so ... well, we been breathing in here ..."

"Almost two months." Jessamy's hands drifted to her belly. Her pregnancy was blatant now, her baby's body rounding her own as it grew.

"Suppose utilities ain't paid ... crap," Joe sighed, then shrugged. "We might got to walk home," he told Love, "but we'll get there. We might got to do a lot of things, but we'll do them."

"I have to keep Hum safe." Urgency raised the pitch of Love's words.

"Yeah, you do that and I'll look after you," Joe returned, his voice even and sure. "We'll figure it out."

Bella shook her head and punched Joe's shoulder.

"You should just take a cab."

"I look like I'm made of money?" Joe glared. "I ain't no fancy drug dealer like some people around here."

"Oh, I'm not really a drug dealer."

The bar grew stiflingly still.

"What?" Joe scrubbed at his ear with his index finger. "You're not a dealer now? What're you instead? Other than a liar?"

"I'm a regular." Bella tossed her hair as she said it and tipped her chin up, too. "And as such, I don't see that I need so much cash as I'm carrying, so ..."

She extracted a few bills from her coat and waved them at Joe.

"What the ever-loving ..."

"Take it," Bella demanded, advancing on Joe. "If you won't take it for you, take it for her and her cat."

When Joe, his finger still angled slightly toward his ear, only stood and stared, Bella snorted.

"Dumbass." The word resounded in the silent bar, disparaging and kind—a sloppy, beautiful blend. Bella stepped forward and tucked the money into the front pocket of Joe's shirt.

He moved belatedly, trying to push her hand away. Bella smacked him for his efforts and made another withdrawal from her coat's deep pocket.

"You, too, Jessamy. And if you won't take it for you ..."

"I'll take it." Jessamy allowed Bella to press the cash against her open palm. "I'll take it for me, my baby, and Shadow. We all thank you."

She grabbed Bella in a hug before the other woman determined her intent.

"Whoever you are, whatever you do … you're good. You've helped more than you know," Jessamy whispered. "Thank you!"

When she released Bella, those sharp, jaded eyes bored into her own.

"Don't you ever let a man hit you again, you hear?" Bella hissed. "Or a woman, either."

"I won't." Jessamy summoned a smile in spite of Bella's fierceness—or because of it. "I promise."

"Ha! That's the spirit." Bella pulled Jessamy back toward her with one hand, touching Jessamy's cheek lightly with the other.

When Bella released Jessamy this time, they both looked at the bar, where Warren, Joe, and Love stared.

"What?" In a single word, Bella managed to convey the notion that she'd caught the other three doing something distinctly inappropriate, if not outright appalling.

Joe opened his mouth but shut it without speaking. Warren looked at Bella, and Bella winked. In the continuing silence, Jessamy's stomach growled menacingly.

"I think we should have breakfast now," Love said.

Jessamy covered her smile with her hand.

"Definitely." Her stomach rumbled a second time. "And the sooner, the better."

As Love, Joe, and Jessamy settled at the table next to Sandman's, the bartender wordlessly picked up her notepad and moved around the bar.

"Did she say it to you?" Joe asked, elbowing Jessamy and pointing to the bartender.

"What?"

"She ain't said it to me, but Iri ... Love says she said it to her."

Lost, Jessamy looked at Love.

"'Time for you to go,'" Love intoned solemnly. "She said it to me, but she didn't say it to Joe."

"She didn't say it to me, either." Jessamy's eyes flickered to the bartender as the woman glided in, pencil raised expectantly.

The bartender stopped next to the table and cocked her head, waiting.

"What does it mean?"

"For the love of Pete, how should I know? Maybe it don't mean nothing."

"Thought you were going to eat, but maybe you're just going to talk?" Bella sniped from the bar.

"You buying? If you're not, maybe you don't got nothing to say about it."

"How soon they forget," Warren commented dramatically to Bella.

"No kidding."

"Dumbass," Joe called.

"Idiot!" Warren and Bella replied perfectly together this time, resounding in stereo.

"I want an omelet," Love said. "Is that okay, Joe?"

"That's fine." But to Jessamy, Joe's innocuous words seemed overburdened with worry.

Preparation

After its inauspicious beginning, breakfast became a lively affair.

"Gonna find my car," Joe proclaimed. "Figure where it got towed and get it back with Bella's laundry money, or ransom money, or fake money, or ..."

"I can take that back," Bella threatened.

"Nuh-uh. Not unless you're going diving in my drawers."

Bella smirked. "You want me to?"

Joe didn't answer and Warren laughed.

Joe glared, then shoveled the rest of his omelet into his mouth. "Cahnt uh man et 'is friggin' bruckfust?"

"Joe, don't talk with your mouth full," Love admonished.

Joe rolled his eyes at Jessamy and she coughed, reaching hastily for her water glass.

"Good food?" Bella asked, all innocence.

"Yes," Jessamy replied when she was able. "Eli really does make the best skillet."

"Best omelet, too," Joe added.

"Best ever!" Love agreed.

"It is pretty good," Warren told Bella. "You should try it sometime."

"I don't have that much money," Bella huffed, and then, raising her voice, she added, "in spite of what some people think."

"Whatever." Joe waved one hand in Bella's general direction. "Jessamy, you need to find the truck you come here in."

"It's not mine. And I don't want it."

"Don't matter. Got your babe on the way and a cat already here. Truck's big enough to sleep in if you got to and you can sell it if you need."

Jessamy shook her head. "It's all in Lucas' name."

"Here's the thing," Bella interjected. "He left you. He walked off, and that's what you say. It's true and details don't matter to the truth. You know everything in the truck so you can describe all of it. You tell the part of the story where he left, you list what's in the truck, and they believe you because it's the truth and the truth makes sense."

Bella's gestures became more expansive as she went on, but her voice stayed steady and certain.

"They're going to hand that truck over to you in the end and even if they don't, they're still likely to give you the stuff in it. Especially in a small town ... rules are different than a big city because people get to know you in a small town."

"You come in here in the middle of nowhere, right?" Joe leveled his empty fork at Jessamy.

"Yes, but ..."

"Stop with the buts. In a little place, it don't take long for people to feel like they've known you forever. They'll want to help."

"Just think about it, Jessamy," Warren said. "Don't think about it too long, but do think about it. We're just telling you to try, especially if you end up staying nearby."

Jessamy frowned at her plate.

"I can't imagine staying ... but I guess I can't go far without a car of my own. And I don't really have anywhere to go."

"And you have Shadow."

284

"That's right." Jessamy smiled at Love. "I'll need to think of something fast." She could feel the edges of her smile melting away as she said it, and tried to will her lips back into alignment.

"We all got to figure something out fast," Joe said. "Not too fast, because that's the crap that got us here in to begin with."

Bella sniffed and turned away. "It's not as hard as all that."

"Yes, it is," Jessamy disagreed. She didn't allow Bella to launch another offensive, continuing to speak, "but it isn't, too."

"Here we go again." Bella elbowed Warren.

"It does get peculiar around here," he replied.

"You ain't the ones going." Joe flinched after the words left his mouth. "Well, it's true. It's easy for you to talk."

"I have a friend who likes to say, 'If the truth hurts, it's still the fucking truth,'" Bella said. "He's not here now, of course, but he's got me trained so it's all good."

"What's the last town you seen, Jessamy? Before you come to Between."

Jessamy stared at Joe, but the confusion in her mind didn't lessen even as quiet erupted and deepened around her.

"I don't remember," she finally admitted. "I was thinking about ... " Her hand fluttered up toward her temple and she pulled it back down. "I was distracted."

"You were hurting." Love said it with startling severity.

"Say it," Bella admonished from her perch. "Don't dance around like it wasn't what it was. You weren't 'distracted.' You were abused. Never pretend it was something else. Never."

"My head hurt. Because ..." Jessamy began, with effort. "Because ..."

She didn't want to say it but she also felt like she had to. So when it seemed as if Between itself held its breath waiting, Jessamy started over. This time, she pushed out the abhorrent words that had shaped her reality—it fit like the perfect glove instead of a giant's mitten.

"My head hurt because Lucas hit me. So I don't remember where we were, exactly. Just that it was in the basin in Wyoming."

The labor of speaking the truth could surely be no worse than birthing an actual child, Jessamy felt. But the intense and certain deliverance of relief followed instantly, suffusing her from core to extremities.

"Was that so hard?" Bella cast the words over her shoulder.

"Yes! But it was right."

"It was right," Love agreed. "It was true."

"'If the truth hurts ...'" Bella began, but Warren interrupted her.

"Truth is good and right, and Between is cryptic. I think that covers it."

"Cryptic? Like where they keep the dead folks above ground?" Joe pressed a bill on the table between his plate and Love's.

"Why, Joe, you old idiot. That was almost funny. I didn't know you had it in you." Warren raised his glass to his friend.

"I don't. You bring out the worst in me, dumbass."

Joe fixed Love with over-bright eyes and when he spoke again, he forced his voice out with false good humor. "You done? Best get the cat."

"Okay. Are you ready, too?" Love asked Jessamy, rising.

"I guess. Close enough." The baby kicked as Jessamy stood, making her brave even so close to their impending departure, a foreboding loss as distended and heavy as the stench of rotting fruit.

Love led Jessamy up the stairs, her plodding step remarkably light today. It was one of those times in life, Jessamy decided, composed of feelings that didn't fit ... sadness and loss blended with excitement and anticipation, lumpy and imperfect, but with a solid realness that made it memorable.

"What are you wishing for? I'm wishing for a night in my own bed, with Hum next to me and Joe down the hall. Joe hasn't been sleeping in a bed even since he started breathing, you know. Just at the table with Sandman; I don't know what makes him want to do that. Maybe he's wishing for a night in his own bed, too."

Love's speculation about Joe's wishes gave Jessamy time to consider her own.

"I'm wishing for my own home. I don't care if it's just one room—I want my own place this time ... mine, my baby's, and my kitten's."

Love paused outside Zane's room. "That's a good wish."

"Thank you. Your wish is good, too."

The chunky, emotional mess underlying their simple desires tempered their expressions, muting them.

Truth is good and right, and Between is cryptic.

Remembering Warren's words, Jessamy's smile emerged fully.

"Let's go get Shadow and Hum, and say goodbye to Zane, Eclipse, and Mister Bananas."

Love nodded, and opened the door.

Zane looked up as they entered, his narrow face shifting from amused to serious in an instant.

"You're leaving?" he asked, though he began nodding as he spoke and proceeded to answer to his own question. "Yes, you're leaving."

Love sat on the floor next to Zane as Hum extracted himself from underneath the bed.

"Hum will miss Shadow and Mister Bananas. But Hum will have me, Shadow will have Jessamy, and Mister Bananas will have you."

"You and Eclipse," Jessamy added, sitting next to Eclipse and Shadow on the bed. She reached out to Eclipse and the cat tilted her head, purring in anticipation of the caresses Jessamy hurried to bestow.

"Yeah." Zane's voice was glum. His head drooped but his hands moved constantly, weaving about with tapping fingers that now served as toys for Mister Bananas rather than timekeepers of an unimaginable interlude in Between.

"It'll be all right, Zane." Jessamy watched Zane's long digits as they enticed Mister Bananas into a crouch. The kitten locked his eyes on the hand mostly obscured just behind the bend of Zane's knee, and wriggled his butt as he prepared to strike.

They all laughed.

"Mister Bananas is a lucky cat to have you," Love said.

Hum launched over the edge of Love's skirt, landing awkwardly in the parachute-like center, which promptly sank in under his weight.

"I'm lucky." Zane lifted his head. "I count Mister Bananas' days instead of mine. It's better. It's a lot better."

Jessamy blinked at the sudden fullness of her eyes. Poignancy lay beneath Zane's short speech, holding it up as sturdily as rebar supported skyscrapers.

"It's better for all of us," she said, when she thought she could, "to count someone else's days instead of our own. It keeps us connected."

"Connected. Instead of between?"

Jessamy tried to decide whether Zane meant the bar or the spaces barely separating their lives. The terms seemed interchangeable in this instance.

"Connected and between," she said.

"We're all the 'and,'" Love intoned, lifting Hum into the air and touching her nose to his. "We only think we're the 'or.'"

288

Shadow, sitting with her feet primly placed together and the tip of her fuzzy tail draped over her toes, tilted her whole head then. Jessamy giggled, even though she wanted to hold onto the idea Love's words encapsulated—the notion of being connected regardless of whether or not she felt it.

"What?" Love asked.

"Oh, it's Shadow." Jessamy scooped the little cat into her arms. Kitteny fullness would soon give way to the gawky length of adolescence in a pattern Jessamy remembered from Ruthie's youth. She delighted in imagining this progression in her child's life as well.

"If I get a tattoo," Jessamy declared, "I'm going to get 'and, not or.'"

Love settled Hum on her shoulder and glanced from Zane to Jessamy.

"Where?"

"On my wrist." Jessamy set Shadow back on the bed and extended her left arm, palm up. "Right here."

"That would hurt," Zane said.

"Yes, but it would be wonderful, too."

"I'll get the boxes." Love transitioned to standing with care, Hum wobbling and latching his claws into her shoulder, making her wince.

"You might need a thicker shirt," Jessamy observed. She reached out to pet Shadow, who paced the bed between Jessamy and Eclipse as if both anxious and reluctant to leave.

"Or a scarf," Love exclaimed, rubbing Hum's front foot gently until he relaxed his grip.

"Scarf?" Zane levitated to his feet and dashed over to the desk they'd moved next to the wall. There, he opened a drawer and pulled out a seemingly endless length of pilled gray material. After extracting the ombré scarf in its entirety, he carried it to Love and circled her twice, draping it loosely around her neck.

"Zane!" Love stared at him, and then craned her neck to see Hum, who obligingly moved onto the layers. The kitten sniffed and massaged the fabric—it appeared he approved.

"It's okay. It was mine, but now it's yours. Mister Bananas won't ride on my shoulder like Hum rides yours."

"Are you sure?"

"Yeah." Zane nodded. He turned to Jessamy, shrugging. "I don't have one for you."

"I don't need a scarf, but thank you. Shadow likes to be in my arms. I don't think she wants to ride."

"I can get a leash for Mister Bananas someday. He doesn't like to ride or be carried; he likes to walk. Or run."

Love touched the ends of the scarf on her chest and glanced at Hum out of the corner of her eye again.

"That's very nice of you, Zane. Thank you, from Hum and from me."

"You're welcome." Zane looked away as if embarrassed. "You should go. I ... Mister Bananas, I mean, might get sad otherwise. So you should go."

Love ducked her head and moved toward the door.

"The boxes are in my room," she told Jessamy, who hesitated.

"I'll meet you there."

Love smiled, nodded, and left the room with Hum hanging on to the scarf and apparently having the time of his young life.

"I know how Mister Bananas feels," Jessamy said after the door clicked shut. Her voice barely fit around the lump in her throat. "I'm glad you and Mister Bananas will be here to help Eclipse, too."

"Yeah." Zane brightened. "I'll keep taking care of them."

"It's like a job," Jessamy said. "An easy job, though, because they both love you."

Zane nodded, then frowned.

"Easy, except for the litter box," he confided.

"Well," Jessamy gathered Shadow to her, "nobody really likes taking care of the litter box. That's okay."

"Yeah. That's okay."

Departure

Love let Hum ride her shoulder down the stairs while Jessamy carried Shadow in the crook of her arm. Rather than spooking or struggling to escape as she took in new sights and smells, Shadow absorbed it all with active but seemingly objective interest.

Hum alternated his time between surfing for balance and gnawing Love's hair.

"I think you might end up with shorter hair," Jessamy said as she followed Love to the bar. The box dangling from Jessamy's other arm bumped against a chair as she passed Sandman's table, resounding like a poorly-crafted drum. She pushed the box onto the bar next to Love's.

Love giggled.

"Hum wants to give me a haircut."

"You got to get that critter in the box," Joe frowned.

"I will. Right before we go."

"I ain't no spring chicken to get him back if he gets down so take care. He do look happy where he is, though."

"He does," Jessamy agreed. Now that Love paused in her movements, Hum peered through the tangles of her hair, nose twitching, staring at Joe in particular.

Joe stretched, directing his hand to Hum, and the kitten watched its approach, intensifying his sniffles.

Jessamy found a grin tugging at her lips. "I think he likes you."

"Watch out." Love's warning came a moment too late, just as Hum nipped Joe's finger.

292

"Ouch! Feisty bugger." Joe pulled his hand back, inspecting the indentations left by Hum's fangs. "Didn't break the skin."

"He plays rough," Zane said from behind them, just as Eclipse leaned her body around Jessamy's ankles and then threaded the needle's eye between like a skilled seamstress.

Zane spoke again. "Eclipse wants to go."

Jessamy looked down past Shadow, who regarded her mother with all the seriousness a fluffy body could assume.

"Are you sure?"

Zane nodded. "Won't be as much to clean." He sounded like he was trying to convince himself that Eclipse's leaving was a good thing.

He sounded like he was failing the task.

"I think she's safer here. I don't want her to go, either, Zane." Jessamy watched Zane's downcast face as she spoke. "But if it's time ... I guess it's time."

"She wants to go with you, not stay with me."

Jessamy shook her head. "We came in Between around the same time, even though we weren't together. We might have to leave around the same time. Maybe she knows."

"Do you know?" Zane asked.

"I don't." And Jessamy felt every single fear of not-knowing compressed tightly into that instant. "I'm scared. But we can't stay, even if I'm scared. I know that now."

It seemed significant, saying those words. Bella's eyes narrowed but Jessamy saw the other woman smile; she replayed the short speech in her mind and awareness dawned.

"Oh!"

"Yeah," Bella said. "'Oh.'"

"'Oh' what?" Joe's thick brows came down over his eyes like clouds over darkening hills.

"Idiot," Warren sighed. "You want one for the road?"

Distracted, Joe regarded his old friend. His lips tightened under the turmoil reflected in his eyes.

"Nuh-uh-uh." The phrase cracked, and Joe cleared his throat. "Nuh-uh, dumbass." He softened the refusal by clasping an arm around Warren's shoulders. "Got to get home safe," he added, looking at Love. "If her can stay off the sauce, I guess I can, too."

"Well, then." Warren stood, moving as if all his decades in Between suddenly caught up with him and beat him with their weight. "A toast."

"A toast!" Bella pounded her hand against the bar. "Eli ... Eli, get out here, we got regulars fixing to leave us." She downed what remained in her own glass and flung one arm expansively toward the bartender, calling for another round.

Hum ducked, having caught her gesture through the veil of Love's hair, which he still battled. His small back limbs churned as he lost the sureness of his grip, but Joe gave him a boost underneath his rear.

"Easy, there."

Eli peeked from the kitchen and, spotting the group and apparently verifying their intent, exited his sanctuary. While he always appeared serious to Jessamy, his countenance now looked as solemn as a clergyman giving last rites.

Eclipse meowed, pacing near Between's door.

"Let her go," Joe said while the bartender prepared the drinks, most of them water.

Jessamy shook her head. "I think she'll be in time with us, so I want to go with her. Maybe she'll come with me and Shadow."

Zane looked at Eclipse. "She will."

Eclipse meowed again, tail lashing.

"A toast," Warren began, reaching for the nearest glass—a beer. Bella intercepted him and slapped his hand, shoving a whiskey into it as an appeasement.

"That was mine." She shrugged when Warren raised his brows.

"Joe, there's the water." Jessamy angled her head to the five glasses filled with the banal beverage.

Joe hastily secured glasses for himself and Love, and Eli arrived next to Jessamy to claim the third. Zane picked up one more, and Jessamy took the last.

"Are we ready now?" Bella asked.

"Ready." Hum bobbed his head on Love's shoulder as if agreeing with her.

"Warren?" Bella turned to him, and Jessamy watched as Warren's emotions blustered across his face. It was an intense, jumbled assortment, scrawling over the paleness of his lifeless cheeks, written in magnified script on his crinkled forehead.

Anticipation, sorrow, relief, fear, frustration, loss ...

And, Jessamy thought, the tiniest blossom of abiding *hope.*

"To friendship." Warren struggled to speak even in the absence of a dry throat or lack of oxygen. "And to the happiest of trails."

"To happy trials! I mean, trails. What does it matter as long as they're happy?" Bella laughed over her error and tossed back her drink with the ease of regularity.

"Happy trails." Jessamy clinked glasses with Love and Eli, who were nearest her, and then with Zane, who again sought each available glass against which to tap his own—even Bella's empty one—before he drank.

Joe drank his water, which he obviously didn't have any interest in doing and looked at Warren. Warren stared back, frowning.

"What are you looking at, idiot?"

Joe swallowed visibly.

"My friend. My best friend ... "

"You," Warren said, leaning forward and knocking his whiskey so hard against the water Joe still held that Jessamy gasped, thinking the glass might break, "better get going then, and make some new friends."

"Who ain't dumbasses." Joe pushed back and made Warren's whiskey slosh.

"That's right. Go. It's a mess but it's life, and it's worth living."

"God." Bella banged her own glass against the bar. "I'm going to need another drink. Or two."

"Come on, Hum." Love reached awkwardly for the kitten on her shoulder.

"I got him." Joe set his glass on the bar and grasped Hum. The little cat tightened his grip on the scarf, unspiraling it from Love's neck as Joe moved him into his box.

"He can keep the scarf until we get home," Love said as Joe tried to extract it from Hum's claws. "It's okay, Hum. It's time to go, that's all." She tucked the kitten's head gently underneath the cardboard as Joe folded the box shut.

At the door, Eclipse raised her voice and so Jessamy packaged Shadow into the other box.

"I'll let you out as soon as I can, Shadow."

Shadow, placid and seemingly unconcerned, sniffed the side of the box and ducked as Jessamy closed the lid.

"I'm ready." Love picked up Hum's box. She licked her lips, looking to Jessamy. "Are you?"

"I guess."

Eclipse yowled.

"You're ready." Joe nodded to Love. "Jessamy's guessing she's ready, I'm ready, and the cat's past ready." He inclined his head toward the door. "So let's go."

Joe laid his arm across Warren's shoulders one last time, patting his friend's shoulder repeatedly before withdrawing.

"See you, Warren." Then Joe jumped as Zane slapped his back.

"See you!"

"Parrot," Joe snapped, but he mussed Zane's hair like a genial uncle.

"Are they leaving or not?" Bella nudged Warren. "Seems like a good time to see the upstairs, Warren; what do you say? You ever been up?"

Warren abandoned his detailed study of his drink.

"Once, I think. A long time ago." He stood, his jaw clenching and unclenching, and shook his head. With determined movements only slightly more fluid than a moment earlier, he bent his arm into a crook and offered it to Bella. "I'll escort you."

"Escort?" Bella winked at Jessamy. "Don't mind if I do." She downed her next drink before passing her arm through Warren's.

Jessamy watched the pair make their way to the stairs until Eli blocked her view.

"You are ready." Eli added the slightest emphasis to "are." "And you are healing. Continue with these things—you will be well."

"Thank you, Eli." Jessamy felt her eyes filling. "Goodbye."

"Until we meet again," Eli intoned, and then walked away.

Jessamy stared after him, following his purposeful progress all the way to the kitchen.

He did not look back.

"Until we meet again."

Again?

As Eli disappeared into the kitchen, Jessamy blinked, half-turning to Joe. He looked away, shrugging, as if Eli's final words to Jessamy had no real significance … or he wished they didn't.

"I got to go up," Zane said. "Make sure Warren and Bella meet Mister Bananas proper, so he doesn't bite them. Bye, Jessamy. Bye, Love."

"Goodbye, Zane," Love and Jessamy spoke together, and Zane acknowledged their reply with a final wave as he propelled his lanky frame toward the stairs.

Eclipse meowed, frustrated, and stretched out her body, scratching at the door frame.

"Taking longer to leave than it done to stay." Joe's resignation blended to perfection with his annoyance.

"We can go now," Love said.

"Yeah, but will we?" Joe snorted.

"We will." Jessamy settled her box gently, aware of Shadow's off-center weight. "We are."

She glanced over at the bartender, meeting those mysteriously old eyes.

"Thank you for visiting Between," the bartender said, looking directly at Jessamy. The music of her voice was strong when she began to speak, but by the time she said "Between," Jessamy felt the beauty fade like a troubadour walking away.

The bartender repeated the same farewell to Joe, and lastly, to Love. Her voice—while still lovely—sounded flat without its musical resonance and it made Jessamy shiver. The end of her time in Between seemed more defined with every seemingly insignificant change, making Eli's words even more foreboding.

"Thank you," Jessamy whispered back. The bartender nodded, but her focus already shifted to her perpetual task, eradicating invisible spots from the glassware.

Except ... Jessamy saw there were spots after all. The bar's wood didn't glisten, but instead oozed a dull sheen; the glasses lining the shelves didn't sparkle, but rather gritted like transparent and brittle teeth. The wall of names, when Jessamy looked at it, exuded an impression more like a mass grave than a living thing that could capture a person's essence in her name, singing it when the majesty of *being* had been forgotten.

"We have to hurry." Jessamy advanced past Love and Joe, who seemed spellbound, too.

"Yes, we do—come on, Joe!"

"Don't got to tell me twice." Joe inserted his body between theirs and sped past them to open the door.

"It's beautiful out." Love stopped next to Joe. "I'll miss you Jessamy; good luck."

"Good luck to you, Love, and you, Joe," Jessamy replied, overwhelmed by the impending transition ... afraid, excited, and alert to her restoration to the world she'd exited all unawares ...

"Go!" Joe urged, waving her ahead. "Me and Love got to go together."

"Eclipse?" Jessamy looked down at the cat, who in spite of her earlier urgency, paused on Between's threshold.

Eclipse turned her head to regard Jessamy, then redirected it to the world outside. She took a single step forward.

"Go! Go, go, g- ..."

The sound of Joe's voice shut off like a switch when Jessamy stepped outside Between, with Eclipse surging ahead.

Jessamy steeled herself and stepped off the bar's threshold, feeling the blazing Wyoming sunlight like a balm against her skin and the cutting edge of its wind as a cleansing blast. Her heart raced but Jessamy kept walking, following Eclipse across gravel, pavement, and back to gravel again.

When they stepped into the stubs of vegetation fringing the road's edges, the cat stopped and sat, swiveling to stare over her shoulder. Although Jessamy knew what she would—wouldn't— see, she turned, too.

Between was gone.

Epilogue

"**O**rder up!"

Jessamy raised her hand to arrest Mark Girard, not even halfway through an enthusiastic rant about the latest travesty of justice, as he saw it, wrought by the Wyoming Department of Game & Fish.

"Go ahead." Mark clucked his tongue. "Story'll keep. Hot food won't."

"Thanks, Mark." Jessamy smiled at the older man. Crossroads had many loyal customers but even among those, Mark exhibited dedication bordering on devotion. "I'll be right back."

Mark nodded, sipping his coffee ... just another Thursday night, Jessamy reflected, and even if the new cook—what was her name?—used the same phrase to announce a prepared order, she was certainly no Eli.

Jessamy carried the plate past Cindy Miller and her latest beau, a burly roughneck who went by the unlikely pseudonym of "Prince." She paused next to their table.

"What do you think, Cindy? Prince? Should we keep her?"

"Oh, hell yes!" Cindy spoke awkwardly around the mouthful she'd just taken, and then covered her grin with her hand. "S'good!"

Prince took the time to swallow the bite he'd been working on. "Real good."

Jessamy smiled at the pair, squeezed side-by-side into a booth barely large enough to accommodate such behavior in thin folks, much less stocky ones. They either enjoyed each other's company that much or simply determined to give such an impression; Jessamy, for one, believed that it was true love and it delighted her, for Cindy rarely brought a man to Crossroads more than once.

"Just let me know if you need anything else."

Most booths were occupied, which would have been unusual at this time of week except when the town geared up for its annual Pioneer Days. The influx still impressed Jessamy on this, her sixth year in Dry Fork.

"Here's your steak, Mavis. Make sure it's good and red, now." Jessamy placed the barely-warmed slab with its steaming baked potato and green bean sides in front of the local, self-defined food critic.

"Best be," Mavis sniffed, picking up her knife and fork and carefully slicing a sample. "I know you know what I want, but that new cook of yours ..." she let her voice trail off as she lifted what must surely be the rarest morsel of beef to ever exit a kitchen.

"We'll get her trained," Jessamy assured, biting her lip to prevent a smile from forming. "Not everyone's got as sensitive a palate as you." She used Mavis' own choice expression advisedly and by the sudden gleam in the other woman's eyes, Mavis approved the phrasing.

Mavis nodded as she chewed, an expression of careful consideration molded into her furrowed brow and pinched lips.

"Not bad. Not perfect, mind you, but I do have hope for her. What's her name, again?"

Jessamy, who'd been thinking frantically from the instant Mavis deemed the steak "not bad"—the highest praise Jessamy ever heard her offer—frowned.

"Let me think ... it starts with a 'J' ... Judy ... Julie ... Juliet! It's Juliet."

Mavis quirked one eyebrow, elevating it to nearly touch the ever-present quiff that swooped across her forehead no matter the time of year or weather conditions.

"That's an exalted name, isn't it?"

"If it helps, her last name's 'Smith,'" Darla Lawson said, draping her arm over the booth bordering Mavis's.

Jessamy moved past Mavis to take Darla's plate. "Anything else for you, Darla?"

"Nothing for me, though I expect Jack here might want pie." Darla tipped her head toward her nephew, who kicked his feet up against the bottom of the table top. "Which he can have, but only if he stops kicking."

Jack let his limbs descend back down, dangling above the floor he could not reach without stretching in spite of all his determination. He nodded vigorously, which set his brand-new Mohawk haircut flopping. "Apple pie!"

"I'll get it right away." Jessamy grinned at his enthusiasm and energy.

"Darla Lawson. Kindly remove your arm from my booth."

"It's my booth, too." Even as Darla spoke, she did as Mavis bid, but winked at Jessamy.

"What's your precious little girl up to these days, Jessamy?"

"She starts first grade in the fall," Jessamy sighed. "And every time I turn around, she grows an inch, I swear."

Jack's eyes rounded. "A whole one inch?"

"It just seems that way," Jessamy confided.

"First grade," Darla exclaimed. "Why, I remember the day Little Miss Muffet arrived ... all legs and lungs, that one."

Jessamy smiled at the old nickname.

"We were lucky to have you and Doctor Owens in delivery." Memories flashed through Jessamy's mind as clear as the night she'd delivered Lucille.

302

"Still remember every little detail?"

"Barely any, and that's the way I like it!" Darla laughed at that. "I do remember when you put Lucille in my arms ... that's the part I love to remember."

Darla pressed one hand against her chest, her face lit with warmth, and Jessamy knew she recalled that moment, too.

"I'll be right back with Jack's pie."

Jessamy stopped to speak to another customer on her way, and nodded to two more at Angela's tables. Angela was prepping two slices of pie when Jessamy got back behind the counter.

"While you're at it, would you get me an order of the apple, please?" Jessamy settled the dishes she'd collected and reached for a new pie plate.

"No problem," Angela replied, taking the plate. "With whip or without?"

"It's for Jack, so go crazy and drown it."

"Of course." Well acquainted with Jack's love of sweets, Angela covered the pie so thoroughly it could barely be seen peeking out underneath its fluffy burden.

"Perfect."

Jessamy waited for Angela to precede her, and then started back to Darla and Jack's table.

"Hey ..." an unfamiliar voice rasped as she passed the counter's edge. But Jessamy could see Jack watching her progress, and so she patted the new customer's arm gently and kept moving.

"Be right with you—I promise," she called over her shoulder.

"I got the guy at the counter," Angela said, already on her way back.

"Thanks."

Jessamy settled the whipped cream mountain—with its nearly-hidden apple-pie core–in front of Jack with a flourish.

"Wow. Thanks!" Jack didn't lift his gaze from the pie, but that only magnified his appreciation.

"Thank you, Jessamy." Laughter wrapped Darla's words. "You always make Jack feel so special. You make everyone feel special."

"It's not me; it's Dry Fork," Jessamy answered, but Darla's words might as well have been chiming bells for the joy they inspired.

Behind Darla, Mavis snorted.

"Dry Fork? Hardly. It's you."

"Why, Mavis. It's not even Christmas and I do believe your heart just grew three sizes." Darla announced, turning Cindy's and Prince's heads.

"Bull hockey." Mavis' voice sounded as smooth as the whipped cream Jack licked from the edges of his fork.

Darla cackled, thumping her hand on the seat back.

"Darla!"

"I know, I know. Kindly removing my arm, again."

Jessamy grinned—Darla and Mavis reminded her so much of ... of ...

Crossroads might as well have vanished in the instant realization struck.

"Would you excuse me?" The words formed automatically and Jessamy turned away before Darla even answered. It seemed to take a long time to scan the small restaurant, to locate the man whose voice had faded from memory.

But there he was, watching her, his once-whiskered face now clean-shaven, his scruffy hair largely unchanged but for additional gray coloring.

"Joe?" Jessamy whispered it, her feet moving faster as she neared him. "Joe!"

"Found you, Jessamy girl … starting to wonder if you was real at all," he answered, bright eyes sharpening. She thought she saw a flicker of surprise there as she flew at him, wrapping him in a hug. "Don't go making the rest of the folk here jealous ..."

"Sometimes I wondered if you were real, too," Jessamy gasped, caught between laughter and tears. As she pulled back, laughter won out. "This is my old friend, Joe." Keeping one arm around him, she waved to the rest of the restaurant and saw Prince and a few others wave in response. "I ... we haven't seen each other in years ... Joe!" She blinked to clear her vision. "I'm so glad you ..."

And then, Joe's expression crystallized in Jessamy's mind and it occurred to her that their reunion wasn't the only thing glazing his eyes. "Wait ... where's ... no. Oh, no."

Joe nodded, all the lines of his face sagging. Jessamy tightened her grip on his shoulders and held out her free arm to Angela, transfixed behind the counter.

"Angela ... could you ..."

"Of course. Take whatever time you need."

"Thank you, it's ..."

"No need to explain," Angela said, wiping her hands on a towel before clasping the hand Jessamy continued to extend. "I've got this."

"Thanks." Jessamy squeezed Angela's hands. "Joe, come outside with me; there's a table around the back."

Rising slowly, Joe scrubbed his face with his sleeve and moved to the door with Jessamy. He didn't lean on her as they walked, but she knew she supported him.

The picnic table where Angela worked Sudoku puzzles on breaks—weather permitting—squatted underneath a yard light, but the setting sun suffused the atmosphere, rendering artificial illumination redundant. Jessamy and Joe faced the street with the table at their backs, and Jessamy rubbed Joe's shoulder.

"You don't have to tell me ..." Jessamy began, finally, because it seemed like he was waiting for her to speak.

"She died." He spoke just after she did, so she knew he'd been gathering the strength to say it. "Nothing to do. Cancer."

"I'm so sorry." Jessamy's voice broke on the words.

"She had her way with folks, you know? I don't understand it—never did—but she had it." Joe stared down at his hands, limp in his lap. Jessamy released his shoulder and picked up his hand. "We wanted to find you, but there was never time for me to get away from the shop. Then she got sick ..."

"It's okay. I ... well, my job's like that. No benefits except the people."

"People're all right. When they're not dumbasses." Joe bumped his shoulder against hers.

"Or idiots." Jessamy nudged him back.

They sat quietly for a bit, and then Joe spoke.

"You had your babe?"

"I did. Her name is Lucille. I know what it sounds like, but I named her Lucille for me, not for ... well. Mama and I used to watch 'I Love Lucy' reruns when I was little ... I ran all the way home from school to get there in time. And I always wanted a girl named Lucy. Mind you, my girl doesn't want to be called anything but 'Lucille.' But that's all right, I guess."

The edge of Joe's smile reappeared.

"And the cat?"

"Shadow? Or Eclipse?"

"Both. Hum's still with me. He's home with my next door neighbor checking in on him. Hum's okay, but he don't like me the way he liked her."

Jessamy nodded, pressing her lips together at the intensity of loss.

"Eclipse's not getting around as well these days, but she curls up with Shadow at night and they're both really patient with Lucille."

"Big name for a little girl."

Jessamy let that remark settle before she spoke.

"She only wants to be called Lucille, but sometimes ..."

Joe's eyes flared, catching the dying sunlight as he turned to Jessamy, expectant.

"... sometimes, I call her Love," Jessamy finished.

"She'd like that." Joe's voice tightened, in the way of gratitude even more than sorrow. "Love'd like that. Someday your little girl'll like it, too, I bet."

"I hope so."

They didn't speak for a long time after that, but the sounds of approaching night filled the void. An occasional car moved along its limited options within Dry Fork's "city" limits, and the distant highway murmured as it carried most travelers past the single, sharp exit to the only town within 60 miles in any direction. The wind whispered, light and lovely today, lulling all who felt its caress into a false sense of security—forecasters predicted it would accelerate its pace tomorrow.

"You ever think about if you could go back?" Joe's question startled Jessamy from communion with the quiet calm of the outdoor symphony.

"Go back? To Between?" She didn't take time to consider hiding her shock, didn't realize how much would carry in her words until it did.

Joe snorted.

"I expect not, young as you are. And with your little girl."

He looked up, over the lines of the houses behind Crossroads and blinked slowly, like a cat expressing affection. Then he sighed.

"I'm alone now. Nobody but the cat, even if he's a feisty bugger and older than his own ma now ... I ain't about to bother with the math. But I ain't got no friends, Jessamy, other than you and you're special, but ..."

"I'm not Warren," Jessamy finished, squeezing Joe's hand. "I know what you mean. Everything was stronger in Between. We weren't even alive but there was something about being ... between ... life and death that made all the things in life seem important. It's easier to forget what's important when you're just trying to keep up with being alive."

Joe laughed.

"Something like that."

"I don't think about going back, not really. And it is probably because of Lucille. She's so ... so open to everything. She doesn't anticipate trouble, though she's learning to, I suppose. I guess it's that she doesn't get stuck on problems the way I do. She just keeps going, finding reasons to smile, ways to help.

When Eclipse stopped being able to jump up to the windowsill, Lucille asked me for boxes so she could make stairs. We ended up using a few bricks and a chair, because it didn't move around so much, but Lucille figured it out mostly by herself, how to help. Instead of just thinking that Eclipse was getting older, like I did."

"Ain't all you did." Joe sounded as if he was scolding, prompting Jessamy to giggle even under the burden of her somber thoughts. "You helped Lucille."

"What I mean is Lucille doesn't get stuck thinking like I do."

"Maybe that's the reason kids never go to Between, never get trapped." Joe extracted his hand from Jessamy's and rubbed his chin.

308

"That and it's a bar?"

"That, too," Joe admitted. "But it's a bar and grill."

"It is. Speaking of a grill, I haven't had supper yet, have you?"

"Now that you say so, I could eat. And you owe me dinner." Joe summoned a dramatic wink as if he'd been saving it for just this moment.

"I owe you dinner? Since when?"

"You know exactly since when, girl, tell you what ... I seen the pie you got for the youngster in the back, and if you'd make me a piece just like it, I expect I'll forget about dinner."

"You don't know how right you are," Jessamy laughed, standing.

Joe stood, too, his expression becoming severe.

"I'm gonna find it."

It seemed to Jessamy as if everything stopped—like the whole world caught its breath at Joe's daring vow. The spell held until his eyes refocused, coming back to the natural now from the supernatural past, and he grinned.

"Like to have that pie and maybe meet your Lucille before I head out."

Jessamy smiled back but took her time deciding whether to address the former or latter part of what Joe said.

"Let's get you some pie," she smiled. "And you can come to Pioneer Days tomorrow with me and Lucille."

"Deal."

Jessamy turned, leading the way to Crossroads' front door.

"Look at that—a shooting star!"

Jessamy whirled on her heel, but the meteor's trail had evanesced.

Author's Comments

As with my first novel, *Here & Now*, a certain element of serendipity interceded as *Between*'s story unfolded. Which is to say, I didn't necessarily write the novel I set out to write.

In the beginning, I expected my characters to work harder at discerning the "how" and "why" of their entrapment; I was certain that revelations of an extrinsic—not intrinsic—nature would permeate their experience. But as with so many of us out here in the "real world," the work for Jessamy and her cohorts turned out to be more about "who" and "what," and Love served as the catalyst for helping me understand that.

The other sentiment that unfolded for me as a writer is one that I hope also emerged for the reader: each person has struggles, but each also has gifts. Together, we are more than the sum of either our weaknesses or our strengths … we bring out either the best or worst in others by our engagement in life, our shared epiphanies, and our shared trials.

I hope you enjoyed your stay in Between.

Acknowledgments

Thanks gratefully given to:

- Jayne, for your consistent encouragement.

- Jean and Gary, who are authors not only of their shared destiny but of their own books as well: A Memoir of Holstein: An Engineer Traces His Origins and Seven Summers with Peregrines: Finding Midlife Adventures. I am lucky that I get to call my most dedicated fans "Mom" and "Dad."

- Janis, who is an honest and supportive beta-reader.

- Dean, for verifying my memory of field trials.

- Janette, for her constant enthusiasm.

- Fred, for his artistic gifts and singular vision.

- Kristy, for contributions above and beyond the call of duty.

- Chris, who read on, even when she realized I wasn't going to explain everything.

- Gordon, for the loan of his last name.

- Angela, who never stopped asking, "How's the book coming?"

- La Crosse Women Writers and Women Writers Ink (WWInk), who bring more to everything. Without you, I would be less courageous, and distinctly less happy.

- All readers—beta and beyond—for your willingness to pick up, peruse, and hopefully enjoy my efforts. Thank you for choosing *Between*!

About The Author

Gayle C. Edlin lives in rural Wisconsin, crafting detailed technical literature by light of day and spinning fanciful tales of her own imaginings in the darker hours that remain. She has previously served as columnist and factotum for the national literary magazine, *2nd & Church*, and as a contributor for *Coulee Region Women* and other regional magazines. She is a member of the La Crosse Area Women Writers and a board member for Women Writers Ink.

Find Gayle C. Edlin online:
gcedlin (Facebook)
@gcedlin (Twitter)
@gcedlin (Instagram)
gcedlin@gmail.com (E-mail)

Other Books by Gayle C. Edlin

Structure, Organization, and Pacing: ★ ★ ★ ★
Spelling, Punctuation, and Grammar: ★ ★ ★ ★
Production Quality and Cover Design: ★ ★ ★ ★
Plot and Story Appeal: ★ ★ ★ ★
Character Appeal and Development: ★ ★ ★ ★
Voice and Writing Style: ★ ★ ★ ★
—Judge, 24th Annual Writer's Digest Self-Published Book Awards

From first-time published novelist Gayle C. Edlin comes *Here & Now*, a story about a self-sufficient writer with a decidedly supernatural muse

Lila Dawkins spins her fictional tales out of the real-life threads of experiences she absorbs by touching significant artifacts of other people's lives. But Lila's secret ability isn't a free gift: she struggles to maintain her physical and emotional health with increasingly frequent trips to her remote Wyoming cabin.

This time, the buffering silence of Lila's private escape is shattered by the death of an old friend, a persistent calico cat, two new neighbors, and the vibrations of surfacing memories tied to an object that is somehow reaching out to Lila rather than revealing itself during chance encounter.

The landscape of the past integrates with the stories that Lila tells herself about how she must live her unusual life. Is the solution she created for herself the only way out, or is there another? What part—if any—will either of Lila's new neighbors play in her future? And is there a way to make peace with known and unknown, past and present, her own and others ... for Lila to find herself, for once, staunchly grounded *Here & Now*?

HERE & NOW
By Gayle C. Edlin
December 18, 2014
ISBN: 9780990973607
$12.99
355 pages